ELAINE FOX

BEDTIME
FOR
BONSAI

AVON

An Imprint of HarperCollins*Publishers*

This is a work of fiction. Names, characters, places, and incidents are products of the author's imagination or are used fictitiously and are not to be construed as real. Any resemblance to actual events, locales, organizations, or persons, living or dead, is entirely coincidental.

AVON BOOKS
An Imprint of HarperCollins*Publishers*
10 East 53rd Street
New York, New York 10022-5299

First Avon Books paperback printing: December 2008

Avon Trademark Reg. U.S. Pat. Off. and in Other Countries, Marca Registrada, Hecho en U.S.A.
HarperCollins® is a registered trademark of HarperCollins Publishers.

Printed in the U.S.A.

10 9 8 7 6 5 4 3 2 1

"You're a stran_____

I can't figure you out at all."

"No doubt you're putting too much thought into it." He backed up a step.

The puppy writhed in Penelope's arms toward him.

"See? He likes you better!"

Dylan stopped bouncing the clay tool in his fingers. "No, he likes this thing better than both of us."

"He does not."

He tossed the stick across the room and the dog immediately struggled to go after it. Dylan raised his brows at Penelope.

She laughed. "Thank you." After a moment's hesitation, she stepped toward him, put a hand on his forearm, and looked up at him with those dark, lush eyes.

He found he couldn't move. "For what?"

"For being so nice." She rose up on tiptoe and kissed his cheek. It was a soft, lingering press of her lips, a moment that lasted far longer than it should have.

Or it felt that way to Dylan.

Which was why he raised his hands to her upper arms, above the puppy, and pulled Penelope closer. He paused a split second, brain registering that she did not even remotely resist, his eyes meeting hers squarely—a question, a challenge, a *mistake,* then captured her lips with his.

Acknowledgments

First, I need to thank the wonderful women in my writers' group, who encouraged, cajoled, supported, counseled, brainstormed, pushed, pulled, and generally compelled me to be my best at every turn in the writing of this book. (Actually, make that nearly *every* book I've written.) Marsha Nuccio, Mary Blayney, and Lavinia Klein—I don't know what I would do without you.

Thanks, also, to Rick Hubbell for the shower test—among other fascinating glimpses into the male psyche—to David Voorhies for his pottery expertise, and to Finch for introducing me to the bizarre world of little dogs.

Chapter 1

Penelope Porter pulled her car up in front of her ex-husband's house.

Her friends were going to kill her. Her family might disown her. Her father, in particular, would call her the worst kind of fool. But they would all, she knew, come around in the end.

Once she and Glenn had gotten back together.

Her heart pounded and her palms were damp as she ran them back and forth over the top of the steering wheel, looking toward the glowing windows of the house.

Only one window on the first floor shone with light, and none on the second floor.

Penelope grabbed her purse off the seat beside her

and rummaged inside until she found her brush. Running it through her hair, she practiced: *Glenn, I was driving by, saw the lights on and thought I'd stop by. I haven't been in the house for so long—I wanted to see if you kept the yellow kitchen.*

With that she would smile her gentlest smile, recalling with him how they'd argued about the color. He'd wanted red—claiming that restaurants were always red—but all her life she'd had a yellow kitchen. She even had one now. She'd finally managed to win that long-ago battle by saying yellow put her in an amorous mood more than any other color in the spectrum. He hadn't believed her, but he *had* laughed as he'd conceded and told her she'd be called upon to prove it once the painting was complete.

She had. That part of their life together had been good, at least in the beginning.

Penelope plopped the brush back into her purse and looked resolutely at the house. First she'd have to make sure he didn't have any company. Then she could implement her plan.

She got out of the car, closing the door with a push instead of a slam—just in case—and walked across the lawn. The air was warm, fallen leaves still few and far between this early in October.

The curtains on the front window were drawn, but there was a gap that she'd be able to see through if she could get in close. It would require pushing past the bushes, but that was okay. She had dressed carefully, wearing jeans and a light sweater with her brand-new boots. She could wrestle with a bush or two without coming out the worse for wear.

She hefted her purse up higher on her shoulder with one hand while holding branches back with the other. The bushes only came to about her waist, but a few ragged stems protruded and what was low was thick. Glad of the darkness, for fear of neighbors thinking she was an intruder, she peered through the window into the lit room where Glenn sat—alone—in a recliner, a remote control resting in one hand on his thigh.

She sighed and watched him a moment. Was he lonely? His curly hair was mussed, but he still wore his suit pants and button-down shirt from work, though the tie was gone and the collar open at the neck. Underneath she could see his white tee-shirt. He hated wearing shirts without a tee-shirt underneath because he loathed the way some men got sweat stains in their armpits.

Or was it she who had hated that? In any case, he still wore the undershirt.

She smiled to herself, turned to push back out of the bushes and dropped her keys. She heard them hit the ground with a soft *clink* and backed up a step. The stacked heel of her brand-new boots hit something solid and her car horn blasted to life, jarring as a marching band in a library.

She jumped and spun on her heel, looking down into the brush at her feet. She'd obviously stepped on the panic button and there was no stopping the damn thing until she could find her key fob and hit it again.

As the horn honked over and over and over, head- and taillights flashing in time with the noise, Penelope struggled not to panic.

"*Noooo*," she wailed, her voice—now needlessly—quiet. "No no no no no."

She squatted in the bushes, hands scrabbling in the mulch. Nothing. She rose up and stomped around with her boots again, reasoning if she'd turned it on that way the reverse could work too. But they were nowhere.

What if she'd buried them when she'd stepped on them? She bent down again, digging under the branches, dirt shoving up her fingernails and azalea branches catching at her hair. She'd *planted* these damn bushes, she thought. Why had he let them get so big?

A minute later, the worst happened. From her position near the ground she saw light spill across the front porch.

Glenn had opened the door.

Staying low, her fingers crawling through the mulch like spiders, she kept her eyes trained on his feet. He'd never see her here.

But then, he *would* see her car. Her silver Mercedes Benz C-Class sport sedan—not altogether common—flashing like a UFO directly in front of the house.

Dammit.

Still, he *might* think it belonged to somebody else, especially if she could find her keys and get the damn thing turned off. Her fingers continued to sift through the dirt around her feet.

Glenn's legs stepped out onto the porch. She could tell from the way his feet moved that he was looking up and down the street. He thought it was her car, she just knew it.

Did she come out now and confess? Or did she wait and hope he went back inside? Who came outside to investigate a car alarm, anyway? They went off all the time. A nuisance, mostly.

On the other hand, this was a quiet neighborhood, and the neighbors might come out soon too.

But how could she reveal herself? What reason could she possibly have for being in the bushes, other than that she'd been looking at him through the window?

She had the truth—which was not so awful, she told herself. He'd understand that she had not wanted to interrupt if he had company, and they could laugh about it later.

With a deep breath, she rose and backed out of the bushes.

"Penelope?" His voice was incredulous. And loud.

It had to be, over the noise the car was making.

She looked up as if she hadn't seen him there. "Oh! Glenn! Hi." She gave him her brightest smile. Not that he could necessarily see it in the dim light.

"*What on earth are you doing?* Shut that thing off, will you?"

Okay, this was not the best start.

She brushed her long hair back from her shoulders, pulled a small twig from near her ear, and tried to remain upbeat.

"I can't. I was just about to knock on your door, but I dropped my keys and—and the panic button got pushed and then—then all hell broke loose." She threw a hand toward the car with a laugh.

"How did you drop your keys *in the bushes*?"

She laughed again; her nervous laugh. "I don't know exactly. You know how that happens sometimes, you drop something and somehow it goes really far—"

He stomped down the steps and moved around her, diving into the bushes himself. A second later he emerged with the keys, handing them to her like they were a piece of dirty laundry she'd left behind.

She grabbed the fob, hit the panic button and dropped her hands by her sides.

"I'm sorry," she said into the reverberating silence. "Really, I didn't mean to be so intrusive."

He looked at her suspiciously as he ran a hand

through his hair. His shirt came partly untucked with the motion.

"What are you doing here, Penelope?"

"Um. Well, I was just in the neighborhood and thought I'd stop by. I saw your lights were on and . . . am I interrupting anything?"

Glenn looked at her a long moment. "No. But you probably already knew that."

It was on the tip of her tongue to say something about scouting for company, but it suddenly sounded weird to her, so she let it pass.

"It's just that I haven't seen the house for so long." She gazed up at the façade, smiling as confidently as she could. "It's looking good. Is the kitchen still yellow?"

He looked at her as if she were nuts. "The kitchen? No, it's white. Why?"

Her smile faltered. "Um, okay. Well, uh, can I come in?"

He hesitated.

"Just for a minute?" She put her hands in her jeans pockets, hunching her shoulders against some imaginary cold.

"I guess. For a minute. It's kind of a mess." He turned for the stairs, rubbing a hand along the back of his neck.

If she'd thought the place would look as it had when they'd been together she was dead wrong. It was nothing like it had been. The furniture—what there was of it—was worn and masculine. There was the recliner—blue, ripped at the right arm—a couple of narrow armchairs with flat seat cushions and a small table between them. Spots marred the off-white wall-to-wall carpeting that now covered her carefully tended hardwood, and the vague outline of several now-absent pictures could be made out against the dimming white paint. The largest piece of furniture in the room was a flat-screen TV, sitting on what looked like a computer cart.

Suddenly she didn't want to see the kitchen.

"So Glenn. I was thinking about, well, I was *hoping* that we could, or that you'd *want* to—" She interrupted herself with another nervous laugh as he turned to look at her. "Sorry, I'm really botching this up."

"Botching what up?" His arms were crossed over his chest. He did not sit down.

For no reason at all she noted that he'd put on a little bit of a belly. It looked strange on his tall frame.

"Well, I wanted to ask if we could get together sometime," she forced out. "Just to, you know, catch up."

His eyes moved over her face but he was otherwise motionless.

"Pen, last time we 'got together' you told me I was the biggest mistake of your life and you were glad I was out of it."

"I—I know, I'm s—"

"And I'm thinking I don't need a repeat of that. I mean, I get it. I'm a shit. I did you wrong. I ruined your life." He cleared his throat and added, "So was there something else you wanted to talk about, or can we just leave it at that?"

He was right. She *had* said all those things. And she'd said them right after he'd told her he loved her, that he'd never *stopped* loving her.

The trouble was, she hadn't been ready to listen. Not then. Then she still had not gotten over all he'd done. How he'd gotten married three months after their divorce.

How he'd had a child with *her*, the new woman. Abigail. Even though he'd refused to have one with Penelope.

How he'd come back to Penelope only after the other woman had left him.

But he was hurting now, she could see that. Despite everything, she wanted to make him feel better.

"Actually, yes, there is something more I wanted to talk about." She straightened her spine. "I'm sorry I was so, uh, *harsh*, at our last meeting. There were reasons. I wasn't ready to hear you. I was . . . surprised by you, by everything you said. Probably a lot like you are with me now." She chuckled awkwardly.

Glenn was silent, but she thought his expression had grown softer.

"I appreciate that," he said finally.

She exhaled.

"So can we get together?" Her hands gripped her purse at her side and she forcibly relaxed them. "You know? Catch up?"

"Penelope, we're together now. Why don't you just tell me what's up?"

He moved to the recliner he'd been in when she'd looked through the window and sat down with a huff.

She tried to gather her thoughts, but she had a hard time getting past the fact that he hadn't asked her to sit down. He just sat there like a judge before a defendant.

"Penelope, I know you. I know how you are. We don't need to try to be friends, if that's what you're thinking. We don't have to play the annual catch-up game so you don't feel like you've been mean, or irresponsible, or whatever."

"I don't feel irresponsible, Glenn. I'm not doing this because I feel *guilty* about anything. I was just thinking about our last meeting. About what we talked about. And I'm sorry I closed the door so firmly that day. I . . . I would like to talk about it now. I mean, you know, not *here*. But soon. If you want to, that is. Still."

He frowned, eyebrows drawing together over skeptical blue eyes. "Are you talking about the meeting where I put my heart on the table and you shoved it back down my throat?"

"Okay, I suppose I deserve that. But, for me, I'm talking about the meeting where you made a suggestion that I was not sufficiently over our history to consider."

There, she thought. That said it. Maybe things could be different this time around, because *she* was different. She was stronger. Smarter.

"Are you 'over' our history now?" His brows rose.

"I believe so." She made an effort to maintain eye contact. "Would you like to come over for dinner?"

That clearly took him by surprise. "Dinner? At your house?"

"Yes. Dinner, at my house. I'll cook."

"When?" He asked the question as if she'd informed him of a murder he hadn't known about.

"Friday night?" Inexplicably, Penelope's confidence had returned. Keeping Glenn off balance seemed to be good for her. She hadn't planned on dinner, but once the invitation was out it seemed like an excellent idea. Dinner, on her turf. She was a good cook.

"I, uh, I'll have to get back to you on that," he said slowly. One palm rubbed along the side of his pants, as if his hands had gone sweaty. "I was supposed to babysit that night, but Abigail said something about wanting to switch week-ends with me. I can let you know tomorrow." He looked back up at her.

Babysit.

She ignored the emotional speed bump and smiled. "Okay. Let me know."

"Okay. Well, uh, thanks. I guess."

"You're welcome." She turned and took a few steps toward the door, knowing full well her butt looked fabulous in these jeans. "I'll talk to you tomorrow then."

"Yeah, sure, tomorrow."

He watched her go, she could feel his eyes on her, so she turned at the door and flashed him a smile, swinging her hair just a little more than necessary, and stepped out into the balmy fall night.

Victory, from the jaws of defeat, she thought, practically skipping down the walk to her car. Now all she had to do was plan the perfect menu, and she'd be on her way.

"Pen, you've got to give this little guy a name," Lily Tyler said as the puppy squirmed in her hands. "He's like a giant cotton ball!"

"I know," Penelope said, smiling into the dog's bearded face. "But I just can't find the one that fits. Griffin?" She leaned toward the brown-and-white fuzz ball. "Jiminy? Scout? He doesn't respond to anything."

"Of course he doesn't." Georgia used one hand

to pull her curly blonde hair behind her head in the fall breeze. "He doesn't know it's his name yet. You've gotta drill it into his head like a mantra. He's a male, you know. It's gonna take some time."

"Wimbledon responded right off the bat to his name," Pen said, remembering her late Labrador wistfully. He had died, far too young, of cancer the previous June.

"So did Peyton." Megan, the veterinarian, nodded.

"What kind is he again?" Lily asked.

"A Havanese. From Havana. Cuba. Well, not him. But the breed," Penelope explained.

"Maybe you should call him Fidel," Georgia said. "Or Castro."

"I am not naming this little innocent puppy Castro!" Penelope laughed.

The four of them sat at the picnic table at the dog park, a warm breeze blowing leaves and the occasional bit of trash across the open space. Lily's French bulldog, Doug, pursued every blustering thing maniacally.

Penelope's puppy—Chopin? Sunday? Heck, *Fluffy*?—watched intently with his birdlike eyes, but did not chase anything even though Lily had placed him back on the ground near Penelope's feet. He was intimidated, Pen thought, by the bigger dogs.

Lily leaned her back against the table, watching her dog run in the enclosed space.

"You look so happy, Lily." Penelope gazed at her friend's contented face. "Like you're enveloped in a cloud of peace."

Lily glanced over at her, startled. "Do I? A cloud of peace? I mostly feel enveloped in dog hair at the moment. I was just thinking I should have worn a different shirt." Laughing, she brushed at the front of her black shirt, where a sprinkling of white Doug-hairs lay.

"I think it's the engagement." Penelope smiled.

No hard feelings, the smile said. No unhappiness here, that they had in fact tried to set up Lily's fiancé with *her*, Penelope, first, only to have Lily fall for him. And he for her. No frustration that once again it had been one of Penelope's friends—nearly the last single one she had, other than Georgia, who, it had to be admitted, was a committed floozy—who had found her soul mate and was getting married.

And she *wasn't* bitter, not about Lily. She was thrilled for her and even knew that Brady would never have been the right man for herself. But still . . . it would be nice if the lightning bolt would strike her, too.

"You've got the Brady glow," Penelope added.

Lily, predictably, snorted. "Wouldn't he love to hear that."

"No, I think she's right," Megan said. "You are glowing."

"Maybe it's just the reflection offa that *rock*."

Georgia raised a brow at Lily's enormous diamond ring. "Every time I look at that thing I get an urge to find my ice skates."

Lily tried to suppress a smile, failed, and looked down at her hand. "I have to admit I am pretty happy."

Penelope sighed, apparently loudly because all three of them turned to look at her.

Lily's face was concerned. "You know, I was thinking about setting you up with Brady's brother, Penelope. He's such a nice guy and *so* handsome."

"The TV guy?" Megan asked.

"He *wrote* for TV, but now he's doing books," Lily explained. She turned back to Penelope. "But he's really into this psychologist woman. If I didn't like her so much, I'd introduce you anyway, but I've got to say, I think they're in it for the long haul." She scrunched her face wryly.

"No, no." Penelope waved a hand and laughed. "It's clear I'm not destined to have any of the men in that family. They are too well situated where they are."

If she were ever going to tell them about her impending dinner with Glenn, now would be the time. But she had no desire to see their shocked faces and be the victim of their strained optimism on her behalf. Strained, because she knew that every last one of them would think it was a colossally bad idea to initiate anything with her ex-husband.

They'd spent years hating him for her. Or rather, *with* her.

Truth to tell, getting together with Glenn did feel a little like leftovers in place of a gourmet meal when she looked at Megan and Lily and how happy they were with their men. Not that they hadn't had gone through a trial or two getting together with them, initially, but neither of them had had to recycle an old boyfriend—let alone husband—just to come up with a date.

Their freshness would wear off too, though—she knew. She and Glenn had had all the wonderful glowy times themselves; they'd just been fifteen years ago . . .

"Hey, have you started that book I gave you?" Lily asked.

"*Pride and Prejudice*?" Penelope stalled. It was sitting on her bedside table, looking thick, small-printed, and very much like a textbook. "I, uh . . . not yet. I'm waiting until I have a good, long stretch of time. To give it my undivided attention, you know."

Lily smiled knowingly. She taught a college course on Jane Austen so she'd probably heard every excuse ever invented. "Just read the first chapter. If you're not hooked after that, you can give it back. Not that you couldn't give it back anyway, but . . ."

"No, no. I will, I'll read it, I promise."

"You'll love it. It's just like—"

"Sweet mother of all things sweaty," Georgia interrupted, rising from her seat at the picnic table and shading her eyes with a hand to look toward the canal path. Standing, the Great Dane tee-shirt she wore was clearly visible—head and front legs on the front, back legs, butt and tail on the back. Georgia was never caught without some article of dog-related clothing on. To this she added Great Dane earrings, watch, socks and a Great Dane silk-screened bag.

Penelope, Megan, and Lily looked toward the path too.

"That's a torso I don't recognize at all." Georgia reached up and removed the ponytail holder from her hair. "And I recognize all the chests worth knowing in this town. Any of you know who that is?"

"For heaven's sake, Georgia," Penelope said, "it could be anyone. This town's growing by thousands probably every day. He could even be a student at the college. Try to control yourself."

Penelope met Lily's rolling eyes and the two of them laughed. "As if that's ever an option," Lily said.

"That's no student." Megan squinted her eyes in the guy's direction as he jogged up the path next to the fenced-in dog park. "He's older than that. Thirty, maybe, I'd say."

"I agree," Georgia concurred. "You've just got

blinders on, Pen, if you don't think that's a new face worth gettin' to know. Look at those abs. I'd put him at about thirty-two, which is just the right age for a guy, if you ask me."

It was true: The guy jogging by did have a nice, carved abdomen and well-muscled legs, even though he was lanky. And Penelope liked the way his dark blond hair shone in the sun. So many guys didn't know how to keep their hair clean. He was tall, too, which she preferred.

But he was bare-chested where a gentleman would have been wearing a tee-shirt, and that hair, lovely as it was, was a shade too long. Plus he was too young.

It didn't matter anyway. Georgia was on him like a hawk on a mouse.

"Hello there!" she called, waltzing across the dog park toward the adjacent path, waving her hand in the air as her blonde curls bounced in the breeze. Beside her loped her gunmetal gray Great Dane, Sage. "Excuse me! Hello?"

The guy glanced her way, then slowed to a halt and bent over at the waist, breathing heavily.

"Ooh, he's panting. Georgia will like that." Megan laughed.

After a second, he straightened up, and though the girls were too far away to hear the conversation, Penelope could easily read the expression of confusion, then amusement on the guy's face.

Georgia must have introduced herself, because they shook hands and a moment later Georgia was sweeping an arm in their direction. The guy glanced at them and inclined his head. Penelope gave a small, half-embarrassed wave that she cut off mid-gesture when she realized neither Megan nor Lily was doing it.

After a minute the fellow took off jogging again and Georgia returned.

"Mercy, mercy me," she said.

She might as well have been licking her chops, Penelope thought.

"Who was it?" Megan asked.

"His name's Mercy, Dylan Mercy, and you were right, he wasn't a student." Georgia swung one leg over the bench seat and sat back down, straddling it. "And he's not a boy, either, though he might be young. He's got a look in his eyes that I like."

"Lust?" Penelope asked.

"Prude." Georgia shot her a grin.

"That's Dylan Mersey?" Megan said. "I should have recognized him."

"You know him?" Georgia asked.

Megan shook her head. "I've only met him once. He's one of Sutter's grant recipients. He's opening a shop in town."

Georgia put her hair back up in a ponytail. "Then you know the look I'm talkin' about, like he's lived some life. That one ain't no babe in the woods."

"You mean he looked like he could handle the indomitable Georgia Darling?" Lily asked.

Georgia shook her head, gazing down the path where "Mercy" had disappeared. Her expression was an uncharacteristic mix of preoccupation and doubt. "Honey, he could handle me anytime he wanted. The question is, could I handle him?"

Chapter 2

Dylan Mersey was accidentally drunk.

He knew how it had happened, but still, it had crept up on him. One minute he'd been setting up his brand-spanking-new shop, the next an old friend—now more of an old associate, really—had stopped by. Then the *next* thing he knew he was balanced on a bar stool doing shots of Don Eduardo tequila.

"What's with this place, man?" Pinky McGann was a belligerent drunk, and despite his own fog, Dylan could see it beginning. Pinky's eyes sharpened and his lips thinned, and Dylan knew that if he didn't get out of there soon, he'd risk being on the receiving end of Pinky's four-fingered fist.

To be fair, Pinky had come by his belligerence honestly. He'd lost the little finger on his right hand in a skateboarding accident when he was eleven and he'd been called "Pinky" ever since. It was a name he hated, and it had added to his toughness over the years.

"You could swing a dozen dead cats around here and not hit any chicks worth looking at. I mean, look around. This place is Deadsville."

"*Deadsville*?" Dylan snorted. "You been hanging out with my mom, Pink? You sound like a hippy."

"Hey, your old lady's all right. Not when she's pullin' a drunk, though." Pinky shook his head, shot back more tequila and sat back on the bar stool.

Dylan winced at Pinky's words, despite—or maybe because of—the truth in them. That was Pinky. Never anything but up-front and out there with the truth. Or at least his version of it.

Pinky was a fireplug, but a well-dressed one. Ever since he'd gotten hooked up with Junior Smith, the Lord of Hot Rocks, in their old neighborhood, Pinky'd been GQ-ing it all over Baltimore. Puttin' the charm back in Charm City, Pinky said. How he'd found Dylan in Fredericksburg was no mystery, however. Dylan's mother got downright chatty when she was drunk. She wasn't exactly a closed book when she was sober, either.

"You gonna be okay out here? I mean this is

positively BFE, man." Pinky swept his eyes up and down Dylan's long, disheveled frame, from his Converse high-tops to his shaggy blond head.

"BFE?" Dylan worked hard to keep his vision straight. He concentrated on the gap between Pinky's front teeth.

"Bum-fucked Egypt, man. I don't know how you even found this town. What did you do, stop for gas and get carjacked?"

"It's . . ." Dylan shrugged. It was nothing he could explain to Pinky, even if he could have accessed all of his vocabulary. "Foley Foundation grant" was *way* beyond his speaking abilities right now. "I'll be all right. I'm good, man. I'm trying something new. A fresh start, you might say."

Pinky fished around in his pocket for his keys. "Fresh start, huh? Sure, I get it. That's cool. You had enough a' takin' care of Sara and she's better off without you anyway."

Dylan laughed once. "That is true."

Without doing anything Dylan made his mother feel guilty for being a drunk. The more guilty she felt, the more she drank, which caused more guilt, then more drink, all of it spiraling together into more and more frustration and anger in Dylan. It was a vicious cycle, and had made his living in her house in Baltimore "to take care of her" a farce.

Dylan followed Pinky from the bar, marveling at how steady his old friend was, while he was having to consciously put one foot in front of the other. Conditioning, he figured. Pinky was master of the drink. Master of virtually any mind-altering substance, and Dylan was out of practice. Intentionally.

It was one reason Dylan had not been happy to see him. Unexpected things happened around Pinky. None of them good.

Pinky had been a friend in the life he'd led long ago growing up in Baltimore, and for better or worse, they were linked for this lifetime. Blood brothers, whether Dylan wanted it or not.

The fact that Pinky had done him a huge favor when he was in a tight spot didn't make it any easier for Dylan to get away from the relationship.

"Listen, man, it's good you're here," Pinky said as they peeled out of their parking spot on William Street.

Dylan's head bounced on the headrest with the car's momentum. If he died as a result of Pinky's drunken driving, the irony of his life would be complete. Dylan considered saying something about slowing down but knew it would only make Pinky worse. He might wrap his car around a telephone pole just to prove he wasn't afraid of it happening.

"I got something I might need you to do," Pinky continued. "Call it a favor."

His brittle eyes shifted to Dylan, making sure Dylan caught his meaning. Dylan did, with a chill down his spine. He owed Pinky. And Pinky was too smart not to collect.

"Sure," was all Dylan could manage. He hoped to God it was at least something he could do back home in Baltimore. He didn't want to stain his new life here by reprising the old role he was so desperately trying to get rid of.

"I'll let you know when it goes down, but be ready, okay? Might be me, might be someone I send you, got it? I think it's gonna work out good you're here."

Dylan clenched his teeth, suddenly sober. It was something he had to do here. Something for which being in Virginia was better for Pinky. Guns, he was betting. Maybe stolen goods.

Dylan's tone was flat. "Got it."

Pinky dropped him off in front of his shop on Caroline Street.

"Here's hoping your fresh start don't go stale," he called out his tinted window with a wicked gap-toothed grin. Then he did a "California crawl"— Dylan's old signature move—throwing the car into reverse, flooring it, then slamming it into drive so hard and fast it left a pair of check marks on the pavement in front of Dylan's new storefront.

Watching it Dylan promptly lost his balance and fell to his ass on the sidewalk as the car's taillights disappeared down the street.

Stunned, he sat for a moment, hating the dizzy,

dreamlike feeling the tequila had produced. He lay back on the sidewalk and felt his jeans pockets. The front, the back, even his breast pocket—which didn't exist because he was wearing a tee-shirt— no keys. He sat back up, pushed himself to his feet, and staggered over to the door of his shop.

Pressing his face against the glass he gazed inside. Boxes, shelves, counters left over from the previous shop, and his potting wheel were the large, obvious objects in the small space. Balled-up newspapers, broken wallboard, and cans of paint were scattered around those things. He could not see his keys, but he knew they were in there.

Then something caught his eye. He tilted his head back, rubbed and then blinked his eyes several times before looking back in. He had not been mistaken. An animal, about the size of a cat, sniffed around the floor near the forward counter. But it wasn't a cat. It was either a guinea pig or a small dog. Neither of which he owned.

Where had it come from? Was he dreaming? Another look confirmed he was not.

How the *hell* did it get in there when he couldn't?

And was there any chance it would retrieve his keys?

Penelope jumped, dropping her pen, and her gaze jerked to the front window of her shop at the sound of squealing tires. She caught sight of a large black car with tinted windows rocketing down the street and a man being hurled to the ground in its wake. Her skin prickled.

Had he been hurt? Penelope panicked. Maybe he'd been shot. Or stabbed. Before she could react, he pushed himself up onto his knees, then to his feet, and walked crookedly toward the closest door—the shop directly across from Penelope's. Once there he paused, and then tried the door.

It was locked, of course. The place had been empty for months, ever since the wine shop had folded.

He appeared unhurt, she was relieved to see, but whether he'd been thrown from the car or just knocked over by it, he'd obviously been the reason for the driver's action.

She headed for the door—she could help the poor man—then froze when she saw him kneel in what looked like an attempt to fiddle with the lock.

Was he trying to break in? She had never witnessed a crime before. She stepped away from the door. With all the lights on, her place was a fishbowl and she was the fish. Eyes on the intruder, she felt her way backward to the light switches on the rear wall and turned them off. The darkness was a relief. He hadn't turned around, hadn't seen her, so she moved back toward the register and the phone at the front. The dial tone was loud in the silent shop, not least because she'd half expected it to be dead, like in every horror movie she'd ever seen.

Which was ridiculous, considering the guy wasn't even trying to break in to *her* place. Still, her heart was hammering.

She dialed the police.

Okay, so Pinky hadn't had to twist his arm to get him drunk, but Dylan blamed him anyway. Dylan drank with him just to shut him up, or shut him out. All he'd accomplished, though, was to lock himself out of his own damn shop. Barred from his own Fresh Start. It would be funny in the morning.

He glanced at his wrist, where his watch wasn't. He'd lost it, he remembered. Somewhere between Baltimore and Fredericksburg, between squalor and succor, between past and present.

He put his hands on his hips and looked up and down the street. Why were there no pay phones anymore? Did everyone in the world have cell phones? Dylan did. Somewhere. Probably with his watch.

A flash of something drew his gaze across the street. Something in the shop across the street. If it was another guinea pig he was giving up. But no, closer inspection told him someone was in there. He distinctly saw a figure moving behind the darkened window.

"Pen Perfect," he read from the sign. A *pen store*?

The rent must have been a helluva lot cheaper than his if they were surviving on selling pens. He squinted and moved closer. Yep, somebody was definitely in there.

He walked in as straight a line as he could muster to the door. Once there he knocked and pressed his face close to the glass to look inside.

"I've called the police!" a female voice yelled.

He jerked back. Was she talking to him? He couldn't see anybody inside, but the voice had definitely come from there.

"Hello?" he called back. "Is somebody in there? I just want to borrow the phone."

Silence. Then, "Tell the police!"

He twisted on the sidewalk and looked around, adrenaline shooting through his veins, counteracting at least some of the tequila. "Shit."

He had to get out of there. His Fresh Start was going to hell in a hurry. He had figured the police would find him eventually, but his first full week in town was too soon. Way too soon.

He turned away from the pen store and strode down the sidewalk. He thought he was moving pretty soberly—*thank you, panic*—when his toe caught on an uneven joint and he pitched forward. His hands shot out in front of him but they didn't stop his chin from hitting the ground and the wind from getting knocked out of him.

For a second, he saw stars.

"*Damn* it," he gasped, sitting up. He looked at his palms and moved his fingers gingerly over the scraped heel of his left hand. It was dark, but he saw blood. "Shit."

He was sobering up rapidly, vowing never to drink again as he did.

A moment later, the flashing cherry top of a police car turned onto Caroline Street and pulled up with a muscular mechanical growl in front of *Pen Perfect*. Dylan stood, aware that escape was impossible now. The cops had obviously caught sight of him. As the two exited the squad car in unison, one of them walked up the sidewalk toward him while the other greeted a woman who opened the door Dylan had just knocked on.

The approaching officer's hand was on his gun, his stride confident but slow, as if trying to trick a stray dog into submission.

"Sir, can I see some identification?" The cop's voice did not inflect this as a question.

Dylan tried to keep from sounding sarcastic. "Is something wrong, officer?"

"I'd just like to see your identification," the cop reiterated.

"If you're wondering why I knocked on that door, I only wanted to use the phone," Dylan said, wondering for the first time who he thought he'd call. A locksmith? The landlord? What time was it? He looked at his bare wrist again.

"We've had a complaint." The cop was upon him now, larger than life in his uniform with belt and badge and bullets and bluster.

Dylan wasn't a short man, but he was lean where the officer was thick. Add to that the super-hero accessories, and the policeman radiated aggression.

"Look, I only knocked on the door. Is that a crime?" He knew he should shut up, just give the guy his wallet, but this was America, damn it. You couldn't just walk up to someone on the street and demand to see their papers.

No matter what their past was.

He touched his stinging chin and his fingers came away sticky with blood. Great.

The cop's expression turned smug. "We have a witness who saw you attempting to break into a building."

Dylan started to laugh. So that was it. He'd spooked a little old lady and these guys were going to play savior.

"Oh yeah? What shop was that? The one right there?" Dylan pointed to his storefront. "*My* shop? Is that the one you mean?"

Behind Officer Large the partner cop approached. A dark-haired woman stood in her doorway peering at them down the sidewalk. She didn't look like a little old lady. In fact, she looked like a model. Long, dark hair, the kind seen only in shampoo commercials, fell past slim shoulders and along a trim torso held erect as a ballet dancer's. She wore a dress that clung to her curves and was the color of peacocks—deep blues and greens, mixed like a watercolor.

She was, he thought slowly, the most beautiful woman he'd ever seen.

Even if she *had* just called the cops on him.

"Good evening, sir," the second cop said pleasantly.

"Ah." Dylan jerked his eyes from the woman. His lips twisted. "The Good Cop."

Officer Large scowled and glanced at his partner. "Says he owns that shop."

Good Cop smiled. "Have you got any identification, sir?"

"What, do they only give you guys one script?" Dylan asked. "Or is there someone behind you pulling a string out of your back? Because that's all Officer Friendly here's been saying too. Last time I checked, though, this was America, and it's not a crime to be walking down a street, or even breaking into your own place."

Idiot. This was why he gave up alcohol. It made him stupid.

Dylan knew in that deep, dark place inside that he was making another uncomfortable bed for himself and he was going to have to lie in it. But he was pissed. Between Pinky and now these guys, he seemed doomed to live the same life no matter where he went.

Good Cop's eyes narrowed. He was definitely the one in charge. "Sir, have you had anything to drink?"

Dylan laughed. "You mean tonight? Or ever? Because—"

"I'm afraid I'm going to have to ask you to come with us." Good Cop folded his arms across his chest, his stance wide, his face implacable with the knowledge that he held all the cards and was making up the game to boot.

The other cop went for his cuffs and Dylan sighed. He should go quietly. Things would go more smoothly if he just went and cleared the whole damn matter up. They might even help him get into his place. The apartment upstairs was accessible only from the shop. He could be home and in bed by midnight.

Instead, he said, "Well, you can ask, Officer, but I don't normally go home with guys I just met."

"I've called the SPCA every hour," Penelope, on the verge of tears, wailed into the phone to her friend Megan. "I've talked to Evan and Nancy and Linda, who all own stores nearby, and none of them has seen anything. I've made up flyers that I'm going to have Lucy distribute when she comes in. I just don't know what else to do! He's disappeared completely and I don't even know how he got out of the car! Megan, I swear, I have never been this irresponsible, ever."

"It's not irresponsible, Pen. Dogs get loose. They run off. He'll turn up, mark my words." Megan Rose, the veterinarian, had presumably heard it all when it came to pets. "I'll put a notice up here, and I'll call the other animal hospitals. Someone will find him."

"But he's just a puppy." Penelope slumped onto the stool behind her counter and put her forehead in her hand. "He's so cute. If anyone finds him they'll just keep him."

"He was wearing a collar, wasn't he?"

Penelope sniffed as a tear dropped onto the countertop. "A collar, yes. But no tag. I hadn't gotten him one yet. I haven't even given him a name, and he's so little, I thought it would be too big for him. What an idiot."

"You just got him. You're not an idiot," Megan said calmly.

"This just proves I'd be a *terrible* mother. What if he'd been a baby? This is why Fate has made sure I'll never have a child."

"Penelope!" Megan protested, laughing. "You're really going overboard here. There's no way you'd have lost a baby."

"What's the difference?" Penelope argued, knowing she should not get into the baby thing, not now, not while her heart was racing with fear. A heart could not simultaneously take breaking and racing without exploding. "A baby, a puppy, they're both helpless beings depending on me to take care of them. And I've proven I'm not up to the task."

"The difference is," Megan, mother of a two-year-old, said sagely, "for one thing, if you put an eight-week-old baby down, it stays where you put it. Puppies are much harder to keep track of."

"Maybe." She took a deep breath. She would *not* make this about parenting. She would not tie this to the fact that all she'd ever wanted was a child and it was becoming increasingly clear she'd never have one.

"Besides, I think someone must have taken him." Penelope clenched her hands together, if only to think about something other than her failures. Better to think about bone and sinew and nails biting into palms. "He was *in the car.* How could he have gotten out of the car by himself? Somebody had to have opened up the door and grabbed him."

Penelope sat up straight. Anger felt better than dejection.

Megan sighed over the line. "I don't know. Puppies do amazing things. I once saw one climb drapes to hide on top of the window valance. Another time I treated one for squeezing through the narrowest of wrought-iron balconies and falling to the patio. He was fine, by the way. Oh, and there was another one that got its head stuck between the slats of an antique Stickley chair and had to be cut out. The dog was fine but the owners were heartbroken over the chair." Megan inhaled. "I could go on and on, Pen. This was not your fault. Did you . . . uh, I guess you didn't have him in a crate."

Penelope could hear the cringe in Megan's voice as she realized she shouldn't have asked the question.

"No," Penelope groaned. "I hadn't gotten one for the car yet. I didn't expect to get a puppy this soon after losing Wimbledon. I meant to go to Petsmart tonight but I had so much work to do, and Wimbledon's old one was too big. Why did I wait so long? I'm such a fool!"

"Penelope stop. These things happen, I keep telling you. It's been a long time since you've had a puppy."

"I was about to leave," Penelope explained, having already been through it in her head a hundred times. "I thought he could be in the car for *five minutes*, five minutes where I wasn't chasing him down to keep him from chewing electrical cords or furniture or merchandise. So I put him in the car to finish my paperwork, but then I saw that guy, that stupid, drunken jerk who's moved in across the street and I got distracted. It's all *his* fault."

Penelope put her head back in her hand, knowing it was not really the new guy's fault but mad at him anyway. He was going to be trouble, she could already tell. He was a drunk with rude friends who left skid marks in the road. What more did she need to know?

Later she planned to talk to Carson, one of the cops who'd come to check out the disturbance the night before, and whom she'd known since she'd moved to town years ago. When she'd moved here with Glenn, young and in love and full of hope . . .

She shook her head. Carson would tell her the truth about the guy. In the meantime, she could not help but think the worst.

"Pen? Shoot, I have to go," Megan said. "I've got an emergency."

Pen gasped. "Is it—?"

"No, it's not a puppy." Megan chuckled slightly. "But I'll call you later, tell you if I've found anything out. He'll turn up. Stop beating yourself up!"

Penelope sniffed. "Okay. I'll call you later."

She hung up the phone and looked anxiously out the window for Lucy, her part-time helper. She said she'd be there by noon to help distribute the flyers, and it was quarter after. In addition to being irritated, Penelope was worried it was too late. The puppy had been gone for over twelve hours. He'd either gotten hit by a car or somebody had decided to keep him.

She ran her fingers back through her hair and closed her eyes. She was a wreck. After being up all night scouring the neighborhood herself, she was tired and scared and cranky.

She hadn't even named the puppy yet! She'd had him all of two days, her cute little cloud of a boy. He was feisty and smart, and was going to be a great companion, but now he was gone. Stolen, it had to be.

She bent to retrieve the tissues stashed underneath the cash register when she heard the door chimes ring. Thank *God*, Lucy had finally arrived.

"You're here!" she said, straightening and wiping her eyes, only to see the lanky, blond guy who'd been jogging the day before on the path. It took her two seconds to put together that he was also the guy who'd started all the trouble the night before. The drunken guy from across the street. "Oh, it's you." She didn't even try to disguise the disappointment in her voice.

He looked vaguely surprised, glanced behind himself as if she might have meant someone else, then said, "Yeah, uh, I wanted to apologize about last night. I was—"

"Fine," she said, dabbing at her eyes. "Please don't bother explaining. Now if you'll excuse me I'm in the middle of a crisis."

In his hands, he held a rolled-up piece of paper. "Okay."

His eyes looked wary. Eyes the color of autumn oak leaves, she noted. Light brown, with dark blond. But who cared.

"I just wondered if I could put this in your window." He raised the paper in his hand. "It's a—"

Lucy came through the door behind him, startling him. He turned.

"Lucy! Thank God you're here," Penelope breathed. She glanced at the blond guy again. "I don't think I can help you, Mr. . . ."

"Mersey. Dylan Mersey. It's just that—"

"That's right. Mersey. As I just said, I'm in the middle of a crisis that I really need to deal with." She gave him an exasperated look—did he have no situational awareness at *all*?—picked up her flyers from the shelf behind her, and put them on the counter.

Lucy stood just inside the door, glancing from Penelope to Dylan Mersey and back again. She was a cute girl, just out of high school, with shoulder-length dark hair and wide blue eyes. She looked shocked by Penelope's rudeness.

Dylan Mersey frowned but didn't leave. "I'm sorry. Is there anything—"

"*Please*, I don't have time for you right now. And haven't you caused me enough trouble for one twenty-four-hour period? This crisis, in fact, is partly your fault. So please excuse me, I need to talk to my assistant."

Somewhere in the back of her mind Penelope knew she was being a bitch, but between agonizing anew about Glenn's response to her overture and then losing her puppy because of this guy's good time, she had no energy left to be polite.

"*My* fault?" His dark brows shot up and those autumn eyes went sharp. "Since I just moved to town and have only known you about three seconds, I have a hard time believing that. But I'll let you go. I can see you've got yourself wound up all over again."

"All over again?" Penelope's back straightened. "*All over again*? What do you mean by that?"

"I mean, you obviously freak yourself out on a regular basis, so I'll leave you to it."

"If you're talking about last night . . ." She put her hands on her hips. "I'd hardly consider having my door pounded on in the middle of the night by a drunken stranger freaking *myself* out."

"It was only like eleven o'clock—"

"It was *quarter to twelve*—"

"All right then, I apologize again. I only wanted to borrow your phone. Who calls the cops over that? But okay." He held up his hands and took a backward step toward the door. "You were scared. Just so you know, though, all it would have taken to be rid of me was a polite 'leave me alone.' Not handcuffs and a police cruiser."

"A polite 'leave me alone' doesn't seem to be working now," she shot back.

He laughed. "Fine. I'll go before your dialing finger gets itchy again."

"Thank you."

Penelope watched as her new neighbor turned, gave Lucy a very frank once-over, and grabbed the door handle.

"Lucy." He nodded to the girl and left.

As he crossed the street Penelope was discouraged to see Lucy's eyes trailing him.

"Stay away from him," Penelope warned. "He was picked up by the police last night."

"Really? What for?" Lucy's eyes went wide.

Penelope watched him stride lazily—no, arrogantly—across the street and felt annoyed all over again.

"Drunk and disorderly." Penelope held out the stack of papers. "Here are the flyers. I think you should hit every store on Caroline and Princess Anne Streets, and maybe hand them out to people who are out walking while you do it."

"Okay." Lucy read one of the flyers. "No picture?" She cast a worried look back up at Penelope.

Penelope slumped in her chair, guilt and dread growing in her chest again. Even Dylan Mersey's rudeness couldn't distract her from it for long. "I had just gotten him. I hadn't had time to take a picture of him. There's a very detailed description on there."

"Of course. Okay," Lucy said quickly. "I'm sorry. I just thought . . ."

"I'm taking one the second I get him back," Penelope vowed. "Right after I get him a crate for the car and a tag. And I'm getting him micro-chipped. I've already told Megan."

"I'm sure that won't be necessary," Lucy said.

Penelope took a deep breath and forced a smile at her assistant. She was trying, poor thing, and Penelope was being a bitch. "I'm sorry. I didn't get much sleep last night. You'd better get going."

"Okay." Lucy looked relieved. "I'll let you know what everyone says."

"Thank you." Penelope watched her turn toward the door, then stopped her. "Oh, and Lucy? You can skip the shop across the street. There's no way Dylan Mersey will be any help with this."

Chapter 3

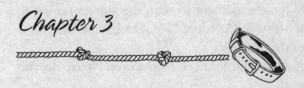

Not fifteen minutes after Lucy left the shop with the flyers, the bells on the door clanged and a short, wiry man with receding slicked-back hair entered. He wore a pale blue dress shirt too tight for his narrow chest and pants that appeared to have been purchased in the boys' department.

"Yes?" She lifted her head.

"Are you Penelope?" His slim-fingered hand gripped one of her flyers, all but her name wadded into his fist. His eyes shifted from her face to her body and back again.

She moved expectantly to meet him. "Yes I am. Have you seen my puppy?" Her hands clasped each other near her belly in a vain attempt to quiet the butterflies there.

He took a moment to scan the store, craning to look around Penelope. "I might have some information."

"Really? Did you see something? What do you mean?"

"I mean, I might know something about your dog."

"You *might*? Are you . . . are you asking for *money*?"

He lifted one hand, palm up, and the shoulder above it. "I wouldn't put it like that. It's more like I'm a private detective, see, and I do things like this for a living. I could find your dog for you. It's what I do. My name's Pond." He extended his hand. "James Pond."

Penelope grimaced. "You're kidding, right?"

Straight faced, hand still outstretched, he said, "About what?"

"Look, I'm not playing around here." She crossed her arms over her chest. "Are you serious about finding my dog?"

He dropped his arm and managed to look offended. "Of course."

"Mr. Pond—"

"Jim."

"All right, *Jim*. You either know something or

you're offering to look into it or you're some kook who's messing with me. Which is it?"

Again with the one-shouldered shrug. "Like I said, I might know something. I mighta seen something. In back. Near your car, last night."

Penelope swallowed, heartbeat accelerating. "I *knew* it. Somebody took him deliberately, didn't they?"

He bobbed his head up and down, side to side, in an indirect admission, and looked around the shop again.

"I'm thinking it was deliberate, yeah."

"Who was it?" Despite the empty store she lowered her voice. "Did you recognize them? Was it someone from in town? Do you know the people around here?"

"I know people." He moved his mouth as if swallowing a piece of gum, and looked her dead in the eye. "So you want my help? A hundred fifty bucks, I can promise you delivery of your dog by tonight. It's an easy job, so I'm giving you the good rate."

She straightened, realization dawning. "You already know where he is. And now you're asking for money to tell me. That's not detective work, that's extortion."

"Hey, I never said I knew where he was. I got a suspicion is all, and I'll check it out for you if you want me to." He took a sideways step closer.

"Tell you what, for you I'll do it for a buck and a quarter."

"A buck and a quarter! Oh, you mean a hundred twenty-five." She studied him until a slight flush hit his cheeks. "I'll tell *you* what. If you bring my puppy back here by tonight I'll give you fifty dollars."

"A hundred," he said, jutting his chin out as he said it.

If he'd simply brought her the dog, she probably would have given him the hundred fifty bucks or more, out of gratitude. This, however, was different. He was not a Good Samaritan deserving of a reward. He was an opportunist bartering for money. She was sure he already knew where the puppy was.

Relief made her strong. If he knew where the dog was, he knew it was okay, and that told her she could get it back.

"Fifty," she returned, eyeing him steadily.

"Lady, you're killing me here. Seventy-five and that's all I can do."

She might have gone with the seventy-five, but the "lady" got her. "Fifty," she said again. "Anything more than that and I might start to think the police would be a better bet. I'm sure they'd be interested in what you 'might have seen.' "

He chuckled and stuck out his hand again. "You're one tough broad. Ten bucks in advance and I'll bring the dog here tonight."

Broad? she thought. That was worse than "lady."

"Five bucks, and you have him here by six."

"Eight o'clock," he promised. "You'll be here?"

"I'll be here." She moved to the register, popped it open and pulled out a five. "And I'll be waiting."

It wasn't until he left that she wondered how he knew which car was hers.

Dylan picked up a shoe from the display on the wall and bounced it in his hand. Feather light. Amazing. The more expensive the running shoe, the less material there seemed to be in it. And the more unintelligible the language that went with it.

Dual-density SSL EVA midsole. Extended SRC Impact Zone. Blown-rubber outsole, Flexion Plate technology, Arch-Lock, TPU external heel counter, rearfoot overlay wrapping, crash pad, impact dispersion.

Then there was the baffling question: Did he pronate or supinate?

Who knew? And what did it all mean?

One thing it meant was that getting back in shape was going to be more expensive than he thought. At least with running all you needed were the shoes, he'd reasoned, having no idea how high-tech these things got. He'd considered biking, but the cost of a new bicycle was prohibitive. He couldn't afford to join a gym and he didn't own any exercise equipment other than a couple of free weights, so running seemed the simplest, most direct route to fitness. Then he'd seen an ad in the paper for a marathon training group. "Beginners Welcome!" it had enthused. When it had gone on to tout a program—actually "The Program," as it repeatedly said—that began with a two-mile "fun run" and promised to have you ready for a marathon in twenty-two weeks, he'd been sold. It had seemed so simple. Not to mention a good way to meet people in town.

Dylan glanced around for a salesperson and noted one standing at the register, studiously ignoring him by leafing through a clipboard full of papers. No doubt he was trying to look busy with inventory. They obviously didn't work on commission here.

Dylan stuffed his hands in his pockets and rocked back on his heels, sighing at the wall of shoes. He didn't need some guy pressuring him anyway, not just yet. He hadn't made up his mind how extravagant he was going to be with his one athletic-equipment purchase. If he bought a cheap pair, it would make it that much easier to quit The Program when he got tired, which he did not want. But if he bought an expensive pair, he knew he'd look like the idiot who goes out and buys all-new stuff for a sport he's never even tried. No matter how high-end his purchase, Dylan knew he was going to be huffing and puffing within a mile.

The one thing he was sure of was that he couldn't run in the ten-year-old sneakers he'd had on last time. He still had shin splints, and it had been *days*. Some woman had stopped him along the canal path and he'd almost kissed her for giving him respite from the misery, he'd been so exhausted. Of course after a mere moment to catch his breath he'd had to sprint off into the sunset looking tireless, just so the group of women she was with wouldn't think he was a wuss.

Still, he had to make a decision soon. The puppy he'd found in his shop needed to be let out of the bathroom he'd barricaded him in, if for no other reason than to pee on Dylan's shoes as he had yesterday.

Another man joined him at the wall, studying the array of sneakers as if they were paintings in an art gallery. Dylan recognized him from the marathon meeting. Another out-of-shape thirtysomething who'd bought into the twenty-two-week miracle cure for couch potato syndrome.

"Hey," Dylan said, "you're in The Program too, aren't you?"

The guy, tall with curly hair and the soft belly of an office worker, glanced at him. "Yeah. You?"

His tone was as resigned and dubious as Dylan felt about the prospect of running a marathon in twenty-two weeks.

Dylan nodded. "Yeah."

They both turned back to the wall of shoes. Dylan marveled how not only was the lone sales guy able to ignore one customer with ease, he was now demonstrating he could overlook two with equal indifference.

"You have any idea what's good here?" Dylan asked.

The guy laughed. "None whatsoever."

"I feel like I'm trying to buy a spacesuit. What's a TPU external heel counter?"

"You got me. I've got half a dozen pairs of tennis shoes, but *Rock*" —the way he said the name made it clear what he thought of the twenty-five-year-old marathon group leader— "told me I might as well strap a couple of pieces of baloney to my feet as run in those."

"I've gotta give him that one," Dylan said. "I ran in basketball shoes the other day and can barely walk now."

The guy glanced at him askance. "You're sure it was the shoes?"

Dylan laughed and shook his head. "That's my story and I'm sticking to it."

"So how come you're doing this marathon thing?"

Dylan shrugged. "I just moved here. I guess I want to start fresh. Get in shape. All that. You?"

A smug smile settled on the other man's face. "I'm doing it because of my ex-wife. I think she's angling to get back together, so I figured I'd tone up. I was in a lot better shape back when we were together."

Dylan nodded.

After a second—during which time he heard his mother saying, *"You've got to make waves to make change"*—Dylan added, holding out his hand, "My name's Dylan. Any chance you'd like to train together during the week sometime? I don't know about you, but I'm going to need all the motivation I can find to get the individual runs done."

"Sure, that'd be great." The other guy extended his hand. "I'm Glenn."

Penelope didn't leave the shop all day in the hope that someone would show up with her puppy, having seen her flyers. James Pond—she scoffed at the name—was a last resort, and worth five dollars as a backup plan.

He may or may not have seen something by her car last night—presuming he actually knew which one was hers—and he may or may not have known where her dog was when he'd made the offer to find him, but at least he *might* be on the trail, and that gave her a modicum of optimism as the day dragged on and nobody else showed up with information.

Plenty of people had shown up to offer sympathy, friends from town who'd seen the flyers, but she'd had the dog so short a time that none but her closest friends had laid eyes on the puppy. And nobody knew what the heck a "Havanese" was. Without her description they'd all be out looking for a cigar.

She spent the afternoon behind the front counter, trying to get into the book Lily had lent her and jumping every time the phone or the door chimes rang. Some sentences she had to read three and four times before they registered, and by then she'd lost the thread of the paragraph.

After a while, when the store was empty and closing time was near, she began reading the words aloud, hoping that by having to voice them—hear them in addition to reading them—she might be able to concentrate. She felt like Melanie Wilkes in *Gone with the Wind*, reading *David Copperfield* aloud to distract the women from worry about their husbands.

Finally, at six o'clock she put the book down and locked the front door. She had paperwork she could do in back until James Pond arrived. Not that she believed he would anymore. The more she thought about it, the more likely it seemed he was just a con artist who used the flyer to cheat her out of some lunch money. At least she could feel good she'd only fallen for it five dollars' worth.

So it was with a frustrated, cynical hope that Penelope emerged from the back room, ten minutes after closing, when she heard someone knocking on the front door.

It was the guy from across the street, she saw glumly. He'd wanted to talk to her about something earlier, but she'd put him off. She supposed she ought to talk now, but she could barely hold a thought beyond that of her missing puppy. Despite all her efforts to remain optimistic, she could not help picturing his little body lying in a gutter somewhere having been hit by a car.

She made a supreme effort to pull herself together as she moved toward the door, and was a mere few feet away when her eye was caught by a blur moving around Dylan Mersey's feet.

She gasped as her eyes took in the little dog. "My puppy!"

She fumbled with the bolt lock, gazing from the puppy jumping on the glass door to Dylan's face, which bore a look of guarded amusement.

The moment she got the door open the dog shot toward her. She squatted and was greeted with wild, furry exuberance. The dog licked her face, her neck, her hands and arms, wherever he could reach as she held him to her and beamed up at Dylan Mersey.

"You found him! Oh thank God. Where was he? Where did you find him?"

Though his smile was small, Dylan looked unquestionably pleased. "Believe it or not, he found me. He was in my shop last night. He'd gotten in somehow, I'm thinking the door must have been ajar, but frankly it's something of a mystery."

"Oh I can't *tell* you how worried I've been. In fact," she said sheepishly, rising with the puppy in her arms, "it's the reason I was so rude to you earlier today. I was beside myself, and I'm sorry about that."

"It's no big deal."

Standing this close to him she could see that his eyes weren't really brown. Or rather, they weren't merely brown. They had flecks of green in them, moss against bark, which made them look deeper, fathomless.

"Actually it is a big deal. I'm usually very polite, I pride myself on it even. But today I just . . . lost it over this little guy." She let the dog lick her on the chin a couple times before moving her head. "You didn't deserve it and I need to learn not to take my frustrations out on others. Forgive me?"

He shook his head, shoved his hands in his pockets and smiled. "Nothing to forgive. I'm sorry I didn't know he was yours earlier. I could have saved you some worry."

Was it just gratitude that had her looking at him with new eyes? He suddenly looked handsome to her—tall and lean, high cheekbones, square chin . . . Was this something like falling in love with the doctor who saved your life?

The puppy squirmed against her and she realized she'd been staring.

"Yes, well, that would have been nice. But you couldn't have known."

He tilted his head. "Actually, when I came in earlier and you, uh, didn't want to talk, it was because I had a sign to put in your window about the dog."

Penelope felt herself blush hot. "Oh. So, hm. I guess I did it to myself then."

He laughed. "I wasn't trying to say that. I just—"

"No, no. You're right. You're absolutely right. It's a lesson learned." She turned away from him and walked to the cash register. "But here. Let me give you the reward."

"No—"

"Please. I *insist*." She pulled out fifty dollars and slammed the drawer shut.

"I don't want your money." He backed toward the door, holding his palms up. He actually looked embarrassed by her offer.

She smiled. "Listen, there was this smarmy guy who came in here earlier and offered to get him back for me for a hundred and fifty dollars. I told him I'd give him fifty, but I'm so glad it was you and not him that I really *want* to give it to you. It'll be worth it just to be able to tell him I did."

One side of Dylan's mouth kicked up and the corners of his eyes crinkled appealingly. His straight blond hair fell in choppy layers to his shirt collar—open flannel over a black tee-shirt—like a good haircut that had grown out for too long.

Not her type, but she had to admit he was cute.

"Tell him you did anyway. Your secret will be safe with me."

Despite herself, she felt a little thrill at the idea of having a secret with Dylan Mersey.

"No, really. Please take it." She held the money out, away from the puppy, who kept nipping at it. "It's good for a few beers, maybe a bite to eat somewhere. Think of it as a gift from" —she lifted the puppy with one elbow— "this guy."

Hands shoved deep in his pockets, he asked, "What's his name, anyway? I was calling him Bonsai 'cause he's so little—hope it didn't stick."

She smiled down at the dog. "I don't know. I only just got him two days ago."

"Then what's your name?"

Her gaze darted to his, surprised. "Oh! I'm Penelope Porter. This is my shop." Her right hand, the one with the money in it, swept the room. Then with a sly smile she extended it to him as if to shake. "And you're Dylan. It's nice to meet you properly."

His lips curved again. "I'll shake your hand," he said, moving closer and gripping her fingers, cash and all, "but I'm not taking your money."

He had large hands. His right enveloped hers in

a firm grip. She tried to grip his back, but since her fingers still held the money she couldn't. He let go.

"Uh-uh." He grinned. "Buy yourself some beer with that money. Better yet, a nice merlot. You seem more like a merlot girl."

Penelope blushed again, this time with pleasure. She did prefer wine. A merlot girl. It sounded so . . . lovely.

He headed back for the door, looking at her over his shoulder. "I've got to go. Keep an eye on that puppy, now."

She tittered—actually *tittered*—a laugh. "I will."

He pushed through the door and headed across the street, his stride long and limber, his too-long hair shifting and shining in the setting sunlight.

He did *not*, she reminded herself as she watched him go, save her life. He wasn't even a doctor.

"Penelope." The cop who entered the store might have looked menacing to anybody else. Penelope marveled at it every time Carson Sellars stopped by. He was as gentle as a Disney bear, she happened to know, but he exuded strength and knew how to intimidate. He also had zero sense of humor.

"Carson, hello. How are you today?" She put down the pen she'd been holding and closed the case on the display she'd been arranging. She gave him a smile, glancing at her one patron, who was scanning the sale items on a shelf toward the back.

"I wanted to follow up with you on your disturbance the other night." One enormous hand rested on his gun holster, the other on his radio, over which a low, staticky conversation seemed to be taking place between distant parties.

"That's not necessary. It's all cleared up now. Just a misunderstanding."

She hoped he wouldn't stay long. Sometimes she wondered who kept track of what cops did all day long, because there were times when Carson would come in and chat—and she used the term generously, mostly he talked without pause in an attention-killing monotone about himself and his gun collection—for hours.

"I wouldn't be so sure about that." He looked around the room. "I've got info on the perp."

"What?" she asked, confused. "What's a perp?"

"Our guy from the other night. Mersey. He isn't near as innocent as he pretended to be. I'm here to tell you to keep away from him. What we know now, he's dangerous. Got a record."

"Oh Carson, what kind of record?" she asked, exasperated. He could be so overprotective. One time he told her she should keep away from a guy because he'd racked up so many parking tickets, his car got booted.

As it turned out, she should have stayed away from him, but not because he was an illegal parker.

"Robbery, I think. Probably armed. Drugs were

involved too." Carson's chest seemed to expand with the words. "Guy served time."

Penelope's stomach dropped. "*Armed* robbery? Like with a gun?"

She tried to picture the lanky blond with his soft flannel shirt and his crinkling eyes wielding a gun.

"I don't know the details. But he served a deuce in the pen up in Maryland."

"A deuce?"

"Two years. Guy could be dangerous, Penelope. I'm not kidding. I want you to be careful. I'm going to up the patrols around here after dark, but keep away from him. Don't give him the time of day if he asks. It's likely he was feeling you out the other night, see if anyone was in here after hours."

"But he said he just wanted to borrow the phone."

"An excuse. Disregard what he says. Bottom line, he's a criminal. Good chance he'll try to bring more of the criminal element in here too. We're keeping an eye on him."

"More of the criminal element? You talk like he's setting up a drug ring or something."

"I don't know what he's doing, but I'm going to find out. You said a vehicle departed before the incident that night at a high rate of speed. Just the kind of thing ex-cons do. They're jumpy. For good reason."

Penelope's heart fluttered. An ex-con. Dylan

Mersey was an ex-con. She'd been flirting with an *ex-con*.

"Surely you're being overdramatic, Carson. Maybe he got in trouble for something small. A youthful indiscretion. Maybe he was just some kid who made a mistake."

"Yeah, sure." Carson had a long face, horselike, with small, hard eyes. Sometimes, to Penelope, he looked prehistoric. "Medium-security prisons hold a lot of kids who 'made mistakes.'"

He actually made quote marks in the air with his fingers. It was the first time Penelope had heard Carson say anything remotely sarcastic, or even use a tone outside of his usual just-the-facts-ma'am drone.

"But I've met him since then," Penelope persisted, refusing to believe she could have thought a dangerous criminal was cute. "He seems like a nice guy. He apologized. He brought me back my puppy!"

Carson actually laughed, like a tiny burst of machine gunfire. "Ever hear of Ted Bundy? Dozens of women said the same thing about him."

"Ted Bundy!" she repeated, appalled.

"Yeah," Carson confirmed. "Nice guy. Good-looking. Serial killer. There's always a catch."

Chapter 4

"He's an *ex-con*," Penelope said, looking direly at Georgia.

Georgia, holding Penelope's puppy, gave her a mischievous look. "Honey, we've all got baggage."

"Baggage!" Penelope repeated. "That's not baggage, that's a moving van."

A saleswoman from a company called Artisans Inc. took catalogs out of her tote bag and laid them on the counter by Penelope's register.

Penelope saw the woman's eyes shift at the words *ex-con*, but she kept to herself.

Business at Pen Perfect had slowed in recent months, so Penelope had begun to think about broadening her inventory with some more affordable artistic items. When the saleswoman from Artisans had cold-called her, Penelope had considered it a sign and told her to come on in.

Georgia leaned close to one of the tall glass cabinets and squinted. On the back of her shirt was the needlepointed face of a Great Dane. "Have I got to get new glasses or is that pen really four *thousand* dollars?"

Foah THOUsin dollahs. Georgia's Southern drawl occasionally became more pronounced, usually when she was flirting, but sometimes when she was appalled.

Penelope sighed. "It's a Tibaldi, a limited edition. Sterling silver. And it's got an eighteen-karat-gold nib."

Georgia looked over her shoulder at Penelope with raised eyebrows. "And a 'nib' is . . . ?"

Penelope chuckled. "Not as interesting as you're making it. People collect these pens, so the limited editions can be very pricey."

"I'll say. Who in this town spends that kind of money on *pens?*"

"Hey, there are a few," Penelope said. "Though I'll admit most of my sales come from the Internet. That's why Shirley here is going to show me what Artisans carries. I want to get more foot traffic in here." She beamed at the older woman, who wore a flowered print dress with a round collar and a salon-sculpted mass of gray curls.

Penelope had to admit Shirley didn't look like a salesperson for a conglomeration of artists, but then salespeople weren't necessarily representative of their products. She'd bought her car, for example, from a man wearing a polyester suit. And her car was very classy.

"Good plan," Georgia said. "And if you want to attract a rich man, I guess you're carrying the right stuff. If rich men shopped for themselves, that is. Which they don't."

She picked up a leather journal and held it just out of reach of the puppy's curious teeth. "I have to say, a guy who spends a fortune on a pen would probably spend a fortune on a woman."

Penelope shrugged. She was tired of thinking about men and their habits and where they might be hiding in the small town in which she lived. "So this guy, my new neighbor, has a record. And I called the police on him. Do you think I should be worried?"

Georgia scratched behind the puppy's ears, fluffing them up. "He'll get over it. Just be sweet to him. I don't think there's a man alive who wouldn't forgive you anything if you were bein' sweet to him. Besides, it was a natural mistake. He was poundin' on the door—how were you supposed to know he only wanted to use the phone?"

Penelope pulled her long, dark hair behind her into a handheld ponytail and looked away from her friend's flattery. "He was nice when he returned the puppy to me. I just wish I had a man around. You know, to discourage anyone who might think I was . . . vulnerable."

She thought about Glenn and glanced at the catalogs Shirley was laying out as neatly as if she were arranging magazines on a coffee table.

"Oh, I *agree*." Shirley nodded. She sat on the stool behind the register and took out an order pad and Bic ballpoint. "You can't be too careful. For all you knew he was coming to rob you."

"That's true." Penelope shared a look with Shirley.

"You need to get your husband to come by more often. Make his presence known. If that man's been in *prison*, he's obviously a *very dangerous character*. You don't owe him an apology for what you did. Any man worth his salt knows a woman has to protect herself."

Penelope pulled a catalog toward her and began leafing through it. Maybe she should encourage Glenn to come by a couple of times a week. Maybe they could do lunch. She liked the way it felt to think she had someone to call on.

"That's right. Thank you, Shirley," she said. "If Dylan Mersey were a gentleman, he'd understand."

"It's been my experience that if you have to rely on a man bein' a gentleman, you're settin' yourself up for disappointment." Georgia turned from the display with a flip of her curly blond hair and moved toward the front window to gaze across the street.

Penelope slumped, one hip against the counter.

"Then have your husband talk to him," Shirley said. "Warn him that he's got his eye on him. That's what I'd do. I make my husband talk to all those people. Mechanics, plumbers, homeless people, you name it. Some men only listen to other men, and an ex-con has got to be one of them."

"I don't have a husband." Penelope trained her attention on the catalog in her hands. "Not at the moment."

She felt, rather than saw, Georgia turn and look at her.

"No husband? A pretty girl like you?" Shirley sounded overly surprised. "Then have your boyfriend talk to him."

Penelope pressed her lips together. She could say she'd have Glenn talk to him but she didn't want to get into it with Georgia. Not yet.

"Your father?" Shirley's voice trailed off.

"There's no reason to talk to him." Penelope closed the catalog and pushed it away from her. "Not really. We had a misunderstanding, then he returned my dog and we had a pleasant conversation. I'm just being paranoid." Penelope raised her chin. "Besides, I've been taking care of myself for a long time now. If he ever needs talking to I can do it myself."

"That's the spirit," Georgia said.

"Of course you can." Shirley patted her hand. "You've been alone this long, I'm sure you know how to handle yourself. But you know, that might be a little part of your problem. Men like to feel needed, like they can take care of you. If you're too self-sufficient you'll never get a husband."

Penelope hated that she had to defend her man-catching abilities, but she couldn't let Shirley's comment stand.

"I *had* a husband. There are men out there who like capable women. It just . . . it wasn't the right time for that relationship. Things are much better now."

Shirley gave her a look that said *too self-sufficient*.

Georgia turned surprised eyes on her.

"But I don't want to talk about it," Penelope said to both of them.

"You don't want to talk about *what*?" Georgia moved back toward her. "Penelope Porter, have you met someone without tellin' the rest of us? That's not like you to be secretive. Who is it? Where did you find him?"

"I just said I didn't want to talk about it," Penelope said. She looked at Shirley, who was safer, and shook her head with a smile.

Georgia threw the hand not holding the puppy up in the air. "Why not? It sounds like good news!"

"It's not. I mean, well, it's not new."

Georgia's eyes narrowed.

"I mean it's not *news*." Penelope blushed and picked up another catalog.

"Not new?" Georgia neared the counter. "Penelope, tell me you're not doin' something stupid."

"Stupid?"

"Don't play dumb with me, missy. You're not cavin' in to Glenn's advances, are you?" She glanced at Shirley and added, "Her rat dog of an ex-husband."

Shirley blinked. "Oh my."

Penelope dropped the catalog to her lap. "What's wrong with Glenn?"

Georgia's eyes looked as if they might pop out of her head. "*What's wrong with Glenn?*" She turned again to Shirley. "This guy cheated on her. Lied to her. Treated her like dirt. Said he never wanted children then ran off and had one with the next woman who came along. Glenn is as low—"

"He is *not* that bad!" Penelope objected. "He made mistakes. I made mistakes. We *all* make mistakes."

"Honey." Georgia leaned over and grabbed Penelope's hand in a strong grip. It felt much less patronizing and more urgent than Shirley's condescending pats. "You do not need to go backwards.

Glenn Owens is a good-lookin' guy, sure. And I'm sure he knows how to be nice every now and then. But if you are seein' him again, at least promise me it's just for the sex."

Shirley gasped.

Penelope burst out laughing. "Georgia, you do know how to put things in perspective."

Georgia did not relinquish her hand. "Promise me."

"All right. I'll promise not to do anything rash."

Georgia sighed and let go. "I guess that'll have to do."

Penelope looked down at the catalog and flipped a few pages. "Hm, these are interesting. Witches' balls."

Georgia made a noise in the back of her throat. "I thought only warlocks had those."

Penelope smiled. She knew that would get her off the topic. "These are handblown—"

Georgia guffawed.

Shirley's cheeks reddened.

"*Glass balls*," Penelope overrode Georgia loudly, "designed to hang in a window to capture witches that try to enter your home."

Georgia raised her brows at Shirley. "Order me a dozen of those."

God knew Penelope loved Georgia, and knew her friend cared about her, but really, Georgia had no room to talk about what was or wasn't stupid in relationships. Just last year she'd been caught *in flagrante* in a car with the mayor—the *married* mayor.

Shirley's stout, short-nailed fingers pulled one catalog after another out of the stack she'd brought with her, one covered with ceramic rabbits, another with commemorative plates, and a third filled with tiny, palm-sized baby dolls. In none of them could Penelope find anything she liked.

Maybe the problem was her, she thought. Maybe she was incapable of change. Look at what she was doing in her personal life. Instead of forging ahead into something new, she was trying to go backward, to her old husband, her old life.

But you couldn't force yourself to adopt something you didn't believe in, could you?

Sighing, Penelope shook her head. "Thank you, Shirley, but I don't think any of this goes with the nature of my shop." She swept a hand around her, toward the Tibaldi pen case, the Aurora Piquadro collection of leather pen holders, the teak pen chests starting at three hundred and seventy dollars. "I'm sorry to have wasted your time."

Shirley snapped back the pages of her order pad and stacked up her catalogs. "Well, if that's your decision, it's your decision."

Penelope frowned. "Thank you for understanding." She extended her hand toward the door to walk Shirley out.

Georgia, who had moved back to the front window, thrust an arm out in front of them. "Wait!"

Penelope nearly plowed into Shirley as the older woman stopped and gave that little gasp again.

"There he is." Georgia leaned toward the window.

Penelope's gaze shot out the window. Across the street the door of the empty shop swung shut behind Dylan Mersey. He wore jeans and a tee-shirt, untucked.

"Yep, cute as I remember," Georgia said. "Nice shoulders. And look at how he moves. I love that kind of jock walk."

"He does *not* look like a jock." Penelope had known her share. She'd dated three out of the four football captains in high school and all of them had worn deck shoes and rugby shirts, *tucked in*. She frowned at the guy loping toward the sandwich shop on the corner. "His hair's too long. And look at that tee-shirt."

"Honey, the place isn't open yet." Georgia glanced back at her. "He's probably doin' work on it before he opens it up. Paintin' and all that. Give the poor guy a break."

The three were silent a second before Georgia murmured, "Too bad he's not wearin' a tool belt. I love a man in a tool belt."

"I'm sure he's got one he can put on for you." Penelope ushered Shirley around Georgia and opened the door.

Shirley gave Georgia a steely-eyed gaze as she passed. "He's too young for you." Turning back to Penelope she added, "Call me if you change your mind, dear. You know, sometimes one can be a little too picky in life."

Penelope sucked in her breath as the woman disappeared down the sidewalk. "Did you hear that? I know what she meant by that. The *nerve* of her!"

"Shoot, she's probably right," Georgia said, looking at the spot where the ex-con had been a moment before.

"Hey, I've had a husband already and I'm perfectly capable of getting another one. I am *not* too picky."

Georgia laughed and gave Penelope's arm a squeeze. The puppy squirmed toward her. "I meant she's right, he's probably too young for me." She tilted her head and studied Penelope with a pensive smile. "But not for you, honey. Heck, he's probably just about perfect for *you*."

Dylan jogged up the alley to the back door of his shop, his final steps labored now that he was out of the public eye. Glenn had cut off just above Princess Anne Street to go to his house, and though

Dylan could have stopped—and on one level desperately wanted to—he was determined to collapse only once he'd gotten home.

It might be shallow, this pride, but it was the only thing that kept him from giving up when it got tough. Glenn, the bastard, had wanted to chat while they ran, mostly about some impending date with his ex-wife, but Dylan had been capable of little but a sympathetic grunt every paragraph or two.

The run had only been four miles, had not lasted an hour, but, as he had at the end of the other runs the two of them had done this week, Dylan felt enormously proud of himself.

Toxins begone, he thought. He'd been eating healthy, barely drank, never smoked anymore, and was nearly ready to open his business just in time for the fall pre-holiday season. He was on a roll.

He'd also been working a lot, beefing up his stock. The fact that he could barely move after his runs because of sore muscles might have had something to do with this. Sitting at the potting wheel was a lot more comfortable than moving around setting up shelves, sorting through stock, and installing light fixtures. He was also glad he'd gotten all the painting done before he began The Program in earnest.

Once he'd regained his breath outside the back door, he untied his key from his shoelace and unlocked the shop. He already loved the welcoming smell of his back room, where the clay and the wheel and the two small electric kilns were. It was starting to feel like home.

He tossed the key onto the table along the back wall—a heavy Masonite-surfaced piece where he wedged the clay—and headed for the mini-fridge he'd picked up at a yard sale. As he pulled out a refilled bottle of water, his eye was caught by a movement under the table.

He took two steps back, thinking *rat*, but immediately saw that it was the guinea pig again. A.k.a., the puppy belonging to Pen Perfect's Penelope.

"Damn," he said softly, "I gotta figure out how you get in here."

He squatted, clapped his hands lightly and the puppy writhed over to him, fluffy tail going double time and low growls of pleasure coming from his throat. Dylan picked him up, fingers sinking into feather-soft hair to a bony, birdlike body.

"You're just a little bonsai guy, aren't you?" he said, holding him up and looking him in the eye. "Bet you're a giant pain in the ass, though."

He scratched the dog's head and noticed that he'd gotten hold of one of Dylan's tools, a small wooden spatula used for scoring the clay. No matter. He had a million of them.

He pulled on the stick, playing tug-of-war, as he moved toward the front of the store. Someone knocked on the glass and he smiled to himself, knowing exactly who he would find there.

Sure enough, Penelope Perfect stood wringing her hands on the sidewalk, peering worriedly through the glass. As usual, she was dressed to the nines. A tailored skirt skimmed her slim hips and spike heels showed off her long legs. Her hair, though loose, looked as if not a strand was out of place as it cascaded over the shoulders of her silk shirt with a hairspray-free ease.

Still, despite all the polish and perfection, she smoldered like embers about to take to flame. Was it her eyes? Dark and thickly lashed, they were hard to look away from. Or was it her poise, so restrained but with a dormant athleticism about it?

It was all too easy to imagine her being a hellcat in bed.

When she saw him with her dog, her whole body went slack and she smiled. Despite himself, Dylan felt that smile soak into him like water on a dry sponge.

Which was the last thing he needed. He'd seen the look in her eyes when he'd returned her puppy and he'd recognized it immediately. Surprised interest. Surprised because he was not her usual type—not rich, not educated, not classy. Surprised because she found herself considering him as a man, despite her prejudices against him.

It had disappointed him, frankly. He liked her better when she knew she didn't like him. The last thing he needed was to be slumming grounds for a princess. A transient experience for the temporarily intrigued. Or worse—a fancy girl's *project*.

About two feet from the door, he stopped. "Good thing I'm not dialing the police right now, huh?"

Her beam of gratitude turned wry. "Good thing it's not midnight."

He chuckled and unlocked the door. The puppy squirmed in his arm, but he held it tight. "Can I help you?"

She crossed her arms over her chest but he could tell she was just itching to reach out and grab the dog. "I believe you have something of mine."

"Do you, now? Because he seems to think he belongs to me. Why do you think that is?" He continued scratching the dog behind the ears and, as if coached, the puppy looked up and licked him on the chin. Dylan grinned.

Penelope's face darkened and for an awful moment he thought she might cry.

"Very funny," she managed. "No doubt he likes it here because it's such a mess. He's not allowed to chew things up at my store."

She snatched the clay tool from the puppy's mouth. The dog yipped once at the game, tail wagging.

"Do you know what this could do to him?" She wagged the stick at Dylan. The puppy snapped at the air trying to get it.

"Give him hours of chewing pleasure?" Dylan guessed.

"It could splinter, and those splinters could perforate his intestine and cause him to bleed internally. Or he could swallow too big a piece and create a blockage."

"And think of the cholesterol," Dylan added. "He could die of a heart attack in thirty years."

Penelope stuck out her hands, a silent demand. "I'm sorry he got into your store. I won't let it happen again."

"How does he keep getting out of yours?" Dylan handed the dog over.

"I don't know. I think he followed a customer out the front door this time, but I can't be sure." Penelope handed back the clay tool.

"I'd have thought after last time you'd have him chained to the front desk, or at least be watching him like a hawk."

Why did he feel such a need to antagonize her? It wasn't as if she would ever fall for a guy like him, even if she did exhibit temporary interest. She was doctor's-wife material. Junior League. Garden Club. The whole nine yards. He bet the moment she got a husband she'd give up her business and head for the maternity ward.

"I *was* watching him like a hawk," she snapped, and here again, she looked on the verge of tears. "I only took my eyes off him for a second. But you can be sure he'll be chained to the front desk from now on."

The puppy wriggled toward Dylan and the stick he was tapping on one hand with the other.

"I'm just kidding," he said, reaching out again to pet the dog. "Don't tie him up. I don't mind him coming over."

"Well, I do." She turned to the door.

This time he heard her voice break. Without thinking he took her elbow. "Hey, hang on," he said gently. "Look, I was being a jerk. I don't think you're doing anything wrong. The little guy's just smart."

Penelope bowed her head and he heard her sniff. He dropped his hand and she turned around to look at him, big doe eyes watery. *Shit*, he thought.

She took a wavering breath. "It's not you. It's . . . he just likes you better." That sentence ended on a high, uncertain note.

Dylan scowled. "No he doesn't. Believe me, *no one* would like me better than you. Least of all this guy." He tousled the dog's curly fur.

Penelope looked at him a long time. Too long. Dylan thought he should say something to offset the moment, but for some reason he could think of nothing.

"You're a strange man, Dylan Mersey," she said finally. "I can't figure you out at all."

"No doubt you're putting too much thought into it." He backed up a step.

The puppy writhed in her arms toward him.

"See? He likes you better!" She held the dog up, looking at it worriedly.

He stopped bouncing the clay tool in his fingers. "No, he likes this thing better than both of us."

"He does not." She looked down at the puppy, her fingers playing with its feet.

He tossed the stick across the room and the dog immediately struggled to go after it. Dylan raised his brows at her.

She laughed. After a moment's hesitation she stepped toward him, put a hand on his forearm and looked up at him with those dark, lush eyes. "Thank you."

He found he couldn't move. "For what?"

"For being so nice." She rose up on tiptoe and kissed his cheek. Only it wasn't a quick little peck, it was a soft, lingering press of her lips, a moment that lasted far longer than it should have.

Or it felt that way to Dylan.

Which was why, he'd tell himself later, he raised his hands to her upper arms, above where they bent around the puppy, and pulled her closer. He paused a split second, brain registering that she did not even remotely resist, his eyes meeting hers squarely—a question, a challenge, a *mistake*—then captured her lips with his.

Chapter 5

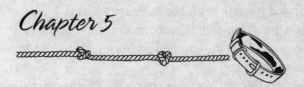

Had she asked for it? He was sure of it.

Had *he*? He had no idea.

Penelope's mouth opened immediately to his tongue and he was swept into a current he knew would drown him if he didn't escape from it.

Still, he dove into her mouth, raising one hand to her hair—*impossibly soft*—and turning the kiss to a dare, an invitation to her to leapfrog across the tracks to the bad-boy side of town.

For being so nice . . .

He wasn't *nice*. He wanted her. Wanted her body in his bed, her pristine princess skin soft against his, her debutante sensibility tumbled into a skid row of passion. He wanted her to want him, to understand him, to meet his difficult psyche and wounded passion with the strength to heal.

He wanted her to be someone she could never be.

He pushed back, watched as her eyes worked to focus on his face.

"Seems I'm not so nice after all." His tone was harder than he'd intended, but so be it.

Her cheeks turned red and her eyes shifted. She clutched the puppy closer.

"I—I better go." She looked up at him one last time, eyes pleading for something. Something romantic, he thought, or apologetic. Something an Ivy Leaguer would say at the end of a date at the club, when a little too much champagne produced a little too much passion.

He lowered his lids and gazed down at her. "I guess you'd better."

She hesitated just a moment, then she spun on her heel and walked swiftly out the door and across the street.

Dylan watched her go. Not his type, he told himself. *Not his type, not his type, not his type.*

And yet, he could still feel her skin on his palms, her hair in his fingers, her mouth against his.

He could still feel his heart hammering inside his rib cage, harder than it had pounded on any of his runs yet.

* * *

Good *God*, she'd kissed Dylan Mersey! Kissed him like her mouth was on fire and his tongue was the only thing that could put it out.

Penelope marched across the street on wooden legs, sure he was watching her, and not in a good way. Tears stung her eyes, making her mad. Whenever she was overwhelmed or frustrated or angry, she got assaulted by tears. It made her look weak, which only increased her frustration.

Out of the corner of her eye she spotted someone coming up the sidewalk from the corner at Goolrick's Pharmacy. She brushed angrily at her eyes and tried to straighten her expression. Shifting her gaze she saw it was that odd, smarmy man. *Pond*, she remembered, *James Pond*.

She nearly ran the last steps to her door, not wanting to catch his eye, or worse, talk to him. But he'd seen her, she knew. The question was, how much of her had he seen? Had he happened to be looking at Dylan's shop a moment ago?

She burst through the door of Pen Perfect, hot, flustered, and more sexually coiled than she'd ever been in her life. At the same time, her heart had been chilled to its core by the detachment in Dylan's face when he'd pushed her away.

Megan Rose, standing with her hands on her hips in the middle of the store, turned at the sound of the bells. "There you are—Penelope? What on earth is the matter?" She looked at Penelope as if she wore the whole last ten minutes on her face like a slide show.

"Nothing." Penelope's voice was unsteady. She had been sure the store was empty and almost didn't know how to compose herself upon finding it was not. "I'm just . . . I'm surprised you're here. I was only gone a minute."

Holy cow, might *Megan* have seen something through Dylan's shop window too? She leaned down, letting the curtain of her hair hide her face, and let the puppy run free on the floor, thinking if the dog went back to Dylan, she'd let him keep him before she'd go back over there.

"Where were you?" Megan asked. "I was just getting worried that there was no one here. Are you all right?"

"I'm fine." Penelope forced a smile. "I—the dog just got away again and I had to go get him. He went back over to—" She jerked her thumb in the direction of Dylan's shop. She didn't even want to say his name, had no idea why she'd done what she'd just done.

But—he'd done something too.

She felt confused. Had she just kissed him or had it been the other way around?

Megan's brows rose. "Dylan's?"

Penelope walked as if she were made of glass to perch on the seat by the register. She supposed she could have been robbed while she was gone, it had been longer than she'd anticipated, but thought maybe that would have been preferable to having to act normal in front of Megan's all-too-perceptive eyes.

"Yes." She took another deep breath. It still quavered. "He keeps running off to his place. I don't even know how he gets out. I think he likes *him* better."

She envied Megan's unfettered laugh and gave an unconvincing one herself.

"Puppies love everyone," Megan said. "Witness Twister. He fell in love with Sutter even while Sutter hated him."

Penelope's heart raced. "That only works with dogs, doesn't it? Once people dislike each other it's a done deal." She gave a one-shouldered shrug.

Megan looked at her closely. "What's up with you?" She glanced over at Dylan's shop, now darkened. "Did something . . . happen?"

Penelope's face flushed. "Did you know he's an ex-con? I mean, I know he was one of the Foley Foundation grant winners, so . . ."

Megan exhaled. "Ah, that's it. I thought you looked shocked. Yes. I knew. But it was confidential, so I couldn't say anything. Did he tell you about it?"

Penelope shook her head. "Carson did. After I called the cops on him."

"You *what*?"

Penelope told her the story, finishing with, "And at first, you know, just after that, he was so nice. Then just now he—well, I just don't know what to make of him. And *this* guy . . ."

She bent down to pick up the puppy and looked him in the face. The dog's tail wagged and his tongue lashed out to catch Penelope on the nose.

"He just can't keep away from him. Snuggled right up and licked him on the face."

She spent an uncomfortable moment thinking she'd done the same thing.

"This is the second time he's gone over there," she added. "I just don't know what to do about it. I don't think Dylan's going to be so *nice* about it next time."

She placed the dog back on the floor. *Seems I'm not so nice after all . . .*

"Penelope," Megan interrupted her thoughts, "is anything else going on? You don't seem like yourself. I hope you don't really think your dog—who needs *a name*, by the way—likes Dylan better. He probably just has a stash of bacon bits on the floor or something. As for Dylan not being nice, he is kind of a hard case sometimes. Sutter calls it street charm. But he hasn't been mean, has he?"

Penelope forced a chuckle. "No. I don't know. No. I'm being an idiot. I'm just . . . confused. Sometimes he's nice. Sometimes he's . . ."

Irresistible. And a bastard.

She shook her head.

Megan studied her. "Hmm."

"But it doesn't matter in the slightest. Besides . . ." She bolstered herself up and looked at her watch. "I have to get going. I'm—" She flashed a glance at Megan.

"You're . . . ?"

She sighed and then laughed. At this particular moment, her life really was a mess. But what better way to deflect Megan from what had just happened? "I've invited Glenn over for dinner tonight."

Megan's mouth dropped open. "Your ex-husband? *That* Glenn?"

Penelope splayed her hands. "One and the same."

"But *why?* I mean . . ." Megan laughed. "That's not very polite, is it? What I mean is . . ."

"What you mean is: Why? It's okay. I'll give you the short version. If I'm not going to have children—which it's looking like I won't—then maybe I gave up my marriage for the wrong reason. Maybe we can patch things up and get back to where we were." She ran a hand through her hair. "You know I've never felt good about divorcing him. When I took those vows I meant them. So if I can make things work with Glenn, then . . ." She lifted her shoulders and gave Megan a look of forced hope.

"Then maybe the divorce in a way never happened?" Megan's tone was concerned.

Penelope shrugged, then nodded.

"Pen, can I ask you something and tell you I mean this as your friend, who loves you and would never want to make you mad?"

Penelope gave a reluctant laugh. "Well, that's ominous. Sure."

"Are you sure you're not thinking, or hoping, that now that Glenn has a child with someone else, he might be more open to having one with you?"

Penelope busied herself straightening the pens by the register. "I hope not."

Megan put her purse on the counter. "I just want to make sure you know exactly what you're doing. That you're aware of all the pitfalls."

"I am."

Megan picked the puppy up off the floor, where he had been jumping lightly on her leg. Holding him close, she kissed the top of his head and breathed in. "Oh, there's nothing like the smell of puppy fur. Hey, there was something else I wanted to ask you, aside from when on earth you're going to name this guy."

"I have named him," Penelope said, grateful for the subject change. "He's Mr. Darcy."

Megan's brows rose. "So you read Lily's book?"

Penelope smiled. "Actually, there's a video. It was *great*, by the way, so now I'm reading the book. But go ahead, you said you had another question." Penelope began packing up her bag to go home.

She'd had a standing rib roast in the oven all day, had gone home at lunch to make the sides, and now had to prepare appetizers and get dressed.

How she was going to host Glenn tonight after that tsunami of a kiss with Dylan, she had no idea. All she knew was she had to give it her best shot, because if she was stooping to fall into the arms of someone like Dylan Mersey, she was in real danger of ruining her future.

"Would you consider being my maid of honor?"

Penelope's eyes shot to Megan's face. "Really? Your maid of honor? Of course I will!"

Megan laughed.

Penelope rushed around the counter and embraced her pal, puppy and all, laughing. "Thank you so much. What an honor."

"It's an honor for me," Megan said. "You've been my best friend since I moved here. I don't know what I would have done without you."

"You've repaid it tenfold. But let's not get into that." If nothing else, she'd ripped Penelope's mind away from Dylan. "I'm thrilled. Now tell me, what kind of stripper would you like at your bachelorette party?"

Penelope's hands were sweating and she could feel beads of perspiration along her hairline. She took a deep breath and opened the front door to her ex-husband, bedraggled on the stoop in the rain.

"Come in, come in! When did it start raining?" She looked out the door at the sky after he entered as if she could see it on the clouds.

"About an hour ago. It's been torrential." He shed his raincoat, shaking the wet onto the foyer floor, and hung it on the coat tree.

She closed the door, noted that he had no flowers or wine and was still dressed for work, necktie loose, first button undone.

He looked good, though. That dark, nearly black hair was just mussed enough from the rain, making his eyes even bluer. And he'd lost some of the gaunt, beaten-down look he had when she'd stopped by last week.

She ushered him into the living room and he plopped down on the sofa, one arm along the back, one ankle on top of his knee.

"Can I get you something to drink? I have wine or I can make a martini, if you'd like." She'd been hoping he'd come into the kitchen with her, maybe even volunteer to make the martinis, as he used to, but he just leaned his head back against the couch cushions.

"Martini'd be great. I had a bitch of a day."

Penelope frowned and headed for the kitchen. If this had been a first date she'd have been unimpressed. And wasn't it a first date, for all intents and purposes? Why had he thought she'd invited him over? Did she need to be more explicit?

Did she *want* to be?

She made the drinks and tried not to think about it. She was just reacting to her bizarre afternoon. He'd had a hard day at work. Maybe even a hard week. She wasn't giving him credit for having a difficult job.

She delivered his martini and sat next to him on the couch.

She asked about his day, why it was such "a bitch" and he told her all about it, just like when they were married. She didn't recognize the names of the players like she used to—she used to make an effort to remember every client, every case, and even make small knowing jokes about the more difficult ones, as if she worked there too—but her ability to sympathize and say the right things came right back to her. In fact, she thought she could see him loosening up, lose his wariness about being her guest, about her motives.

He even made the second round of martinis and joked about her yellow kitchen. (So he *did* remember!) He loved the dinner, and actually did most of the talking throughout, which made Penelope happy. She was using all of her mental energy to focus on him, to make sure he was enjoying himself and to *not* think about her earlier mistake kissing Dylan Mersey. Really, what *had* she been thinking?

This was where her future lay. With Glenn.

Granted, it was her past, too, but maybe she and Glenn had had some growing up to do and that's why they'd had to separate for the last four years. She knew she had learned a lot in that time.

Back then, all she'd had was her role as his wife, even though she'd participated in many different charities and clubs. Those had always been as Mrs. Glenn Owens, however, and never as herself. Not that he had insisted on that. No, she had been the Good Wife, who chose to work to make her husband look as good as he could, to focus their life on teamwork as much as possible.

It wasn't until the divorce that she realized the team had only been working for him. She'd given up everything to produce a Glenn Owens the world should respect, but where had Penelope Porter gone?

It had been scary, discovering the sum total of her pursuits had become luxuries she couldn't afford. She needed to work for money, so giving up things like the garden club and the Junior League had been required.

Then she'd opened her shop. And she would never have dreamed, back then, how much happier she would be with her own priorities, her own identity, her own life.

Conversation had slowed by the time she brought dessert out—icebox cake, just like his mother used to make—and she worried she had nothing more to add to the conversation. Was it just because they hadn't seen each other in so long that she had nothing to say to him?

"Oh!" she burst, thinking of something as she took the last bite of her dessert. "Megan Rose asked me to be maid of honor at her wedding today. Isn't that something?"

Glenn's eyes, fatigued a moment ago, lit up at this. "Really? You're going to be maid of honor at Sutter Foley's wedding?"

"Well, Megan Rose's wedding," Penelope chided, gentling it with a smile.

"That's fantastic. You know, talk around town is that that's the invite of the year. Everyone's wondering who's going and who's not." He leaned one elbow on the table, the one closest to her, and looked into her eyes.

She raised her brows and smiled. "I guess I'm one of them. I'm sure Lily and Georgia will be invited too, but I don't know who'll be on Sutter's list. Most of his family's in England, I think."

Glenn nodded, studying her. "He needs more contacts—friends—in town. I bet it's hard, being so rich. How would you know who really had your back and who just wanted to be near you because you're one of the richest men in the country?"

She nodded—that was perceptive. "I never thought about it, but I bet it is hard for him to make friends. Especially since friendship is based on shared experience. Who shares the experience of being a billionaire?"

Glenn grinned. "Nah, he's probably only a millionaire. I could relate to that."

They both laughed.

Glenn was a little tipsy when she walked him to the door, but she attributed that to his probably being nervous and drinking to calm himself down. He certainly had seemed so when he'd arrived. Well, tired and nervous. Or nervousness masking itself with fatigue.

At the door he put on his coat and turned to her. "That was great, Pen."

She smiled and put a hand on his arm. "Thank you for coming, Glenn. I think we—"

He swallowed the rest of her sentence by planting his mouth on hers. She was caught so off guard she'd moved and he'd nearly missed her lips, but he slid his mouth back over to cover hers completely, his arms going around her and pulling her up against his still-damp raincoat.

She wasn't sure what to do, so she submitted. She opened her lips to his, took in his thrusting tongue, his vodka-laced breath. Her neck arched backward as he pressed forward. But when his hands slid under her sweater and moved up and around to her breasts she pushed him away.

He was drunk. He'd been nervous about the

night. He wasn't sure what she'd expected. Still, she was shocked to find him inebriated.

"Glenn." She placed a firm palm on his chest and a prim smile on her face. "Let's save something for the *second* date, shall we? Now let me call you a cab."

"I think this might work out well for me, ultimately. I mean, we've got a history, sure, but we're comfortable together. She seems to feel it too. I bet we end up in bed before too long."

Dylan looked over at Glenn, unsure if he should know who the hell he was talking about. They had just been talking about Rock, The Program leader, who last Saturday had whipped the group through a six-mile run with a combination of challenge, cheerleading, and scorn.

"Who?" Dylan expelled with his breath.

Glenn glanced at him and laughed. "My ex. Remember I had dinner with her the other night? I'm pretty sure she wants it. That might even be why she invited me over. She's the type to go back to someone she knows instead of having to admit to someone new that all she wants is sex. She wouldn't want to risk thinking of herself as someone who'd do that. But she was always hot blooded."

"If all she wants is sex, how come you didn't hook up the other night?"

Glenn blew air out of his cheeks a couple times before answering. "No, see, because there again she'd have to admit that sex was what she wanted. She's telling herself we're dating. That's how she's justifying it to herself. So I've got to finesse things. If there's one thing I know about my ex, it's that she needs to be seduced."

Dylan nodded. "So how do you know she doesn't want something else? Like someone to fix her kitchen sink?"

Glenn's eyes shifted to look at Dylan from the corners. "You ever been married?"

Dylan snorted. "Like I'm marriage material. I've got no money, I live in a tiny apartment, my car barely runs, and my idea of an expensive date is ordering two subs instead of splitting a pizza. Then there's the whole "checkered past" thing. Chicks just don't find that stuff attractive, for some reason."

Glenn laughed. "Hey, there are plenty of women who like that whole bad-boy schtick. They love a man they can save and then recreate. Then there are the ones like my ex. She's more proud of my job than I'll ever be. And she brings up my education like I'm the only guy who ever graduated from Princeton. At least with your creds you know when a woman really wants *you*."

"I don't know about that, but I can say I know the ones who really don't. To be honest, right now a little ex sex would suit me just fine." He thought of Penelope, how hot he'd gotten for her the moment he'd touched her. It'd been too long, that was the only reason. He was starved for it. Because God knew, Penelope Porter was not the type of woman to overlook his "creds."

"That's what I'm saying," Glenn continued. "That's all it is, it has to be. You ever hear of a marriage being successfully rekindled?"

"Gotta say no, man."

"Me neither. So there you go. She *thinks* she wants to give our marriage a second chance, but I know she just wants what I want. A little physical closeness. A fuck buddy."

Dylan was skeptical, or maybe jealous. He didn't know many women who wanted fuck buddies. A few, but not many. Almost every woman he'd ever met had wanted a relationship. Even if they *said* they only wanted sex, they ended up wanting a relationship. That's just the way they were wired.

He'd have said as much but they were running up a hill, heading for the mansions on Washington Avenue, and he had little breath to spare, especially for cynicism. Negativity was a habit he was trying to break.

"Sutter Foley lives up here somewhere, doesn't he?" Dylan asked, once they'd reached the top.

Glenn nodded, panting, and flung out a hand. "Right there. The place is amazing inside. My ex is friends with Foley's fiancée. That's the other thing. If I play my cards right, I can get invited to the wedding. She's maid of honor. The contacts I'd make there could triple my business."

"Yeah?" If Sutter Foley and his friends didn't have teams of attorneys already, making them probably the least likely people to need a small-town lawyer, he'd eat his stupidly expensive shoes.

"Yeah. I'd have an in. The guy's got more money than God and likes to support the local economy."

Dylan kept jogging, looking at the wide brick house that belonged to one of the richest men in America. He had a lot to thank Sutter Foley for— the grant that got him out of Baltimore being the biggest—but it wasn't just that that made him admire the guy. For one thing, being one of the richest men in America, he could live anywhere. Yet here he was, in a small town that was nice enough but still a long way from being what anyone could call a playground for the rich and famous. He had the feeling Foley was the type who worked to keep things real.

Also, Dylan had met his fiancée, Megan Rose, and she was great. The last person on earth who'd ever be called pretentious.

"What about you?" Glenn asked. "You got a girl-friend?"

Dylan stopped short of snorting. "No. I just moved here."

"Didn't leave anybody behind?"

"I left everybody behind."

Glenn laughed. "I know what you mean. I thought about leaving town once. After my first divorce. There was just so much crap with that divorce. We were both in thick with certain social circles, so everybody was talking about us. I thought there was no way I'd ever live that shit down. Then I met my second wife. She wasn't any part of that, but God, what a bitch. Talk about frying pan into the fire."

"You didn't think about leaving town after the second divorce?"

"Oh hell no. That'd be just what she wanted. Besides, she has my daughter." Glenn shrugged. "I figure I should be around to make sure she's not spending my child support on new cars and shit."

The more Glenn talked, the more convinced Dylan became that it was a mistake to make friends in a shoe department. He was entertaining, though.

"Think you'd ever get married again?" Dylan marveled over the fact that this guy had married twice already and he couldn't be much more than thirty-five, and Dylan had yet to make the leap once. In fact, his longest relationship had only been a year. He'd been too busy taking care of his mother, and making sure he didn't get caught doing what he was doing, to pay much attention to girls before jail. Then afterward, he wasn't much of a catch. Broke, trying to make it as an artist (of all things), living in one of the seediest parts of Baltimore *with his mother* . . . Well, there just weren't a lot of women who wanted to be part of that.

Not that women weren't interested in him to begin with. He got some looks, and enough action to keep his hormones in check. Until recently.

"I don't know," Glenn mused. "Maybe. If I really thought it would stick I'd marry someone. No more kids, though, that's for sure. That's where they can really screw you in the divorce."

"Not to mention how the kid gets screwed." Dylan wondered if divorce would have been worse than his dad just disappearing as he had. If fights and paperwork and lawyers and all that would have made him happier than knowing that his father, unencumbered by marriage, had felt disconnected enough to simply walk.

Glenn grunted. "Are you kidding? The kid gets everything. Don't get me wrong, I love my daughter, but I'll be damned if I'm having any more. That's why I got snipped."

"Snipped?" Dylan laughed.

"Yeah. Vasectomy. Shootin' blanks, my friend, and never has an unarmed man been happier."

"Sounds like it'll make your ex happy too." Spermlessness had to be desirable in a fuck buddy. He should think about it. Then again . . .

"One of them," Glenn said. "Abigail, my second

wife, wouldn't want any competition for Brittney. Penelope, on the other hand, all she ever wanted was kids. That's what broke us up."

Dylan nearly stumbled hearing the name. "Penelope?"

"Yeah, my first wife. I won't be mentioning the vasectomy to her, because if the reason she wants me in bed is she'd like to talk me into becoming a daddy again, it'll screw up the whole deal. And if it's not, then no harm, no foul. We all get a good roll in the hay."

Chapter 6

"No, no, no, no, *no!*" Penelope raced across the room and grabbed her dog by the scruff of the neck. She shook him gently, secretly wanting to throttle him. "No, Mr. Darcy! No drapes! No chewing! No no *no!*"

The puppy cowered and she wanted to cry. When had she become such a shrew? What happened to the gentle, controlled corrections she used to give her last dog? When had she gone from Barbara Woodhouse to Mommie Dearest? She let go of the pup, expecting him to slink off in the face of her wrath, but he jumped up, tail wagging, and grinned at her.

She looked at him doubtfully. "That's better."

She started back toward the kitchen, glancing over her shoulder one last time. He'd picked up the corner of the drapes again.

"Darcy, *no!*"

He dropped it, sat back and looked at her, tail still wagging.

"Good boy!" she enthused, then sighed. Was he getting any of this? "I'm watching you."

When did having a puppy get so hard? Her last dog was nine when she'd lost him and he'd been perfect for so long she'd forgotten how he'd gotten that way. Had he been this much trouble?

Lately she spent her days with the pup in a schizophrenic frenzy, often ricocheting from a Minnie Mouse "Good boy!" to an *Exorcist*-like "NOOOOO!" in the same breath.

The phone rang and she continued into the kitchen, standing in the doorway to keep an eye on Mr. Darcy as she picked up the receiver.

It was Suzanne Ruthe. She'd called three times in the last couple of days, and Penelope had meant to call her back every time. She needed to get organized again. It wasn't like her, not to be on top of things like this.

"Listen, I'm calling about Gallery Night," Suzanne began in her no-nonsense way. She had an air of getting straight to the point, even though she could talk a blue streak and rarely let anyone else get a word in. Even so, she had to take a breath sometime, and people must talk to her when she did, because Suzanne always had the latest gossip on everyone in town.

"There have been a few changes, and since you missed the last meeting, I wanted to fill you in," Suzanne added.

Penelope put a hand to her head. She'd missed the last meeting because that was the night Mr. Darcy had gotten away. The first time. Penelope listened as Suzanne ran down the list of business items, thinking about all she was not keeping up with because of the puppy. How could one small dog get so in the way? Five walks a day, for one thing. Not knowing how the heck he kept getting out of the store, for another. And then there was—

"Dylan Mersey's place," Suzanne was saying. "Because he's the newest and needs a grand opening."

"What? What about Dylan Mersey's place?" Penelope asked.

She heard Suzanne sigh and was sure the woman was rolling her eyes. "That's where we're centering Gallery Night, like I said. He's agreed to buy food and we'll provide the wine. He seemed up for it. Have you met him yet?"

Penelope thought about their recent lip lock. "I— uh—yes, we've met."

"Then you know what a nice guy he is. And his pottery's gorgeous, don't you think? Not your typical stuff, though he has plenty of plates and bowls and vases, which, let's face it, you need to survive on your own. If he could stick a Civil War soldier on a few he'd be set. But have you seen his sculptures? Oh, and the raku. Gorgeous."

"No, I actually haven't seen any of his work." Penelope wondered if it had been out last time she'd been there and she hadn't noticed it. She hadn't noticed much of anything but Dylan Mersey's lips.

"His mother does some beautiful work too," Suzanne continued. "You know he's also selling her stuff. That's where he learned the craft, from her. It's interesting how feminine it is, compared to his, and not just in her glaze choices. She does more whitewear, of course, and more lower-temp firings as opposed to his cone tens, but that's not it."

"Sounds like you got quite a tour." Penelope could picture Suzanne oohing and aahing through Dylan's store, asking pertinent questions, being appropriately appreciative, showing off her artistic knowledge.

Not that it would be showing off, exactly, since Suzanne *did* know a lot. Penelope sank her head in her hand. What a sorry creature she was, to be jealous of Suzanne's interaction with Dylan. If she hadn't been so prickly to him she might have gotten a tour too. But she'd gone straight from bitchy to easy, with no pause for artsy along the way.

She was about to ask Suzanne another question when she spied Mr. Darcy speeding through the living room with a throw pillow in his mouth.

She pulled the phone down from her mouth and hollered, "Mr. Darcy! *No!*"

"I'm sorry," Suzanne said, "have you got company? Who's Mr. Darcy? I thought you were seeing your ex-husband again."

Penelope *was* seeing her ex-husband. He was standing at the door to her shop the next morning when she arrived.

"Hey babe." He smiled and grabbed her hand, giving her a kiss—on the cheek when she turned it to him. He looked momentarily disconcerted. "I was in the neighborhood and thought I'd drop by and say hi."

She laughed and pulled her keys from her purse. "You're always in the neighborhood, Glenn. Your office is like four blocks away."

He grinned and shrugged. "I had a good time Friday. Thanks for having me over. And since you mentioned a second date . . ."

"Yes?" She looked at him from the corners of her eyes as she put her key into the lock on the shop's front door.

"I thought maybe you'd like . . ." His voice trailed off as the rumble of a police cruiser neared. They both turned to see the car pull to a stop at the curb in front of them.

Glenn leaned down to look in the window. "Is that

Carson? Jesus, does that guy ever work? He was in our office shooting the shit a couple days ago."

Penelope shushed him, but sure enough, the car door opened and Carson unfolded his full, impressive height from the interior. Penelope marveled again, as she always did, how huge he looked in his uniform and attendant paraphernalia.

He nodded at Glenn but gazed at Penelope. "Mornin'."

"Good morning." Penelope smiled and turned back to the door, pushing it open and motioning for the two men to step inside. "How are you today, Carson?"

Carson shook Glenn's hand, then insisted the smaller man precede him into the shop. "I'd be better if the town were safer."

Glenn laughed. He used to joke about Carson's exaggerated sense of importance, calling him "Cartoon Cop" behind his back. "No rest for the heavily armed, eh?"

Carson's gaze grazed him as if he were no more than a mouthy child. "Got vandals. I think it's the start of something bigger." He hiked his pants up by the belt, then put both hands on his hips.

"What do you mean?" Penelope pushed her purse under the register.

"For one thing, I'd lock up that handbag. Turn your back for one second, it'll be gone."

"What are you talking about, Carson? This town

is the safest place on earth." She smiled and shook her head, punching the code into the register to open it.

"Was," Carson said.

"I heard some cars got a once-over in the new parking garage last week." Glenn leaned a hip on the counter and crossed his arms over his chest. Penelope knew that was his way of trying to seem as big as Carson.

Carson crossed his arms over his chest too. "Not just there. Multiple vehicles on this street were broken into last night. That's why I'm here, Penelope, to tell you to be careful. Pretty sure it's about drugs."

"What do you mean? Why would someone look for drugs in cars around here?" Penelope asked.

"They wouldn't be looking for drugs," Glenn explained, playing the knowledgeable lawyer in front of the beat cop. "They'd be looking for money to buy drugs. Or something they could hock for money."

"He's right." Carson's eyes flicked impersonally to Glenn. "But we got a line on stuff coming up from the South. Think someone here might be preparing to receive it." He raised one brow at Penelope. "If you remember our previous conversation."

Penelope's heart raced. "Are you talking about—?"

"That's right." He nodded once. "Guy's been in contact, we know that. We're watching him."

Glenn looked from Penelope to Carson and back again. "What guy? Who's been in contact?"

Carson's back arched just enough that his chest broadened as he put his hands back on his hips. "That information's priority."

"Priority? What does that mean?" Glenn demanded.

"*Priority* means on a need-to-know basis." Carson gave him a deadpan look. Score one for the cop for confusing the lawyer, he might as well have said out loud.

"Actually, that would be *proprietary*." Glenn scoffed at him. "But *Penelope* knows?"

"She needs to know."

"Hey, if this concerns my wife, *I* need to know." Glenn poked a finger to his own chest and took a step toward Carson.

If it weren't so ludicrous to think of Glenn fighting the giant man, Penelope would have thought she needed to intervene. Instead she wanted to laugh at the posturing.

"*Ex*-wife," was all she said.

Carson flicked his head back toward the door. "Guy across the street's got a past. And connections. We're watching him."

Glenn's eyes trailed across the street to where a new sign proclaimed MERSEY POTS NOW OPEN.

"*That* guy? Dylan?" he asked, incredulously.

"You *know* him?" Penelope asked Glenn, equally incredulous. Panic flapped in her breast.

"I can't say any more," Carson said. "But we're watching him. I suggest you do too." He directed this last to Penelope in such an ominous way that she wondered if even *he* might have seen her kissing Dylan the other night.

"I—I will," she mumbled, her cheeks on fire as she looked at Glenn. "How do *you* know him?"

"I run with him. He's in the marathon training program with me," Glenn said. "He's not a criminal. Or if he is, I can't believe he'd be any good. He doesn't strike me as the cunning type."

"Doesn't matter how he strikes you," Carson said.

Penelope could swear there was a sneer in his otherwise toneless voice.

"How does he—how do you—I mean, do you run with him a lot?" she asked Glenn.

"Yeah, couple times a week. In fact I know him pretty well. Well enough that my impressions should carry some weight, but far be it from me to tell Officer Sellars how to do his job." He smiled coldly at Carson.

Carson gazed at him with dead shark eyes. "I'll report to my superiors that you like him. Thanks for your help." Then he turned to Penelope, said, "I'll keep you informed," and left the store.

Penelope looked at Glenn, stomach knotted and

her heart in her throat. "So . . . what do you and Dylan Mersey talk about?"

Dylan straightened his back and rolled his head from side to side to try to get the stiffness out of his neck and shoulders. He'd been throwing mugs off the hump all day, and he'd do more tomorrow. Though technically he had already opened, long hours were required to get ready for the grand-opening sale he was planning for Gallery Night.

The good news was that his shop was doing well. He'd had a pretty good inventory when he'd opened, but had sold enough that he now had to play catch-up to have enough merchandise to look good for Gallery Night's reception.

His mother too was working hard, according to her latest note, and planned on sending a vanload of merchandise the next time her friend with the van was heading this way—presumably in the next week or two, but her "friends" were less than reliable. If he didn't see the stuff by then, he'd rent a truck and go get it himself, but he was hoping to avoid the expense.

Behind him, the phone rang and he wiped his hands on the clay-stained rag on his lap.

"Mersey Pots," he said, all business. Nobody he knew ever called him, it was always a salesperson or unpaid utility or, less frequently, someone wanting to know what his hours were. At just after his

6-P.M. closing, it was late for any of those calls, but you never knew.

"You know who this is?" The low male voice on the other end of the line was unmistakable and made Dylan's heart sink. Pinky. He never identified himself or anyone else, in case the phones were tapped, and he limited himself to under three minutes.

"Yeah," Dylan said, his voice going flat.

"I'm just checkin' in. Hope you're good, man."

"I'm good. Thanks." Dylan rubbed a spot near his solar plexus.

"Good. Remember that favor we talked about? The one you owe me? It's been hanging out there awhile now."

Dylan inhaled deeply. It would do no good to deny remembering it. He'd have to forget a lot more than that night Pinky was in Fredericksburg if he were to get out of it. "I remember."

"It's coming due. Soon. I wanted you to be ready. It won't be much. Just being a point man, one time, for a transaction. Going on right in your neck of the woods, so it won't be no trouble. You got me?"

Every inch of Dylan's skin crawled. Not now, he thought. Not here. Why hadn't he done this "favor" for Pinky before he'd come here, before he'd begun his new life, before he'd left Baltimore? At least there he'd had some people who'd watch his back. Here, there was no one. Here they'd bust him without a second thought about who else they might get.

"I got you. But listen, you know I want to help, you know I remember, but I . . ." How to say it? How to get sympathy from someone like Pinky McGann? Especially after what he'd done for Dylan.

"Spill it, man. I got limited time." His voice had hardened.

"I'm trying to stay clean," Dylan asserted. "I know I owe you. Believe me, I haven't forgotten, but I can't do something that's gonna bring down everything I've worked for the last five years. Understand?"

Silence greeted this, a long, painful silence.

"You saying you won't do it? You letting me down?"

Dylan expelled a breath. *Yes*, his mind said. *Yes, fuck it, yes. Come kill me if you have to, but I'm out of this.*

"No." His voice was low. He rubbed his forehead. "No, you know I wouldn't do that."

"You do me this favor, we're good," Pinky said. "You don't . . . well, I'm gonna assume you don't remember who your friends are. I'm gonna assume you forgot where you came from. Maybe you don't care about me, maybe you don't even care about your old lady. Maybe you think you can forget all about your old life, but you got debt, man. So what's

it gonna be? We gonna be good? Or am I gonna
have to find another way to get paid back?"

Dylan sighed. "I haven't forgotten anything."

"I'll be in touch." Pinky hung up.

Dylan pulled the phone slowly from his ear and
pushed the OFF button. He'd just have to be careful. He'd have to watch his own back. He'd have to
cover his tracks very, very carefully. And very, very
thoroughly.

He placed a hand on the back of his neck and
lowered his head. He didn't want to live like this
anymore. Didn't want to wonder who knew what
about him. Didn't want to be looking over his
shoulder all the time.

For some reason he thought of Penelope and
a surge of regret washed over him. For what, he
wasn't sure.

A second later he was startled by a movement
from the corner near the basement door. An uncharacteristic jolt of adrenaline coursed through
him, until he laid eyes on the furry white puppy
bounding toward him. Damn it, the old paranoia
was back already.

Despite himself, he smiled wanly. "Bonsai."

Predictably, half an hour later, the door chimes
rang and Dylan emerged from the back room to
find Penelope Porter in his shop. He'd thought
about taking the dog back to her, but he was in such

a foul mood after Pinky's call that he'd decided to wait, knowing she'd be by sooner or later—hopefully after he'd regained some equilibrium.

She stood with her arms crossed over her chest, looking around the shop. She was obviously uncomfortable, no doubt because the last time she was here they'd gone to a place neither of them had intended to go.

Dylan put the dog down and he ran out in front of him. "I thought it might be you."

"I barricaded him in the stockroom this time. There's no way he got out the front door. And I can't believe he went all the way down the alley and around the block." Her voice was combative but her eyes looked apprehensive.

He shrugged. "I don't know what to tell you. Maybe he's a ghost."

The joke blew past her. "You *really* don't know how he gets in here?"

"No." He pushed his hands into his pockets, willing himself not to take the bait. After being asked to become something he used to be, he did not feel kindly toward anyone accusing him of what he wasn't: a dog napper. "Do you?"

"Of course not." She threw her hands out in frustration. "Why would I let it keep happening if I knew? I've done everything I can think of to keep him in my store except tie him to my belt. And that's next."

"Sounds like that'll work. Though I have to say I'll miss the little guy."

The pup ran back to him.

"Mr. Darcy, no!" she said, taking one step forward.

Dylan bent to pick him up, ruffling his ears, and Penelope stopped.

"If you miss him, you can just come get him. Is that why he's always over here, Dylan? Because you're lonely?"

He laughed. "You think he feels sorry for me? Is he that perceptive?"

"Maybe *I'm* that perceptive," she said quietly. Her gaze was steady on his. "And I want you to know . . . if you're in some kind of trouble, or if you need help—"

He narrowed his eyes. "Am I being accused of something?"

She hesitated. "Look, if you want him to visit every once in a while, I'm okay with that. You don't have to . . . I mean, he doesn't have to sneak over here. And I know how hard it is to get a business started. It takes a lot of hard work, and long hours, and it can be lonely. So if you . . ."

He approached her, legs suddenly feeling wooden, an inappropriate amount of adrenaline coursing through him. He looked into her eyes. She backed up a step.

"You think I'm *taking* him? You think I

somehow—what—" Dylan was so appalled he couldn't even form a question. But his mind was flooded with them.

"Maybe it's because you want a visitor? Look, I'm not judging, I just can't take the worry. Or the confusion. Just tell me how—"

Dylan thrust the dog at her so abruptly she had to grab for him. He turned away, heading for the back of the shop. Anger threatened to blow the top of his head off.

"I'm not *stealing your dog*, Penelope," he spat, as he strode away. He pushed his hands through his hair, then spun back to face her. "Why the *hell* would I take your dog? Especially since you know just where to find him? What on earth would—"

The light dawned.

"Ahh. I get it." He gave a twisted smile and sauntered back toward her. The whole scene played out in his mind. The cops coming to report on what they'd found, just to "warn" her, the good citizen, the defenseless woman, about the bad element who'd moved to town. They'd discovered his record and couldn't wait to tell her about it. So now she knew he was a criminal. And once a criminal, always a criminal.

"Are you that much of a snob?" he asked, bending toward her as if to keep her secret. "Is it so hard to believe that a guy who just happens to be from a poorer neighborhood than you, who has a little rougher past than you can understand, can actually be a decent person? You think *I'm* a thief because you can't keep track of your *own god-damn dog?* So you have to blame the guy with no money?" His voice rose. "What, are guys like me just in the habit of stealing shit? Is that what you think?"

His anger was only partly at her, he knew. If he hadn't just been caught in the criminal undertow of his own past, the threat of his old life coming back to swallow him up, he might not have reacted so vehemently. But between Pinky's request and her belief that he was a thief, he suddenly saw that there was no escaping who he'd been, who she thought he still was. There was no fresh start here.

She had tried to interrupt him several times but now she grabbed his arm with one hand. The puppy cowered in her other arm. "Dylan, stop! I just—"

He stopped ranting and glared at her. She seemed startled by his silence.

"I only thought," she began again, face flaming, "that you might, you know, like him." She hefted the dog slightly. "And I thought maybe you wanted—company—a little . . . but it doesn't matter. I was wrong—"

"You're damn right you were wrong. Though I have to say I wouldn't have thought you'd have had the balls to come over here and actually accuse me. You strike me as a cower-behind-the-door-and-call-the-cops type. Maybe that's because— oh yeah, you already did that. I'm also impressed you'd come back over after . . ." He gave a short laugh, the truth slapping him hard across the face. "Of course. I see now."

He hated the nausea that ran through his stomach.

"What?" She looked afraid, and that pissed him off more than anything. She held the dog so tightly he whined and squirmed out of her arms, jumping to the floor. She made no move to get him, her eyes fixed on Dylan's face.

"You did it because of the kiss. You were ashamed to have kissed me." He looked at her hard and came toward her, standing too close. His voice was quiet. "You know I'm a thief. Don't you? In your heart of hearts, you know it, you always have. Since that first day you called the cops. And now you're embarrassed. You just can't believe you lowered yourself enough to kiss a criminal. You're ashamed to know you've got it in you."

She looked up at him, attempting a defiant expression. "No I'm not. I mean I—"

"What an idiot I was not to have seen it," he marveled quietly. Her perfume, soft and feminine, fluttered into his senses. "You freaked yourself out, coming on to me like that, and maybe, just maybe, getting a response you weren't prepared for. But now you're embarrassed. Maybe a little afraid of what I might do next. So you need a reason to disapprove of me, to write me off as a close call. Like a walk through a bad neighborhood, where you only just barely outran the scary men who followed you and your tight little good-girl ass." With these last words he grabbed her hips and pulled her into him.

Her hands flew to his chest but she did not push him away. Was she too afraid?

He didn't want to scare her, he wanted her chastened. Ashamed of what she'd thought. But all he was doing was taunting her with her worst fears. Did she deserve it? Probably not. But if he was going to go down in flames for his past, either with the law or with this one opinionated woman, he was going to make damn sure he deserved it.

He pulled her in tighter, judging the expression on her face as part intimidation and another part arousal, and lifted one hand to the back of her head.

"If you came here looking for trouble, Penelope Porter," he said low, his fingers threading through her hair then squeezing tight, "you found it."

He lowered his mouth to hers.

Chapter 7

Penelope had never felt so attracted to anyone in her life. Her entire body melded itself to his—no shy pretense here, no coy pushing away, no pretending not to be part of the inferno the two of them created.

She'd meant to get the truth out of him, that he somehow encouraged the dog to come here, lured him, maybe even came and got him. Because he was lonely, she thought, not because he had a record.

She *felt* for him. She did. She didn't believe he was a bad person, and after Carson had left the other day, she thought that she too should have said something in his defense, the way Glenn had.

Glenn. She'd also intended to find out from Dylan

how much he'd told her ex-husband about his . . . uh . . . dealings with her. Had he mentioned that they'd kissed? No, obviously not, because Glenn would have been all over her about it. He was always the jealous type. As her mother said, the cheaters always were.

But instead of doing any of that, she was kissing him. Kissing Dylan Mersey. She knew nothing about him, nothing about what had passed between him and Glenn, nothing of whether he was involved with her dog's disappearances beyond being his destination.

All she knew was, she could not get close enough to him. And she wanted his hands all over her, everywhere.

His arms tightened around her, one along the small of her back, the other in her hair, and his kiss deepened, consuming and powerful.

She gripped his tee-shirt near the collar, pulling pulling pulling. Her hips pushed forward into his, her body responding to this sensual awakening as if it were the one thing it had been waiting for all her life.

Dylan pushed her up against the counter. An old cash register a few feet away rattled as she put one hand behind her for balance. His hands moved to her waist and he hiked her up onto the surface, their mouths on a level now. She wrapped her legs around his hips.

He pulled her into him, and she felt the hardness forming within his jeans. She tilted her pelvis slightly, letting it rub against him, just where she longed for contact.

His hands slid up her sides, stopping beneath her arms, the heels of his palms pushing inward against her breasts. She wrested her mouth from his and threw her head back with a gasp. Her breath was gone, her heart thundering as if she were fleeing a predator. And yet, if anything, she was running headlong into danger. She longed to be touched, was dying to whip her shirt off and let him stroke her flesh, let his mouth . . .

His lips trailed down her neck, sending shivers of almost painful pleasure shooting through her. She wanted him. Oh, how she wanted him. But it was dark out, she suddenly realized, and inside the lights were on. They were in a fishbowl.

"Dylan," she breathed. She could smell the mild scent of his shampoo and raised her hands to touch his hair, to encourage him to look at her.

His mouth slowed on her neck and his head bent forward, forehead on her shoulder. He took a long, shuddering breath.

She wondered if he was sorry, if he regretted already what was happening, but when he lifted his head his eyes glittered with something else. Passion, certainly, but also, maybe, defiance?

Their eyes met and Penelope's held his gaze as

she tried to see into his head, his heart. Her chest rose and fell rapidly, her body still tingled though his hands now rested benignly on her hip bones.

She didn't know if it was the fact that his defiance seemed constructed of pain, or if it was her body's completely foreign and unstoppable response to him, but though she knew she should have said, *We have to stop*, instead the words that emerged were, "Turn off the lights."

His expression was startled, then he leaned over without taking his eyes off her and flipped the switch on the wall.

Darkness fell like cold water.

What had she done? What was she *doing*?

She could hear Mr. Darcy in the back room, tags jingling the way they did when he was chewing on something.

Dylan stood motionless, his hands lightly on her thighs. When her eyes adjusted to the dark, she could see his, reflecting the glow of the streetlights. Neither of them said anything, and yet she felt he was waiting for her to make a decision. But hadn't she just done that? The pause was uncomfortable. What did she want? What would this mean? She forced herself to ask the questions, but she could barely think about the answers over the humming of her body. He'd awakened in her something no one had ever come close to arousing. The hunger deep inside felt primal.

She reached out, her fingers catching his tee-shirt. Gently, slowly, she pulled him back to her. He moved forward but did not reinstigate what they'd been doing. Her fingers moved up his chest, over the hard rise of his pectorals, to the warm skin of his neck. Hands brushed by the softness of his hair, she pulled his face toward hers and kissed him.

He responded gently, his lips touching hers, the upper, and then the lower. Small, simple kisses, his breath grazing hers. His hands rose to her arms, his grip hardening, until he reached into her hair and opened his mouth against hers.

Their tongues met, the frenzy in Penelope's blood returning twofold, and yet he kept it gentle, teasing. Penelope's hands lowered to his hips and pulled him closer, tightening her legs around him. He was still hard and she moved against him.

He pulled his head back and expelled a breath. Under her hands, she could feel him controlling himself, the coiled muscles, the hot blood.

Then he turned away, moving silently across the room to the far window. She felt a cold draft with him gone, but he moved so swiftly she grasped immediately what he was doing: ensuring privacy. He pulled wide shades down over the two front plate-glass windows and briefly checked the angle from the door. They were out of view of the street. Someone would have to press their face against it to see them.

The moment he made it back to her his hands found the buttons on her shirt. She reached for his tee-shirt, pulled it up and went for the button on his jeans. They were all buttons, she found, instead of a zipper, but they came undone easily. And when her hand moved in to cup the hardened heat within, she inhaled sharply at the feel of it. He laid his head back briefly, his hands pausing near her breasts.

Then he pulled off his tee-shirt as she undid the rest of her shirt buttons, and they were kissing again. He undid her bra, then laid her back along the counter, his lips finding her bare nipples. His hands swept up and down her sides, feeling her curves, caressing her skin. She was naked. A moment later, he was too.

He took her by the hips as he raised himself onto the counter with her. She giggled and heard a low chuckle in return. But there was no time for talk, because the moment he was on top of her, he was inside. She gasped at the swiftness and yet her body was more than ready for him.

He devoured her, from his mouth to his pounding hips. She was only vaguely aware of the register trembling behind them, of the creaking of the old countertop. Mostly she was consumed by the slick hardness of him moving in and out, pummeling her, hot hands holding her shoulders, keeping her under him, their bodies in a hard fist of passion.

It was exactly what she needed, what she wanted, what her body demanded. His reckless abandon answered her desperate, driving passion stroke by stroke by stroke. She made fists in his hair, holding his head to hers as they kissed, their tongues thrusting to match their bodies' moves, their breathing hard and determined.

Finally Dylan groaned deep and low, his hips pressing forward, forward again, and once more as deeply as he could, before letting his head drop and lowering himself slowly on top of her.

Penelope could barely think. He held himself lightly upon her, and yet she still worked to catch her breath. Her fingers gripped his back and yet her body was spent. She swallowed hard. She'd never felt like this before. She'd never wanted to consume anyone whole, never wanted to push her body so far into someone else's that they physically became one. Even now she couldn't let go of him.

He rested his forehead on her shoulder, his arms still tense above her, his passion still deep inside of her.

"I'm sorry," he breathed so softly into her neck she almost didn't hear him. "Sorry, sorry, sorry." He muttered it, almost a chant.

It confused her. He wasn't apologizing, it didn't sound like that. And yet the words . . .

She turned her head slightly toward him. "What?" The word came out on a breath.

He pushed himself up, letting his hands drift down her body, his eyes following them. His face in the dark was all planes and angles, dark, glittering depths where his eyes were. He was not looking at her. Or rather, he was not looking at her face. His gaze seemed to trail her body, watching his own fingers trace the line of her breast, then her rib cage, then along a line from her hip to the soft, private curls at the base of her abdomen.

He moved back away from her and picked up his jeans. She sat up, confused by his refusal to meet her eyes.

"Dylan," she said softly.

He pulled up his jeans, and buttoned them, looking down. "Yeah."

"Why did you apologize?"

He looked up at her and she thought he looked startled. Then he bent down and retrieved her clothes and handed them to her.

"I didn't mean for this to happen," he said, the statement ending on a tentative note. Then he added, "Maybe you should get back. You're better off with your husband."

She should have explained. She *wanted* to explain. But there was something in his demeanor that did not invite talk. He was telling her to go, not asking what her status was with Glenn. She felt his desire to be rid of her like an invisible hand on her back, urging her toward the door.

Still, as she stood with the knob in one hand and her dog in the other, looking back at him where he stood in the middle of his shop with his hands in his pockets—as if that's where they should have stayed, as if vowing that that's where they would stay from now on—she couldn't help saying, "He's my *ex*-husband."

Then she left. She would explain later, she told herself. She'd come back after things had cooled off, after his mood had returned to normal, when he could look her in the damn eyes again, and she would tell him she was not with Glenn, not really. She would tell him . . . what? That she wanted him? That she wanted Dylan Mersey, ex-con and starving artist, to be her boyfriend? Her lover? Her husband?

He didn't seem the type for any of those things.

And yet . . . what were all those sorrys for? That wasn't the response of a man used to casual sexual encounters. That was a man who regretted what he'd done. The question was, why?

"What is *with* you? Would you slow down a minute?" Glenn choked the words out as Dylan charged up the hill on Lafayette Boulevard, legs beyond fatigue, lungs straining. He turned left onto

Lee Drive and ran about fifty yards up the tree-lined street before he slowed, then stopped, leaning over with hands on his thighs, gasping for air.

"Jesus Christ, are you trying to kill yourself?" Glenn asked, lumbering over to him a minute later. "Or me?"

Dylan stared at his shoes, adrenaline still coursing through his body, and tried to focus. Nothing, it seemed, was going to stop it. He was going to be charged like this forever, body buzzing and mind spinning with images, denials, disbelief. All because of Penelope. All because of how awful he had been to her.

"I want to . . . push myself. Trying to . . . clean out my system." His voice was hoarse, his breath short. "I've been lazy the last few days."

Lazy and stupid and oh by the way I fucked your ex-wife last night. Did I mention that?

Not that he was worried what Glenn would say to him. He frankly didn't give a damn what Glenn thought. Dylan didn't owe him anything. He was more concerned with what it would do to Penelope.

Ultimately, Penelope wanted to get her ex-husband back, and that was just what she ought to do, in Dylan's opinion. Glenn was her type. Well, sort of. He was selfish and egotistical and, for sure, a dog where women were concerned, but he was educated and had a good job and probably owned more than one suit. Those things alone made him a better match for Penelope.

Dylan, on the other hand, didn't want a relationship, especially not with the princess next door. When he found a woman, the right woman for him, she'd be tough and savvy and she'd know how to deal with a life like Dylan's. She wouldn't make him feel inferior because of the mistakes he'd made, or experiences he'd had, or where he grew up. And she definitely wouldn't be someone who'd call the cops because someone she didn't know knocked on her door.

No, Penelope wanted Glenn and Dylan wanted her to have him. As long as Glenn was in the picture, nothing could be expected of Dylan.

Unfortunately, Dylan knew that because Penelope was a woman, she was probably telling herself last night meant more than it did, but he knew it didn't. It was a misstep on both of their parts, nothing more than the satisfaction of mutual curiosity.

The problem was, he couldn't stop picturing Penelope's lean, pale body, the curve of her waist, the thrust of her breasts. He couldn't help remembering the way his heart leaped to his throat the moment he touched her, the feeling in his gut when he kissed her. And he knew, try though he might to recast it in the light of day, that when she'd looked at him he'd felt her gaze slice right through him.

He put a hand to his forehead, then back through his hair and straightened. "We got two more miles. You ready?"

"No. Jesus." Glenn was leaning against a tree trunk, rubbing the back of one calf. "I want some of whatever you're taking, dude. You're an animal today."

Dylan didn't repress a cynical laugh. "I bet you do," he said. He could enjoy the joke for the one-time opportunity it was.

One thing was certain: he was steering clear of Penelope Porter from now on. She was trouble. And he would bet she thought the same thing about him.

He just wished he could have done better. The thought whispered out from the back of his mind. He'd gone so fast, wanted her so badly. It had been too long, that was why. Months—a year—since the last time he'd been with a woman. With Penelope, it should have been gentler.

But it didn't matter. It wasn't *her* that had made his knees weak afterward. It was the unfamiliar exertion. That's why he needed to run, and to keep on running until he was a million miles away from last night.

"I'm outta here," he said to Glenn. "I'll meet you at the tennis courts."

He took off, but not before Glenn groaned and

said, "Fuck you." Shortly thereafter he heard Glenn's heavy footfalls behind him.

Penelope knocked on the back door of the veterinary clinic and peered through the window. She could see the vet tech, Brandy, cleaning out cages, but no Megan. She opened the door and stepped in.

"Hi Brandy, it's me, Penelope," she said before the girl could get startled. "Is Megan around?"

"Sure. She's in her office," Brandy said, waving in the general direction. Penelope knew the path well and was relieved Megan wasn't with a client.

"Come in." Megan's voice sounded fatigued answering Penelope's knock.

Penelope opened the door and peered around its edge. "It's just me."

Megan broke into a smile. "Penelope, hi. I thought it was Brandy with another problem in the kennels. We've had more dogs soiling their kennels than I can ever remember. It's like one does it and word passes all the way down the line that it's okay."

"They probably do smell it and, you know, it puts them all in the mood." Penelope sat down in the chair next to Megan's desk, unconsciously letting out a long sigh.

Megan leaned back. "Tough day?"

Penelope laughed and absently massaged the top

of one thigh. She was sore today, as if she'd exercised. "Actually yes. One of the toughest."

"So you've masterminded an escape from retail hell. Is Lucy watching the store?"

"Yes, thank God." Penelope leaned her head back and pulled her hair up into a temporary ponytail. "Some days I wish I had a job where I didn't have to see another human soul. It's like people are just trying to be annoying. It's worse since I've gotten the new merchandise."

She let her hair drop and clasped her hands together in her lap. Why did she feel so nervous? She didn't *have* to tell Megan anything if she didn't want to. Then again, if she didn't talk to somebody she'd burst. She had no idea how to think about all she was feeling in the wake of the night before. In the wake of Dylan Mersey.

"You're dealing with the riffraff now." Megan grinned. "That's what you get for lowering your prices."

Penelope looked down to where her hands twined together. She rubbed at an ink stain on her thumb. "I know, I know."

Silence fell for a moment.

"So what's up? Is something wrong?" Megan, ever perceptive, spoke gently. "You seem preoccupied. And it's not like you to leave the store in young Lucy's hands, though I personally think you should do it more often."

Penelope looked up and Megan smiled.

"I . . ." She glanced at the paperwork on Megan's desk. "I shouldn't bother you with this right now. Look at all you have to do!"

It was best to keep it to herself, Penelope thought. She could sort things out. She didn't need to burden Megan with the bubbling cauldron that was her head today.

But Megan said, "Don't be silly. This pile never changes, trust me. If I don't do it now, I'll do it later. Either way, there'll always be something waiting for me to do." She swept her hand through the air over the pile as if to make it disappear.

Penelope took a deep breath. "Well, okay. It's just that . . ." She massaged the top of her thigh again.

"Spill it, sister," Megan joked.

"I think I've made the biggest mistake of my life!" Penelope blurted.

Megan's eyes widened. "You wh—?"

"But it *wasn't* a mistake," Penelope continued, her voice an octave higher than usual. "It felt . . . I don't know . . . inevitable. Like it was the most right thing I've ever done. But it was stupid and impulsive and not *at all* what I'd planned, so how could that be the right thing? And yet . . ." She shook her head, looking inward, marveling at herself and unable to articulate why. "But Megan, there wasn't a condom. And oh my God, how stupid is *that*? But for so long now I've thought I'm not going to have children after all, I've constructed a whole future around not having children so I wasn't even *thinking* about it. All I've thought about was Glenn, and that's why I thought that would work, because I'd decided to go along with what he wanted and I already knew him and all. But then this just *happened* and I—it—"

"Hang on, wait, just a minute, Penelope." Megan held her hands up. "Please start at the beginning. Did you *sleep* with Glenn? I thought you were going to take it slow. Not that I'm judging, because we all know—"

"Not Glenn," Penelope said, "*Dylan*."

For a second Megan appeared nonplussed, as if she couldn't place who "Dylan" was. Then her head jerked and her mouth popped open.

"Dylan Mersey? You *slept* with Dylan Mersey?" When Penelope just nodded, Megan added, "I didn't even know you knew him! I mean, I know you knew him sort of, because he's right across the street, but—but—how long have you been seeing each other? How did I not know this?"

"Because we haven't been seeing each other. That's the thing. We've been dealing with Mr. Darcy, who keeps running over to his place. Although he calls him Bonsai, which annoys me because Mr. Darcy now thinks his name really *is* Bonsai, but that's just what he does. Dylan, that is. He teases me, torments me, actually. I think he goes out of his way to provoke me. But one day he kissed me. Or I kissed him, I'm not sure which." Penelope waved a hand. "But eventually we were *both* kissing. And then last night . . ."

She laid her head back and sighed. "Last night . . . was utterly amazing."

"Last night, when you slept with him," Megan repeated, like a reporter getting the story right. A reporter who can't quite believe what she's hearing.

"I went over to get Mr. Darcy and" —she stopped and looked Megan dead in the eye— "It was the most incredible sexual experience I've ever had. I mean, *ever*. Is that how you felt about Sutter? Just . . . blown away by it? Because I'm telling you, I think I'm falling for him."

Megan appeared to be momentarily frozen. Penelope had never seen her so off guard.

"I've really shocked you, haven't I?" Penelope laughed nervously.

Megan shook herself. "No! No no no. Well, *yes*. But I've got so many questions I don't know where to start. First, when is your period due? How stupid was this mistake?"

Penelope blushed. "Not that stupid. I'm not in the middle of my cycle or anything. In fact I'm right at the beginning. I don't think I have to worry. After all, I tried for a time with Glenn and it never happened, even in the best circumstances."

"No, but as I myself have proven, it's not impossible, even when you think it's impossible." Worry was clear on Megan's face and Penelope knew why. After years of thinking she was infertile, Megan had become pregnant while dating her now-fiancé Sutter.

"But look at how well that turned out," Penelope said. "Not that I'm thinking that should happen to me, but Megan, what if—what if—?"

She couldn't even voice the words, they sounded so silly. What if this was destiny? What if all her longing for a child for so many years had manifested itself *this* way? In the man she might have deemed least likely to be The One?

As if reading her mind, Megan leaned forward, grabbed one of Penelope's hands and squeezed it hard. "Penelope, I know you know this, but I have to say it: *Sex is not love*. Sex is not even 'like.'" She let go and leaned back again. "In fact, I know some people who'd say you can only really have mind-blowing sex with people you have no chance of a relationship with. It releases your inhibitions."

"That wasn't how it was. I really don't think it was." Penelope bit her lip. "It was different. Special. Didn't you feel this way with Sutter?"

Megan's answer was more on her face than in her words, a small private smile that seemed to light her from within. But she said, "Of course I think so now, in retrospect, but it could have gone either way back then. But here's the thing, Pen. I just don't know if Dylan is your type. I mean, he's a nice guy, he really is, but . . ." She tilted her head and thought for a long moment.

"But what?" Penelope's heart sank, but she kept her voice steady. "What do you know that you're not telling me?"

"Nothing!" Megan's face was all innocence. "You know about the jail time, that's the big thing. I just . . . he's tough as nails, you know? I see you more with someone like . . ." She shook her head, thinking. "Well, Brady Cole. Remember when I thought you'd be good together? Because he's funny and likable and, you know, light. But of course now he's marrying Lily, so that's out. The thing is, I think Dylan's got a real dark side."

Penelope frowned. "I can have a dark side too."

Megan laughed, then saw Penelope's face and squelched it. "I know. I'm not saying you're unidimensional or anything—"

"Unidimensional!"

Megan laughed again. "I said I'm *not* saying that. Penelope, you're wonderful and smart and kind and gentle and caring. But Dylan, he's what I'd call . . . *hardened*. I think it would be really difficult to get into his head, to know what he's thinking or what's driving him. He's private, in that totally walled-off and bricked-over kind of way.

Like maybe even *he* doesn't know what's going on inside. He's not likely to do a lot of thinking about his inner child, if you know what I mean."

Penelope's gaze dropped to her lap again. Megan was right, everything she said jibed with Penelope's experience with him. He was hard, closed off, and difficult to predict. But she'd also seen that hurt in his eyes, that vulnerability.

Or was that just the sort of thing a woman like her would tell herself to make the bad-boy more approachable?

She exhaled heavily. "I see what you mean. But . . ." She paused, remembering the way he'd looked at her last night, just before turning off the lights. Amazed and doubtful, and completely, intensely, focused on her. "Last night was just so incredible. I've never felt so connected to someone. I felt close to him, not just physically but emotionally. I think there's something in him that wants to be opened up."

Megan was quiet a moment, then said, "Why do we never choose the easy ones, huh? Why do we all think we love a challenge so much?"

"It's irresistible." Penelope shrugged and they both sighed.

"So he was good, huh?" Mischief lit Megan's eyes.

Penelope chuckled. "I can't even describe."

"So how did you leave it? What happened at the end?"

Heat shot to Penelope's cheeks and she looked away again. This was the rub. This was where all her ideas about his vulnerability and her reaching some core place in him turned to dust.

"He bricked up that wall," she said, "and he sent me home."

Chapter 8

That night Penelope decided to pamper herself. Aside from the fact that she did not know what to do about Dylan—and wasn't even sure how what had happened, had *happened*—she was also tense about Glenn and her business and Gallery Night.

She stopped at a shop called Unearthly Delights, two doors away on Caroline Street, and bought bath salts, foot lotion, microwaveable socks, a manicure set, and a stupidly expensive but decadently thick ballerina-pink robe.

"This looks like a nice evening," Dara, the owner's twentysomething daughter said, giving Penelope one of her impish Irish smiles. She had freckles sprinkled lightly over her nose and cheeks, and her curly blonde hair was cut short and bouncy.

"Are you celebrating?" Dara's eyes glinted as if she knew something.

Penelope's throat closed. How many people might have seen her kissing Dylan the night before through his store windows? Then seen him close the shades and . . . well, the conclusion would have been obvious, wouldn't it?

"No, not really." Penelope toyed with the plush material of the robe. "I'm just needing a night to myself. To treat myself well. I've been really busy lately."

Dara laughed, her fingers tripping over the register keys like a child's pretend dancer. "The rumor mill's been churning about you, girl. I heard you and Glenn were getting back together. He the one who's been taking up all your time?"

Penelope flushed, unsure whether this rumor was preferable or not at this point. "Oh no. Glenn and I . . . we just see each other every now and then. I've mostly been working on the shop. I've got a lot of new merchandise. You should come see. I've branched out a lot."

"Ah." Dara nodded. " 'Cause of Gallery Night?"

"Somewhat," she said, relieved to be off the topic of Glenn. "But I've wanted to expand for a while. I'm doing more home decorative items now. And

I'm totally redoing my display windows this week, to be fresh for Gallery Night. Are you going to be open?"

Dara shook her head, bagging up Penelope's items. "I'm helping at the reception, at the new guy's place. Have you *seen* him?" She raised her brows and widened her eyes. "Oh my God."

"What do you mean?" Penelope pulled her wallet from her purse, slid her Visa from its pocket and held it out.

When she looked up Dara was smiling. "He's *gorgeous*," she breathed. "And so nice! Have you met him? You must have. He's right across the street from you. Don't you think he's amazing? If you ask me, he's the best thing to hit Fredericksburg in *years*."

Penelope swallowed. "Yes, his pottery is beautiful."

Dara rolled her eyes. "Well, sure, that too. But the man. Mm-mm-mm." She slid Penelope's card through the machine, grabbed a pen with a plastic flower taped to it and handed it to her. "And he's *single*."

He's also an ex-con, Penelope wanted to say, but she recognized the pettiness immediately. She didn't need to be jealous. Did she? What was between her and Dylan? Something? Nothing? One weird incident?

"Not that you need to worry about that, now

you've got Glenn back," Dara continued. "Honestly, I never understood why you two broke up in the first place."

A slide show flashed through Penelope's head: a child's red velvet Christmas outfit she bought once when she thought she was pregnant, the stony face Glenn wore for the whole last year of their marriage, the stain left by his throwing a wineglass against the wall during an argument, Megan's car seat littered with animal cracker crumbs, the fingernail marks on her palm from the moment she heard, from a customer, that Glenn's girlfriend was pregnant.

Penelope simply shrugged, offered a weak smile, and gathered up her bag of "comfort items."

"Well, enjoy your evening!" Dara chirped. "I'll see you on Gallery Night, if not before."

"Sure thing." Penelope held the bag to her chest and headed for the door. She was very glad she'd sprung for the robe. She was going to need it.

Two hours later, moist and steamy from her bath, her hair in a towel and her body enfolded in the robe, she sat on her couch, feet tingling from rubbing peppermint lotion on them. Mr. Darcy lay on the seat of the recliner, chewing on a bully stick. She'd tried to keep him off the furniture at first, but he was like a Super Ball. Drop him off a chair and he'd bounce right back up, impervious to her commands. When she got strict and maintained the discipline for half an hour, an hour, sometimes longer, it would produce only a slight pause before he jumped back onto the seat. In the end she decided since he didn't shed, and wasn't going to be very big, he could get on the furniture.

It was failure number two, at least. Number one was not getting him to respond to his name, though she was determined not to cave on that. "Mr. Darcy" was much more to her taste than Dylan's "Bonsai."

She had just painted the nails on her right hand when someone knocked on her front door.

Mr. Darcy was up in a flash, barking and racing for the door, obviously of the opinion that he was a ninety-pound guard dog instead of a twelve-pound cosmetic puff.

Penelope paused, nail brush in the air, and tried to see through the curtained window on the door. All she could make out was a shadowy figure that looked too tall to be one of her girlfriends.

She screwed the cap back on the polish and edged toward the door. This was when she hated living alone. Every story she'd ever heard about men forcing their way in through the doors of unsuspecting single women darted through her head, a montage of gruesome ends flashing before her eyes.

"Who is it?"

Someone, a man, cleared his throat. "Dylan."

Far from calming her down, her pulse shot through the roof. She froze.

Into the ensuing silence, he said, "Penelope? I just want to talk, if that's okay."

She looked down at herself, her left hand grabbing the towel wound on top of her head. She looked ridiculous. The big pink robe suddenly felt like a bunny costume and not only that, but also one that made her look fat.

She shook her right hand, hoping to dry the nails faster and moved toward the door as if approaching the gallows. "Dylan?"

"Yeah, it's me. Can we talk? Just for a minute? I'm sorry I didn't call first, but . . ." He cleared his throat again. "I've been kind of driving around a while, making up my mind."

About what? she wanted to ask. But she couldn't keep him shouting through the door. And it was chilly out, so she couldn't exactly ask him to wait out there while she changed. Could she?

Reading her mind, he added, "Penelope? Can I come in? It's cold as shit out here."

She laughed a little and opened the door, peering around its edge. "I don't look very good," she squeaked.

But *he* sure did. She caught her breath. *Rugged* was the word that sprang to mind. And with the cold adding pink to his cheeks his green-flecked brown eyes stood out like jewels. She hadn't remembered them having such abundant lashes.

She resisted the urge to throw herself at him.

Mr. Darcy had no such compunction. His paws grabbed Dylan's knee and he jumped on his hind legs, doing all he could to climb right up his leg. Dylan chuckled and bent to pet the squirming dog.

"Mr. Darcy," Pen scolded. She squatted, awkwardly trying to preserve her modesty in the robe, and picked the dog up with her left hand.

Straightening with her, Dylan's eyes caught hers and he swallowed. She could see his Adam's apple bob.

"Uh, hi," he said quietly. One corner of his mouth kicked up. It looked reluctant. "Actually you look pretty."

She put her hand to the towel again, then swore and looked at her nails. She'd used the wrong hand. "Shoot. I just painted this hand." She laughed. "But come in, come in. Sorry, it's so cold out there. I wish I'd known you were coming."

She'd have baked herself into a cake.

"Yeah, sorry. Like I said, I was driving." He entered the house, shoving his hands in his pockets and looking around like a stranger on a new planet. "Didn't have my cell phone. Didn't know your number, come to think of it."

"How did you know where I live?"

Did he blush?

"Uh, Glenn mentioned it. We ran by here one day."

Penelope blushed, for sure. Damn it. Why, oh

why, had she brought Glenn back into her life right when something new came along?

"Oh. Well, come on in and sit down. I'm surprised Glenn knew where it was. He's barely been here since we split." She shifted her eyes back to him. "Once or twice, for dinner, is all. We see each other every now and then."

She decided that was all she'd say on the subject, lest lightning strike.

Dylan stepped from the foyer into the living room, his eyes roving over the pale blue walls, the white trim, the built-in shelves, the flowers on the side table. She expected him to say something like "Nice place," but he kept his thoughts to himself.

She moved down the length of the couch and gestured toward it. "Have a seat. Can I get you something to drink?"

Could she really play hostess in a pink robe?

"No, no. That's okay. I just wanted to stop by and . . . uh . . . apologize." His gaze dropped to the floor and he did not sit. "About last night. I was a bastard. And selfish. And I want you to know it'll never happen again."

Penelope stood with her hand still outstretched toward the couch. "Oh."

"Yeah. It's none of my business who you see, either. Like if you get back with Glenn or whatever.

I—can't even believe I said that to you. I just . . ." Finally, his gaze rose from the floor, this time going to the ceiling. He ran a hand through one side of his hair. "I didn't expect any of that. Not that I think you did, but I could have controlled myself better. I shouldn't have—"

"Dylan, it's okay."

"No, it's not. That's not who I am, or who I want to be." His eyes finally met hers. "And you deserve better. So . . . that's all I wanted to say. I just hope you believe me. That I'm sorry to have treated you that way. I didn't—I didn't know what else to do."

Penelope didn't know what to make of this. If she said it was okay, she was saying it was all right for him to treat her in a way he deemed shabby. And if she said it wasn't okay, then she'd be saying she didn't want it to happen again. The before part, that was, not the shabby treatment part.

"We . . . were both caught up," she said finally. "It wasn't just you."

He smiled grimly. "That's nice of you to say. But really, I know when I'm wrong."

"But—"

He held up a hand and turned away. "Nope. I'm not going to let you make excuses for me. I've said what I came to say." He turned at the door, looking startled to find both her and the dog right behind him. "We don't need to talk about this again. I don't want us to be awkward about it. And I'll be

the perfect neighbor from here on out. Promise."
He flashed a smile. "Good night, Penelope."

He opened the door and strode out while the
words *good night* trickled from her mouth.

"We've got to find Penelope a man," Megan whispered to Georgia and Lily, as she poked a piece of
fishing line through the top of one of the blown-
glass witches' balls Penelope had decided to order.

They were helping to dress the front window of
Penelope's shop to reflect the new merchandise, and
Megan took the opportunity to say something while
Penelope secured Mr. Darcy in the back room.

There was something of a push to get things
ready for Gallery Night, even though Penelope's
shop was not technically a gallery. Held at the
beginning of November, the event kicked off the
season of holiday shopping, and Penelope wanted
to be sure people in town knew that she now carried a wider array of products and gifts. Beautiful,
artistic things for the home was how she thought
of it. Unusual things you could buy for your friends
that they wouldn't later see in their local Macy's.

Megan and Lily had offered to help with the
window effort after work; Georgia had just stopped
by to chat and got roped into the effort. But Mr.
Darcy had become so excited by the presence of
all his favorite people that he had to be put away if
they were to get anything done.

Georgia, spreading cotton batting across the base of the window as fake snow, shifted her eyes to Megan. "Are you that worried somethin's goin' to happen with Glenn? Because that's my concern. How could she forget what an utter ass he was to her? I tell you, the worst thing a woman can get is desperate."

Megan snorted, then muttered, "Glenn. I wish."

Georgia sat back on her heels and Lily, unwrapping the witches' balls from their eco-friendly corrugated cardboard wrap, gaped at her. "You wish? What on earth for?"

"Look, I can't say much, I don't want to betray any confidences, but I'm afraid Pen is at risk of being hurt by someone even worse for her than her ex-husband, if you can believe that. Someone totally not her type. So we need to distract her with someone else. Do you guys know anyone?"

Georgia laughed. "Megan, honey, if we knew anyone don't you think we'd'a said somethin' before *now*? I mean, it isn't like we don't talk about this damn near every week."

Megan sighed and went up two rungs on the stepstool, reaching to hang the ball from one of the hooks on the ceiling. "I know. He doesn't have to be perfect, just someone distracting. Someone like Glenn, only honest. Or heck, maybe we should be talking up Glenn."

"I wouldn't know what to say about him," Lily

said. "I mean, other than that he's dependable—in that he's dependably inconsiderate. Who is it you think's going to hurt her?"

Megan grimaced. "I can't say."

"Oh come *on*," Georgia scoffed. "You can't throw a morsel like that out there and not expect us to bite. Tell us."

"Someone new?" Lily asked.

Megan shrugged, looking pained. "Kind of."

"Well, who *is* it? We don't have all day. She's gonna come back in here in a minute. And why didn't she tell us herself?" Georgia huffed.

"It's kind of . . . awkward circumstances." Megan blushed. "I shouldn't be saying anything at all, but I just know he's not the right man for her."

"That's the best kind," Georgia said.

"Think about it this way, we'd be more effective in subtly dissuading her if we knew who it was." Lily's grin was sly.

Megan hesitated. "I don't know." Then she shook her head. "I just can't, you guys. But I'll try to convince her to talk to you all about it, because she *needs* advice. Trust me."

"You've told us this much—" Georgia began, when Megan saw Penelope exit the back room.

"Shh, shh, here she comes," Megan hissed.

"Quick, change the subject." Lily glanced from Megan to Georgia.

Georgia went back to spreading cotton along the

floor of the display window. "I met someone," she said into the floor.

Her voice was muffled, her face turned away from theirs, but despite kneeling on the ground her body language was tense.

Megan and Lily exchanged a look. Georgia usually talked in pronouncements. Was this just a ruse for Penelope? Or was this off-hand mention totally out of character?

"Could you repeat that?" Megan asked.

"What are you guys whispering about?" Penelope asked, joining them. She held another box of merchandise that she lowered to the floor while scanning their faces. On top of the box were several tangled strands of holiday lights.

"I said I met someone." Georgia tossed the last of the batting toward the corner and surveyed her work. "I've been on five dates with him."

"Five dates?" Megan repeated. "Georgia, that's like a major relationship for you. Who is he?"

"And why haven't you said anything before this?" Lily added.

Georgia pressed a blob of cotton into a drift and rolled her eyes at them sideways. "Hang on. I'm not getting married or anything. I just like him."

"You *like* him?" Lily repeated.

"That's wonderful!" Penelope watched her usually outspoken friend avoid their eyes.

Megan stepped back down the ladder and took

another ball from Lily. "How come we didn't hear about him after the first date?"

"He must not have put out." Lily grinned.

To Penelope's surprise, Georgia blushed a deep, uncharacteristic red.

Megan and Lily widened their eyes at each other.

Penelope picked up the lights, dropped one strand on the floor and began untangling the other. "Who is he? Do we know him?"

"I don't think you do." Georgia picked up the other strand. "His name is Leland and he's . . . a bit older."

"Older than what?" Lily asked.

"Don't tell me you're going for the daddy thing," Penelope said. "You've always been one of my most independent friends. Don't ruin it now."

"Very funny. Do I kid you about your wildly inappropriate dating stories?"

They all spoke at once.

"Yes."

"Of course."

"All the time."

"Hey, it's not like you to be sensitive about a guy," Megan said. "Who is this Leland?"

"He's someone I met at the bookstore. He's got gray hair and lines on his face, but he's in great shape and believe it or not, I just really like talking to him." She tossed her hair behind her shoulders and concentrated on the wires in her hands.

"*Talking* to him?" Lily repeated. "Is that a euphemism for something?"

"Okay." Georgia gave up on untangling the lights and picked up the cut-glass Christmas trees that were to stand in the faux snow. "I guess I deserve that. And I know I'm usually the one to make the bad jokes, but I'd appreciate it if you didn't this time."

"Georgia, honey, of course." Penelope leaned over and patted her on the shoulder. "If you like him this much, I for one think he must be someone really special."

"He is. And yes, we've only just talked. So far." Georgia focused on the window display in front of her, placing the glass trees in the faux snow.

"Is that because you want to take things slow, or *he* does?" Megan asked.

Penelope raised a brow and flashed a half smile at Megan, because who ever heard of Georgia wanting to go slowly?

Georgia dropped back onto her heels and looked up at them. "The truth is, I've been dying to have sex with him and he won't do it. I've tried everything. He'll kiss me and hold me, we even slept in the same bed together once, and he won't have sex with me. Instead I get a bunch of . . . poetry."

"You say that like he offered you road kill," Lily said. "Poetry sounds romantic."

"How much older *is* he?" Megan asked. "Could there be a, uh, problem?"

Confused, Penelope glanced at her, then after a second said, "Oh. Right. I didn't think of that."

Georgia looked at them darkly. "There might be. One night, the night we were in my bed, I reached down there for him and there was nothing, no response, not even the hint of a hard-on. And we'd been making out like a couple of teenagers."

"Oh dear." Despite herself, Penelope remembered Dylan's immediate, rock-hard response to her. Would it have been better if they couldn't have gotten carried away? "Sometimes maybe it's good to have to go slow."

Megan glanced at her and smiled.

"Well, there are drugs for things like that," Lily speculated.

"What if he's just old-fashioned?" Megan went back up the ladder. "How old do you think he is?"

"I don't know. Fifty-somethin'. Too young for that kind of problem, I'd have thought." Georgia slumped onto the floor, sitting cross-legged. "But I gotta say, I'll be really disappointed if this relationship has everythin' but sex."

Megan's gaze slid down to Penelope's again. "Better than having nothing *but* sex, don't you think?"

Chapter 9

Penelope stood outside her shop minutes after the girls had left, surveying the display window and thinking about Dylan. It had *not* just been sex, she told herself, wishing she could have said that to Megan. But that would have required explaining everything to Georgia and Lily. Penelope wasn't ready to broadcast her actions yet, the jury still being out on whether or not it was a mistake. While eleven of her inner jury members were on the side of "meaningful," the twelfth was a hold-out for "mistake."

It wasn't like Megan to be judgmental, though, and the fact that her most open-minded friend so adamantly opposed the idea of Penelope and Dylan as a couple gave Penelope pause. She couldn't help thinking Megan knew something she wasn't sharing with her, something bad about Dylan.

Was he a womanizer? She doubted it. Still into whatever put him in jail? Possible. But couldn't a good woman turn a man like that around? Was he emotionally stunted? How would Megan even know that?

She gazed at the fairyland they'd created in her window and felt a stab of longing for the days when she thought the holidays were the most romantic time of the year. She and Glenn used to have an annual party, and they had many friends who hosted parties of their own. They'd gone caroling, to the church socials, to the Christmas concert at St. George's, making the season a swirl of pretty dresses and laughter and friendships she thought would live on forever.

Who knew so many people would move and change and generally fall away from the social circle? And then there were the ones who'd been Glenn's friends first, so he got them after the divorce, and those who simply didn't have parties where a lone woman could show up and not be the odd one out, the ninth wheel at a cocktail party or the woman all the other women strived to keep their husbands away from. One acquaintance had flat-out said something to Penelope, laughing as if of course Penelope would understand, about how she "would have invited you, but you know how some people get about having a pretty, single female at a party."

What might have been a compliment had made Penelope feel like a pariah. Did people really think she'd try to steal their husbands at a party? How desperate did she seem? And she wasn't like Georgia; she didn't have sex with people for recreation.

Which brought her back to Dylan.

How many of those social things would she be doing if the two of them were a couple? How realistic was it to think a man like him would even want to go to a dinner party, or caroling, or to a concert at a church? Maybe he was too different from her in that respect. But it would be wrong not to give him a chance, wouldn't it?

She turned and looked at his shop. He didn't have display windows, just a view into the shop. Though the lights were off in the front, she could see behind his counter the glow of a task lamp near where his potting wheel was. She wondered if he was in there working.

She rubbed her shoulders to ward off the chill. The October night held the promise of winter.

Maybe Dylan would love the chance to have a social life like she could provide. As a businessperson there were people he should know, valuable contacts he could make. Maybe all he needed was the opportunity and he'd discover he *enjoyed* a cocktail party and some Christmas caroling.

Her mind spun with possibilities. She could have the girls and their significant others over for dinner, she thought. He already knew Megan and Sutter. And he'd talked to Georgia, who never made anyone feel uncomfortable, even when she was talking about sex, which was all the time. And Georgia could invite this Leland guy she'd been seeing. And Lily and Brady—Brady got along with absolutely everyone.

That's what she'd do! she decided, her heart quickening. She'd have a party herself and invite Dylan to be her date. It was perfect. She ran back to her door and headed for the phone. First she'd line up the girls. Then she'd invite Dylan.

Half an hour later, she had a party. Sutter was a maybe, as was Leland, but the rest were fairly certain. She felt bad because she'd fudged a little with Megan about who her own date would be— "Oh, I don't know. Maybe Glenn, or maybe I'll even try Dylan [casual laugh]!" —but it wasn't as if she was sure he would come yet. In fact, she had every reason to believe he wouldn't. But she was going on instinct, and her instincts told her he needed to be pulled out of his shell.

She headed for Dylan's door and peered over the "Closed" sign through the window. Though she couldn't see beyond the counter to tell whether he was at his wheel or not, she knocked on the glass. After a second, she pulled on the door. It opened easily, a chime ringing softly toward the back. That was new. He'd been sprucing up.

Dylan rose from the wheel, wiping his hands on a clay-stained towel as she entered. His jeans were coated with clay too, as was his dark blue tee-shirt. His hair was shiny and clean though, and his eyes shone clear and laserlike in his tanned face. She had an uncomfortable thought about how he'd gotten that tan—running with Glenn—but mostly she appreciated how well it suited him. It was hard to believe that she'd once thought him unremarkable, because she now found him electrically handsome. The cheekbones, the direct gaze, the lithe movement of his lanky frame. She felt the stirring of physical desire deep in her core, something she rarely got just looking at a man.

She smiled. "Hi."

He, however, frowned and slowed his pace at the sight of her.

"He's not here." Dylan pushed a corner of the dirty towel into his back pocket. "I haven't seen him at all in a couple of days."

It took Penelope a moment to understand what he was talking about, then her face cleared. "Oh! I'm not here about Mr. Darcy. He's in his crate in my back room. Although," she added conversationally,

"I think I've got the place puppy-proofed now. I've blocked off just about every opening he could conceivably get out of except the door to the basement, but it's not like he can get out of the building from down there so I'm not too worried about that."

Dylan nodded, pushing his hands into his front pockets, much the way he had when he'd sent her home the other night. As if they could not be controlled otherwise. "Good. I'm sure that'll be . . . frustrating for him."

Penelope leaned against the counter that stood between them and was hard-pressed not to think of what they'd done on that spot just a few nights before. The memory made the breath catch in her chest.

"Frustration's what we want," she chirped, then blushed to think how that could be misconstrued. Frustration was certainly *not* what she wanted, not where Dylan was concerned. "So, are you ready for Gallery Night?"

He shrugged. "I've been working my ass—been working myself ragged getting ready, but it's hard to know how much I'll actually need. I've been throwing bowls all day. Tomorrow's mugs, I seem to need a lot of those. I don't think I'm going to get *that* many customers, but then you don't want to have too little. People are not likely to make a return trip because you were out of the thing they wanted."

"It's true. And you'd be surprised how many people might come through. It's a good night, and you're one of the newest shops in town. You'll probably do well. Besides, it's always better to have too much than too little."

"That's what Suzanne said." Dylan nodded again. "So I've upped production. And my mom's sending more stuff down tomorrow."

"I heard her pots were beautiful too. Which ones are hers?" Penelope turned to the displays in the front room. There were shelves on the two side walls, and some tiered tables in the middle of the room. But he could have had more: more shelves, more decorations, more product, it was true. People liked places that were full. Places that overflowed like treasure chests, where they had to look hard to see everything.

"The celadon, there. And the majolica."

"The what?"

"Those with the overglazing, the white and yellow. Some of the red. They're glaze-on-glaze. She likes the colorful stuff."

If she'd hoped he'd come out from behind the counter to show them to her, she'd picked the wrong lure. He stood solidly where he'd been when she'd entered. So much for things not being awkward.

"And these are yours? All the rest?"

She gazed at the darker, earth-toned bowls and platters. A trio of onyxlike vases stood in order of descending size next to some blue-gray platters adorned with geometric patterns. There were plates etched with designs around their rims, and mixing bowls of various size in rich hues of green and blue.

"Yeah. I do a lot of reduction firings. You're not competing with anything mass-produced that way. Stoneware should be individual, you know? You can't do reduction firings industrially because the results can be unpredictable. Makes 'em unique."

She smiled to herself, glad of the way his craft got him talking. She strolled toward his pots, picked one up and held it in her palms.

"This is what I love about pottery," she said, running a hand around the base of the cobalt-blue bowl. "It's so tactile. Your hands commune with the potter's when you hold it. It's a connection to the artist you just don't get with other kinds of art. Don't you think so?"

She glanced over at Dylan to find his eyes studying her hands. She held still and his gaze rose to hers.

"That's true." Her hands were graceful, he noted. Long, slim fingers, the tips painted a pale pink. Like the robe she'd worn. The robe that gaped when she walked, showing lean legs and pale, smooth skin.

Promising never to touch her again had been next to impossible in those circumstances, yet he'd done it. He'd done it and he was proud of himself.

It had been the right thing to do. She didn't need to be caught in his world, with the skeletons in his closet rattling louder than ever.

He moved forward to the counter, glad it was between them, and placed his palms on it, watching her. She picked up his favorites first, running a fingertip along the rim of a vase, a palm cupping the basin of a bowl. He felt her hands on him, the way she'd touched him the other night with fingertips, palms, arms, lips.

He swallowed with a dry mouth.

"You know, Dylan, I was thinking I should introduce you to some people it might be useful for you to know," she was saying. "Now that you're a local businessperson and all."

She looked up at him with a coy smile, her dark eyes flirty. She held a tall, slim vase, one of his own, that used an intricate *sgraffito* technique along the sides. Her open palm rubbed the bottom in a slow, sensuous circle. He felt gripped at the root by that movement. If he moved he knew he would grab her and throw her to the counter as he had the other night.

"You've met some of my friends, and of course you already knew Megan, but I'm having a little gathering at my house and I thought it would be good if you came too."

A long moment of silence jarred him. "You—

what?" He shook himself from his reverie and stared at her. Had she just invited him out?

She put the vase down. He was released.

"I'm inviting you to my house. For dinner. A week from Sunday. You'll know a couple of people there already, and there's a game on—do you watch the Redskins?"

She *was* inviting him out. Didn't he just say last night that they couldn't do, well, anything again? He hadn't put it in so many words, but he had said what had happened between them never would—never could—happen again. Did she not get it? She'd seemed to. Had he blown it somehow?

"The Redskins?" He was an idiot. He sounded like he'd only just learned English.

She wrinkled her nose. God help him, he thought it was cute. He was hot for a Barbie doll.

"You're probably a Ravens fan. But guys like all football, don't they? Anyway, that'll just be on; it doesn't really matter if you watch or not. But it would be good for you to get to know more people in town, don't you think? Is there anything you don't eat?"

He started to shake his head, saw her misinterpret it, and said quickly, "I can't. I can't come to your house."

"Why not? Is the date not good?" She was still, too still. He was hurting her feelings. Again.

He took a deep breath. "Penelope, I thought you and I . . . we talked about this."

Her brows lowered and she looked firm, the way she did when she was ineffectively correcting Bonsai. "I'm not inviting you to sleep over," she said quietly. "I know what you said and I agree with you. What happened the other night was— rash. And precipitous. And all kinds of things that could screw up a good . . . friendship. I'm just asking you to dinner."

"At your house." He was playing stupid again.

"Is that a problem?" She folded her hands together in front of her. The movement appeared very composed, but he could see the fingers gripping each other hard.

"What about Glenn?"

He might as well have smacked her. Her head jerked up, her mouth opened, and her cheeks went red. "What *about* Glenn?"

He crossed his arms over his chest. "Don't play games, Penelope. I know you're seeing him."

"I do see him. I told you. Dinner now and then. Why? What has he said?" She took a step toward him, looking at him like she could read the conversations he'd had with Glenn on his face.

"I don't want to get into gossip—"

"Gossip! How could I be gossiping if it's about myself?"

He ran a hand back through his hair. "I don't

know. It's just clear you've been dating, that's all."

"Dating? Is that what he said? He came to dinner. One time." She held up an index finger. "Once. Just because I saw him once doesn't mean I'm not allowed to do things with other people. Besides, you don't need to protect *him* from *me*."

"Look, I run with the guy. I don't want anything to get—"

"Awkward, I know." She pinned him with her eyes as she walked toward him. "I wouldn't have taken you for the gutless type, Dylan. Is Glenn why you felt so bad about the other night? Because I can tell you, he has no claim on me. We have no claim on each other." She shrugged elaborately. "So if he's the reason you're trying to wriggle out of coming to dinner—"

"I'm not *wriggling out* of anything. I just don't want to step on any toes." He wasn't gutless, for God's sake. If she knew him at all she'd know that.

Her expression softened, looked faintly amused. "Then come for dinner. Glenn can take care of his own toes. It's just dinner, Dylan."

She was close now, right across the counter from him. Both of their hands were flat on the surface where just days ago they'd engaged in the most intimate act a man and woman could perform. He'd been inside her; she'd been all around him, her body soft and strong, her passion explosive. He'd felt like Superman, like he could have leaped tall buildings.

"I'm taking your silence as a yes," she said, unaware of how close she was to being accosted once again.

His hands almost twitched with the desire to touch her. Instead he pressed them harder into the Formica.

"A week from Sunday," he said, rolling the idea around in his head. There were a million reasons to turn her down and only one reason to accept: He didn't know how to say no.

She beamed and it felt like the fucking sun came out. "Six thirty. I'll confirm it next week, okay?"

He scowled. "Okay."

"Don't look so upset," she said perkily, heading for the door, her hair and hips swaying. "You might actually have fun. Did you ever think of that?" She turned back and grinned at him.

He felt himself smile reluctantly in return. It was a mistake, he knew it, but he didn't know how to stop it.

"Fun," he repeated.

"That's right. Good, clean fun." She laughed.

Dylan heard the van before he could see it. And he could picture it from the burbling sound of its engine even before the ancient VW Vanagon bounced up the alley behind his shop, spewing exhaust and threatening to leave parts of itself on the rutted asphalt.

Inside were two of his mother's "friends," which could mean anything from guys she met in a bar to someone she approached on the street because they had a vehicle that could hold pottery and they looked like they needed a couple of bucks. She was the most trusting person alive, and one of the last people who should be. Partly it was bad judgment due to near constant impairment—alcohol was her substance of choice these days—and partly it was a naïve clinging to the love-the-one-you're-with life-style she came of age in.

"If you trust people, Dylan, they'll strive to live up to your expectations," she used to tell him. "But if you treat them like they've already committed a crime, they have nothing to lose by actually committing it."

She'd been convincing when he was younger, and he'd had quite a few naïve years before his father left and his mother departed the realm of reality on a magic carpet of heroin. That's when Dylan had had to step up, and when the world had proven itself patently untrustworthy.

He'd started moving stolen electronics for a local guy when he was fourteen, the only job he could find, and he owed Pinky for finding it. It allowed him to help his mother make ends meet. He graduated to stolen jewelry a few years later, and two weeks after his eighteenth birthday he'd been caught. He didn't have a lot at the time, but the cops believed they had probable cause to search where he lived. When they turned up the heroin— plenty of it, thanks to his mother's boyfriend of the moment—he had the choice of revealing that it belonged to his mother or of owning it as his and taking the rap for her.

It wasn't noble so much as self-preserving to take the rap, he told himself both then and now. She never would have made it in prison, there was no question about it, and he did not want her destruction on his conscience. He loved her too, of course, but mostly he knew that he could not live with himself if he could have saved her and didn't do it.

The one good outcome to the situation was that his mother had been so upset about what had happened to her son—though she was only half aware that she was partly at fault—that she went to rehab. But though she got clean of the heroin, she was an addictive type, and alcohol had been her curse and her crutch ever since.

The one thing that had survived over the years and through all those trials, however, was her trusting nature. She believed in people. She believed in all that "free love" and "flower power" crap of the sixties and seventies she'd grown up on. For her, giving up heroin had been like giving up nuts because of an allergy. She didn't see that it had ruined her son's life and nearly her own. She believed the cops and a set of biased, unfair laws had done that. She had stopped using it only because *the authorities* couldn't understand how "mind expanding" it was, how vital to spirituality, how ultimately benign. But if they could put her son away because of it, she would give it up.

Two men got out of the van and slammed the doors—a thin, tinny sound. They were both short and stocky, and sported patchy, accidental-looking beards. One guy wore a dark blue down vest over his jeans jacket and held a box of Popeyes chicken, which he munched on steadily, while the other sported a faded Orioles ball cap that looked like it hadn't been off his head for a decade.

"Ball Cap" opened the back hatch. "There he is." He jutted his chin in Dylan's direction.

"Chicken Man" turned. Dylan stepped out the back door.

"You guys sent by Sara Mersey?" he asked. No sense not making sure.

Chicken Man dropped the drumstick he'd been holding into the box and extended the same hand to Dylan. "Curtis. And this is Leon."

Dylan shook the offered greasy hand, forcing himself to keep from wiping his hand on his jeans afterward. "Thanks for bringing this stuff down."

Leon rounded the back of the van and attached his narrowed gaze to Dylan's face. "She said you'd pay us. Said we could keep the shit if you didn't, but we don't want it."

Dylan nodded once. "Fifty bucks do it?"

Curtis and Leon glanced at each other. "Each," Leon said.

As he walked to the back of the van, Dylan calculated what it would have cost to have rented a van, driven it round-trip to Baltimore, and lost a day or two of work. Inside it were dozens of newspaper-wrapped bundles, ranging from the size of a cereal bowl to that of a sculptural vase. His mother had been busy. Good.

He shot a glance at Leon, then said to Curtis, "You help unload?"

"Sure, dude," the chicken man said. "I gotta use the can anyway."

"Done." Dylan directed Curtis to the bathroom, then picked up two of the larger pieces and headed inside. "Careful with these things. They're fragile."

"No shit," Leon said in a tone that indicated he'd already been told, probably several dozen times, by Dylan's mother.

Leon and Dylan unloaded the van, taking armloads of wrapped pottery from the alley to the back room, squeezing past each other through the door trip after trip, while Curtis retreated to the bathroom, taking his chicken box with him. He did not return until they were almost finished.

Dylan was taking the newspaper off the first of

the big pots when Curtis lumbered into the room. Tall, elegant vases with majolica glazes told him his mother had used the expensive tin oxide he'd sent her wisely. The work was delicate and assured. He could price these high.

Dylan placed a vase on the counter and Curtis grabbed it in a sausagelike fist.

"Nice." He nodded, turning it. "You get a lotta money for this shit, or what?" His eyes took in the shop.

"I'm just starting out," Dylan said, taking the vase from him. A greasy handprint lingered on the neck. "But it isn't cheap stuff. Costs a lot to make, takes some time. I'll price it high enough that people will appreciate it."

Curtis pointed at the vase he'd just held. "How much for that, say?"

Dylan wiped the neck with his sleeve and glanced at Curtis. If they hadn't already unloaded the van, he'd have been tempted to lie. Not that he could conceive of these two guys hawking hot handmade pottery by the side of the road. "About a hundred. Maybe a buck fifty. Have to see."

Curtis's eyes widened. "No shit?"

"C'mon, man, we gotta go." Leon stood in the back door, face sweating, not interested in the merchandise they'd just hauled. He peeled off his baseball cap with one hand, swiped his arm across his forehead and up over his receding hairline, then replaced the cap. His eyes shifted to Dylan. "You got our money, or what?"

Dylan pulled out his wallet, counted out some bills, and handed half to Curtis. "How do you guys know my mother?"

"No shit," Curtis said again. "That chick's your mother? She don't look old enough."

Dylan shrugged.

"Mutual friends," Leon said, hand outstretched for his pay. Dylan handed it to him. "C'mon, Curtis. We gotta get back."

They left through the back door, each counting his money. Leon started the van, which came to life with a sound like a three-car accident, and hit the accelerator. They bounced down the alley, took the turn too fast, glanced off the corner of a brick building and disappeared.

"Mutual friends," Dylan murmured, not liking the sound of it. He went back inside to unwrap the rest of the pots.

They ran in a group, twenty-six of them, pounding through the streets in a herd, expensive shoes clapping on damp asphalt to the rhythm of fifty-two lungs grasping and expelling air.

It was a Saturday long run, required by The Program. Twelve miles, the most Dylan had ever run at one stretch, this time with the whole group. Rock had given them the obligatory pep talk beforehand

and Dylan had to admit he felt pumped. Over the last five weeks he'd turned a corner in his running. It no longer felt like he was dragging around a bag of cement when he first started out. His muscles didn't groan and resist and make him miserable until he got a mile or two in. He felt light on his feet, energized, ready to go.

Glenn arrived late, missing most of Rock's talk, and stood on the other side of the group from Dylan. Dylan wondered if he knew about the gathering at Penelope's house, that Dylan had been invited, that Penelope had shifted her attention to him. Then it struck him that Glenn might have been invited too. Maybe Penelope was taking this whole thing way more lightly than he thought. After all, he didn't really know her; he just knew how she seemed. The way she'd couched the invitation had sounded pretty casual. Just a group of people he "should meet," going to her house to watch the game. Was it possible she'd invited both himself and Glenn?

Once the group started running, Glenn made his way to Dylan's side with a neutral "Hey" as greeting.

"How you doin'?" Dylan responded, letting off on his pace to allow Glenn to warm up.

"It is way too . . ." Glenn gasped, running beside him, ". . . *fucking* early to be doing this."

Dylan smiled. Glenn didn't seem to be feeling the same light-on-his-feet progress that Dylan was.

"What'd you do last night?"

Glenn shook his head. "Damned if I can remember. I started at La Petite, I know that much. Met this chick who kept buying me Grand Marniers. I don't even like the stuff, but she was hot."

Dylan felt the breath come more easily now. Glenn hadn't been with Penelope. Hadn't, apparently, been thinking about Penelope. Not that Dylan cared, he just didn't need complications in his life. Not right now. Not with having just moved here, starting a business, and trying desperately to shuck an old life.

That was it: He wanted to choose his new life with care. No diving into any unknown situations, most especially a tangled relationship between a man and his ex-wife.

In that spirit, he asked, casually as he could, "Got any plans for the weekend?"

He glanced at Glenn askance as the group turned the corner onto William Street.

Glenn dragged a bandanna across his forehead, already sweating profusely. "Nah. After last night I'm taking it easy tonight."

"Nothing tomorrow?" Dylan turned his head away, as if interested in something in the Ben Franklin five-and-dime window.

"No, why? Did you want to run again?"

Dylan shrugged. "Maybe."

Glenn laughed. "You're a glutton for punishment,

you know that? I'm taking my day of rest after this."

They jogged on, Dylan matching his pace to Glenn's while people passed them in twos and threes.

"Next week I think I'm going to get tickets to a play up in D.C.," Glenn said after a while. "Penelope's been a little standoffish lately. I think she freaked herself out about us. But she's a sucker for dressing up and going out. What she'd really like is to see some opera star caterwauling at the Kennedy Center, but I'll be damned if I'll go that far."

Dylan's steps grew heavier. "She's into that stuff, huh?"

"Oh man. When we were married I got her a subscription to the Kennedy Center. You'd have thought I'd given her the Hope diamond, she was so excited." He chuckled. "Only problem was, I had to go too."

"Yeah, I don't know that I'm the opera type either."

"Most of that kind of stuff she was into was on her own, though, which was fine. You know, lecture series at the college, volunteering, garden club, stuff like that. I was always too busy at work for that and she understood. That's why it worked. That and we both like playing tennis, and golf at the country club. It's good to have stuff to do together."

Golf at the country club. Dylan was grateful for the downhill nature of this stretch of William Street; his energy level had dropped considerably.

"Guess it would be."

They headed onto the bridge over the Rappahannock, heading toward Chatham, and Dylan looked down into the wide, tree-lined depths of the river.

"So, not doing anything this weekend," he said again, just to be sure. "Nothing with Penelope, either?"

He thought he felt Glenn's eyes on him, but he kept his own eyes dead ahead, focused on his breathing, his footfalls, the Toyota passing them on the left.

"No, she said she had too much to do. That's why I'm getting the play tickets. Next weekend's the one, my friend. Nice dinner out, a show . . . she'll be happy. I'll get laid." He laughed.

Dylan smiled and shot him a glance. "Good," he said. "That's good."

But he wasn't talking about the play, and he certainly wasn't talking about Glenn getting laid.

Penelope hadn't invited Glenn to her party. She hadn't even told him about it. And that, for some reason, was good.

Chapter 10

It was a miracle. All six of her guests were coming—seven, including her date. Penelope had thought at the very least Sutter Foley would have to back out—he was famously elusive as a party guest. Fortunately, Megan and Sutter entertained enough that nobody took it personally, but having him to her house unnerved her.

She'd never had a sit-down dinner party for so many people. She'd been working all weekend to have the right drinks, appetizers, sides and entrée. Something elegant but not gratuitously fancy, and not too involved when it came to serving. She'd decided on Cornish game hens, because it was easy to determine how many she'd need for eight people, and she was serving them over wild rice with an apple-brandy glaze. For sides she had scalloped zucchini and *ciabatta* rolls. Vichyssoise was the first course, followed by an Asiago Caesar salad, then the entrée, and she planned to finish with a chocolate mousse cake.

Most of it could be made ahead, so she'd spent Saturday cooking and all of Sunday cleaning and trying to figure out what to wear. In the end she'd opted for a peacock-blue silk tunic over flowy black pants and embroidered ballet flats that reminded her of genie shoes. It looked Bohemian, she decided, which was better than formal or stiff in a skirt or dress.

Brady and Lily arrived first, thank goodness, so Mr. Darcy's conniptions were met with understanding attention. He jumped and barked and ran in circles, making all three of them laugh, and Brady roughhoused a little with him, which Penelope hoped would wear the pup out. She'd have to put him away eventually, but she wanted him to learn to socialize some first.

Penelope put Brady to work making drinks. Martinis for the three of them, and he volunteered to provide for the rest as they arrived.

"The place looks gorgeous," Lily said to her as Penelope rounded the room, martini in one hand and a lighter in the other. The room was sprinkled with candles she had forgotten to light.

Mr. Darcy followed them too, trying to catch the tassels on Penelope's shoes as she walked.

"Thanks, I've been cleaning for days. I'm really nervous about this." She took a sip of her martini.

Lily smiled. "Don't be. The food smells incredible and you know conversation's not going to lag with you, me, Georgia, and Megan here. I'm just anxious to meet this Leland character. Georgia did say he's coming, right?"

"She did. Do you think we'll be able to look at him without thinking about . . . you know?"

"Shrinkage?" Lily offered, holding up a finger and letting it curl down slowly.

The two of them burst into laughter and slid glances toward the door, as if the man might have entered and heard without them knowing.

"What's so funny?" Brady joined them, sliding an arm around Lily's waist. "Have I made the drinks too strong? Giggling usually doesn't happen until after the second martini."

"It's perfect," Penelope said. "Just what I needed to take the edge off. I've never had so many people for a sit-down dinner. Usually if it's over six I go for a buffet. Or a dessert party."

She hadn't even done that since she and Glenn had split. Would she have been as nervous, she wondered, or as excited, if Glenn had been her date tonight? She decided not to think about it.

"I know I couldn't do it," Brady said.

"What, no canned tuna for eight?" Lily teased.

"Hey, they'd eat it and they'd like it," he said, then turned his attention to Penelope. "So what's this I hear about you dating an ex-con? That's a change of pace for Miss Penelope, isn't it?" Brady's brow lifted and he gave Penelope his trademark pirate's grin.

Lily elbowed him. "Brady! I hope you plan to have more discretion when he arrives."

"Oh, you mean like this?" He mimicked Lily's finger motion. "Because that was pretty discreet."

The three of them laughed, with Penelope feeling the guilt first. "We have to stop. I'm sure he's a lovely man and it's none of our business anyway. I'm sure there's a perfectly reasonable explanation for . . . everything."

The doorbell rang and Penelope's heart leaped to her throat. Dylan? She couldn't wait for him to arrive. She wished she'd told him to come earlier, so they could have relaxed over a drink together first. It was bad enough hosting a party for a bunch of people without having to be nervous with your date too. She and Dylan weren't comfortable enough yet to be each other's refuge at a party, the way most significant others were.

But it was Georgia and Leland at the door. Georgia, looking nervous herself, introduced Penelope, then Brady and Lily as they entered the foyer, and shed her coat quickly. She wore a stunning white blouse with ruffles along the neckline, but it was stunning mostly for the amount of cleavage exposed. If she didn't get lucky tonight, it wouldn't be Georgia's fault.

"It's so nice to meet you. And thank you!" Penelope took the bottle of wine Leland offered, then took his hand and shook it warmly. "I've heard so much about you."

He was handsome, to be sure, and dressed like a college professor in a tweed coat complete with elbow patches. His hair was brown with a good bit of gray, but his eyes were a sharp blue and his smile wide and quick. A lean build and pleasant laugh added to his youthfulness. Beside him Georgia positively glowed.

"I've heard much about you, too," he said, then shifted his gaze to Lily. "You girls are quite the pack, as I understand it. Oh, and who is this?"

They all looked down to see Mr. Darcy humping Leland's leg.

Penelope's hand flew to her eyes, as if she could erase the mortifying behavior simply by not seeing it. The dog could not have chosen a worse—or more fitting—target.

She recovered quickly and swept the dog up into her arms, exclaiming, "Oh for heaven's sake! I'm so sorry! That's Mr. Darcy. He does this to everyone, absolutely everyone. He's just a puppy so he has no manners. In fact, I should really have him on a leash."

Behind her, snickers erupted from Lily and Brady.

"Don't worry," Leland said, petting the dog's head as Penelope held him. "It's not as if he's a hundred-pound Great Dane." He shot a wink at Georgia.

Penelope looked apologetically at Georgia and saw to her amazement that her friend was actually blushing. Georgia waved Pen's concern away then put a hand over her own mouth. Penelope, struggling to maintain composure, grabbed her friend's coat and headed for the closet. After a minute she placed Mr. Darcy back on the floor with a low "No humping" command.

Two minutes later the doorbell rang again. Mr. Darcy raced for the door, beating Penelope by seconds, so she was certain it would be Dylan. Sure enough, she opened the door and was caught immediately by those penetrating eyes.

She couldn't stop the smile that broadened across her face. "Dylan, hi."

"Hi." For a moment he looked glad to see her, then his eyes took in her clothes and the people behind her, and the color drained from his face.

It took Penelope a minute to realize he was wearing jeans and a pullover under his canvas barn jacket, and in his hands he held a bag of chips and a can of dip.

"You said we were watching a football game," he said, low. His expression was stricken.

Suddenly her own silk shirt, Leland's tweed coat and Georgia's ruffles seemed like an attack, or a judgment. Like she'd accidentally tricked him. She'd said this was to be casual, but that clearly meant different things to different people. And she *had* mentioned the game—which thankfully Brady had turned on the little kitchen television set—but that wasn't going to mitigate the fact that Dylan was noticeably underdressed.

"We are," Penelope said, infusing her voice with enthusiasm. "Brady's got it on in the kitchen. But I'll warn you, if you go in there he's likely to make you one of these killer martinis."

She held up her glass, but he did not look mollified.

"Come in, Dylan." She reached out and took his arm, afraid he might bolt. "Let me take your coat. And what have you got here? Oh thank goodness you brought chips. I was out and had to substitute crackers, but chips are much better."

He gave her a look that said she was patronizing him, that he was fully aware he'd committed his first *faux pas* before even getting in the door. Penelope had no choice but to ignore it.

She ushered him into the hallway, where Georgia came through like a champion.

"Dylan Mersey, you are a sight for sore eyes." She came forward like she'd known him all her life and planted a big kiss right on his cheek. "I've been tellin' my friend Leland all about you and your work, but I don't know what on earth to call some of those glazes you've got on your pots. He knows about this stuff because he makes a study of art history, you know, and has been very frustrated by my callin' them by the colors, since that apparently tells him nothin'."

"I'll take that." Penelope took the chips and dip from his hands, to keep him from having to walk into the rest of the company with it.

"Is that bean dip?" Georgia grabbed the can from Penelope's hands. "Oh my lord, there are few things in this world I like better than bean dip. Though it doesn't love me, I'll tell you. I'll be tootin' all night if I'm not careful."

That surprised a laugh out of him, for which Penelope was grateful.

"Georgia!" Lily gasped, entering the foyer just in time to hear her last remark. She glanced behind her toward Leland and Brady. "Your date is *right there*."

Georgia followed her gaze. "Oh hell, he isn't gonna sleep with me anyway. He got all the action he probably wants from Mr. Darcy when we walked in the door."

Penelope started to laugh, then noted Georgia's wounded expression.

Lily snorted and lifted her glass to Dylan. "Hi Dylan. I'm Lily. We kind of met once before."

"Hi." Dylan nodded. He still looked like he was in shock, though whether from discovering the party was vastly different than he'd anticipated or from hearing Georgia's revelations about her bodily functions and sexual relations, it was hard to say.

"Let me take your coat. Would you hold this?" Penelope moved to his side, held up her free hand and handed him her martini with the other. As he took the glass, he met her eyes, looking at her with a kind of entreaty she couldn't decipher. Did he want her to let him leave? She leaned closer. "I'm so sorry I didn't tell you—"

Georgia stumbled into her, nearly knocking her over, then righted herself with a firm hand on Penelope's arm. "My lord! I'm just not used to these high heels. And I'm not even drunk yet!"

Penelope looked down at Georgia's feet. They were shoes she wore all the time. But when she started to say it, she received a scorching "shut up" look.

Georgia turned and curled her arm through Dylan's. "C'mon Dylan, let's go get a drink."

Lily edged closer to Penelope as she hung up Dylan's coat. "God, he *is* cute, Pen. But he looks like he's walking into a nest of vipers. Why's he so nervous?"

"Because I misled him. Didn't you notice how he's dressed? I think I might have presented this as a football party and now he's shows up with chips and dip, wearing the wrong clothes. But it's *my* fault, not his."

"Penelope, honey, it's nobody's fault, because nobody's going to notice anything amiss," Lily said. "So he's in jeans, big deal. Brady would be too if I didn't wrestle him into those khakis. Now come on."

Penelope had never been more grateful for her friends.

Dylan, on the other hand, had never so fervently wished he were somewhere—anywhere—else. Penelope's house looked more sophisticated than when she'd been sitting on the couch in her robe and slippers and he'd been apologizing for being a bastard after having sex with her.

Now, looking at her in her cocktail-party clothes, surrounded by her upwardly mobile friends, he could hardly believe she was the same woman he'd had sprawled naked on his counter. She looked like somebody out of a magazine, with her perfectly shiny hair, her china-doll complexion and her expensive but understated jewelry. Hell, her shoes even matched her shirt.

On the other hand, here was old Dylan Mersey with bean dip and his least worn pair of jeans, looking like someone who should be parking cars out front instead of helping himself to a martini.

"So what do you think of Fredericksburg so far?" the guy mixing drinks asked him. Brady, his name was.

"Nice. Quiet. I haven't gotten out and explored much." He sipped the martini, then looked from the glass to Brady. "You put any vermouth in this?"

Brady gave him a conspiratorial smile. "A drop. Why, you want more?"

Dylan chuckled and shook his head. "No, it tastes about right for me tonight. Just don't give me another one or I'm liable to start speaking my mind."

"Dylan." Penelope paused in passing and put a hand to his arm.

Dylan's whole nervous system vibrated under the contact. Jesus, how could he want her when she looked like something he'd been admonished not to touch? She was a museum piece and he was, quite rightly, behind the velvet rope.

"Would you mind lighting the Sterno under that chafing dish?" she asked, with a smile that could melt chocolate. "I don't want that artichoke dip getting cold."

The girl was speaking Greek. If she hadn't looked in the direction of the thing that looked vaguely like a fondue pot he'd never have known what the hell she was talking about.

"Uh, sure." He looked down as she pressed a silver grill lighter into his hand.

She smiled her thanks, squeezing his arm once more before gliding off toward the guy in the tweed coat.

Brady watched him light what Dylan assumed was the Sterno and asked, "So how'd you meet Penelope?"

"My shop's across from hers." Dylan noted the crackers arranged artfully on a plate next to the dip—warmed comfortably in the silver "chafing" dish—and wondered what had become of his Doritos. "She called the cops on me."

No sense misrepresenting himself to this guy. He had that daddy-by-proxy protective look about him.

Brady spluttered into his glass, then swallowed and let out a laugh. "She *what*?"

Dylan rocked back on his heels, glad to have someone else guessing instead of himself. "Yeah, I knocked on her door after dark and scared her. Guess I looked . . . threatening."

Brady tilted his head, sharp eyes regarding him shrewdly. "Pen's a good girl. Some people think she's a snob, but she's not. She's just got a certain way of looking at the world."

Dylan nodded. "No, she's not a snob. But that way of looking at the world . . . it's pretty set."

"You think?" Brady asked, but he wasn't joking.

"Yes. I think."

This guy could have no idea, Dylan thought, draining his drink. This guy had never been judged inappropriately in his life. This guy probably had an MBA, worked in a spiffy, clean office, had a secretary bring him lunch and played golf every Saturday.

"Then what are *you* doing here?" Brady's question caught him off guard. It was combative, but the guy's tone was not.

Dylan's mind reached for a response that wouldn't come.

Brady held his gaze for an extended moment, then shifted it to someone behind Dylan and smiled broadly.

"Leland, what can I get for you? Another martini?"

Leland shook his head as he passed. "Not just yet, but I'll be back."

The doorbell rang. Dylan watched Penelope breeze through the company toward the door. As she passed, she shot him what could only be interpreted as a private smile. It made his insides clench.

What did she expect of him? Was he supposed to play host to her hostess? He'd never been a "date" in this sense, where there were multiple couples and "chafing" dishes and whatever.

"Great." Next to him, Brady muttered the word as he shook another martini.

Dylan glanced at him and Brady frowned ruefully. "Nothing like having your boss at a party."

"Sutter Foley's your boss?"

"Don't get me wrong. He's a good one. But . . ." He shrugged. "Guess I won't be wearing any lampshades tonight."

Dylan laughed. Because of the grant, he'd been feeling like Sutter Foley was *his* boss, too—making him even less of an equal at this party. But this put things in a different light.

"You're in charge of the drinks, buddy." Dylan clapped Brady lightly on the back and set his empty glass on the counter. "I say you get Foley to wear the lampshade."

Brady's burst of laughter followed him as, hands in his pockets, he moved into the living room, which was technically the same room as the kitchen but differentiated by a floor break from ceramic tile to hardwood. Over the hardwood Penelope had an oriental carpet, large and intricate, the colors emphasizing the shift from kitchen yellow to living-room earth tones. He wondered if she'd had a designer do the house.

Lily and Georgia stood together near some French doors that led, presumably, out back.

Lily noticed him first, smiled, then lifted a plate of cut vegetables from the table next to her and offered them to him. "Crudité?"

"What?" The word was out before he could stop it.

"The dip's over there." Georgia pointed with a red fingernail toward the side table. "It's Pen's homemade blue cheese. Fabulous."

Dylan waved off the vegetables. "No, thanks."

"Looks to me like Pen needs some of your bowls and platters," Georgia said. "All this crystal's 'bout to make me blind."

"I don't think Penelope needs anything from me," Dylan said, scanning the room.

"Why would you say a thing like that?" Georgia asked, then tipped her glass up to capture the olive from the bottom. Chewing, she added, "You're about the best thing to happen to Penelope in years."

One side of his mouth kicked up. "You think I've *happened* to Penelope?"

Georgia looked at him speculatively. "What's the matter with you, honey? You look like the dog who's not gettin' any scraps. Aren't you havin' fun? Have yourself another drink and loosen up, that's my advice. It's a party, for heaven's sake."

Dylan glanced at Lily.

"I don't advise you have many more of these."
She raised her glass slightly.

"They're pretty strong. And I *am* having fun," he
told Georgia.

"Then why do you look so mopey?"

Lily laughed. "Georgia, he looks perfectly fine.
Leave the poor guy alone."

"I'm not mopey," Dylan said, thinking yes, he
was. He was walking around acting like the kid
who didn't get as many Christmas presents as everyone else.

Georgia poked him in the chest. "I can see the
thoughts plain as day on your face. You think we're
a bunch of haves to your have-not. Well, let me tell
you somethin'. There's plenty of stuff we haven't
got that you have. Like for example—"

"Oh no," Lily murmured.

"Sex," Georgia said. "I haven't had sex in God
knows how long, and do you know how that makes
me feel? Probably not. You look like the kinda
guy gets sex whenever he wants, and I happen to
know—"

"Georgia!" Lily gasped.

"Well, what? Why dance around it? We all
know—"

"Oh shit!" Lily exclaimed.

Dylan and Georgia watched Lily fly across the
room toward Mr. Darcy, who stood in the middle

of the coffee table, licking the last few bits of bean dip from the bottom of a crystal bowl.

Georgia shifted her gaze from Mr. Darcy to Dylan. "Think we oughta bring him some Doritos?"

Dylan laughed. "Looks like it's bedtime for Bonsai."

So they knew . . . everything, Dylan thought, as they all filed into the dining room. What had Penelope said about it? How were they looking at him now? Could it possibly have made them think better of him or was he the token sex toy? He was pretty sure he knew the answer to that, but after Georgia's accusation of mopery he was determined not to be a baby. So he was Penelope's experiment. He'd treat the whole evening as a trip down the rabbit hole.

Sutter Foley and Megan Rose had arrived with profuse apologies for being late, along with a tale of nanny woes that for some reason had Penelope looking sadder than the story warranted. They'd brought two bottles of wine, which Dylan now recognized as the safe thing to bring to any kind of party from here on out, though he doubted he could afford bottles the likes of which the Foleys had brought.

As he moved into the dining room behind Leland and Georgia, Penelope slid in beside him and took his hand. Her grip was warm and strong.

"Having fun?"

When she looked up at him, her eyes were so hopeful, so unexpectedly vulnerable, he couldn't help squeezing her hand in return. He found himself smiling down at her.

"Sure."

Her other hand rose to his forearm and she leaned into him for one ephemeral moment. "I'm so glad."

She smelled like flowers, just faintly. If they'd been alone he'd have turned to her, taken her silk-sheathed body into his arms, and held her. Just held her. Like a treasure briefly entrusted to him.

Then she was gone, floating to the head of the table with a beatific smile.

"Dylan, you're over here, and Sutter, I hope you don't mind, but I've put you at the head of the table." She held a palm out the way he imagined Martha Stewart would if she were entertaining visiting dignitaries.

Dylan realized as he excused himself through the crowd that she actually had place cards with everyone's name on them. Next to him was Sutter Foley.

As Penelope directed traffic, he sat and picked up the place card, wondering if by chance it was a name tag, too. She'd actually written the names in calligraphy.

As soon as they were seated, Penelope brought

out small bowls of white soup with sprigs of green in the center.

"So, Dylan, are you by chance named after the poet Dylan Thomas?"

Dylan turned his attention from the soup to Georgia's date, who tilted forward in his seat across the table from him.

He cleared his throat. "Uh, no. My mother was, still is really, a dyed-in-the-wool hippy, so she named me after Bob Dylan."

"Some people believe," Leland expounded, directing his gaze around the table, "Bob Dylan chose his pseudonym because of the poet. So I guess that would mean by extension you were named after him."

Dylan smiled. Okay, Dylan Thomas was a poet. "I'll have to look him up, see what I think of his work."

"My mother was a huge Bob Dylan fan too," Georgia said.

"It's actually worse than you think," Dylan added. "My middle name is Joplin."

Everyone laughed. Dylan took a sip of his soup. It was stone cold. He looked around the table to see if anyone else was having the same problem, but they spooned theirs up happily enough. Maybe his was the only one she forgot to microwave.

"Are you serious?" Penelope asked. "Your middle name is Joplin? Dylan Joplin Mersey?"

Dylan smiled. "Not exactly *Mayflower* stuff, huh?"

"Hey, be glad you didn't grow up with everyone thinking you were named for *The Brady Bunch*," Brady said. "At least *Dylan*'s cool."

Dylan laughed.

"I can top both y'all," Georgia said. "My middle name's Virginia. They might as well have called me Eastern Seaboard."

Dylan could hardly believe it, but he was loosening up. It might have been the wine—a red even he could tell was good—but mostly he thought it was the conversation. These people were interesting, and polite about getting everyone involved. In the couple of intervals where conversation lagged, Penelope stepped in with some pertinent detail two of them had in common or some current event everyone could comment on. It was masterful, really. He was impressed.

"Tell me how the store's coming along," Sutter said as Penelope got up to serve the entrées.

Dylan turned to the man on his right. Everything about him screamed *wealth*, from his British accent to his cashmere sweater to his manicured nails.

"So far, so good. But it's still hard to say how business is going to be once the opening is over. This Gallery Night thing looks to be good, but after that . . ." He shrugged. "It's anybody's guess."

Sutter nodded, gazing seriously at his plate. Dylan

wondered if admitting ignorance was a stupid thing to do in front of the one who gave him the money to get started, but he wasn't going to be dishonest. Instead he decided to mention something he'd been rolling around in his head.

"I've been kicking around another idea, though, maybe you could give me your take on it."

"Certainly." Sutter leaned toward him, eyes intent, respectful. One businessman to another. Who'd'a thought?

So he told Sutter Foley, billionaire software mogul, his idea about supplying some of the local bistros with handmade stoneware mugs, plates and bowls, with designs specific to their restaurants. They'd be sold at a discount with the understanding that Dylan's name and contact information be supplied, maybe somewhere on the menu or one of those little informational things you see in the middle of the table sometimes.

"I'm not sure how exactly the restaurants would want to do it, but I figure then people would see my stuff in action, if you know what I mean. They'd get how ceramics and pottery can actually be *used*, not just bought to be decorative, you know?"

Sutter sat back and gave him an assessing look. Rethinking the grant? Dylan wondered. Maybe it was a stupid idea. Pottery in action, of all things.

"I think it's brilliant," Sutter said. "I can think of several establishments off the top of my head that would benefit. They all fancy themselves unique, you know. If they had a signature look to their crockery it would be all the better."

Dylan sat up straighter in his chair. "That's what I thought. I was in that coffee shop the other day . . ."

Before he knew it, Penelope was bringing out the entrées. This just after a weird little glass of sherbet, which thankfully, Dylan had been too engrossed in conversation to question. The entrée carried the same risk, however. They were the smallest chickens he'd ever seen, one to a plate.

Before he could make a fool of himself, Brady cracked, "What'd you do, kill a family of ducklings?"

Lily shushed him, giggling, and said, "They're Cornish game hens. And they look delicious." This last she directed to Penelope, who glowed.

And they *were* delicious, Dylan found. Unwieldy, sure. A little hard to get a decent bite out of, but delicious.

From time to time he'd look up to find Penelope's eyes on him. She'd blush and turn away when he caught her eye, but he wondered what she was thinking. Assessing his performance? He would be if he were her.

He couldn't say he was sorry when the evening ended, though he'd had a much better time than he'd anticipated. He was exhausted. It was tough, socializing, after having been wrapped up in his own head for so long.

When the last two guests, Brady and Lily, said they had to leave, Dylan got their coats and grabbed his own too. Penelope walked the three of them to the door. Thanks were passed around, then Brady and Lily departed, leaving Dylan at the door with Penelope.

Before either of them said a word, both of them became aware of something emanating from the direction of the room just off the foyer—some kind of den, Dylan had seen when he'd volunteered to put the dog away. A smell. A strong, noxious, distinctly dog-poop-like scent.

They looked at each other.

"Oh no," Penelope said.

"The bean dip." Dylan turned and went into the den, where the puppy sat scrunched against the side of his crate, whining. An unsavory mess was in the opposite corner.

Penelope, right behind him, said, "Oh God. He's going to be up all night doing that."

"Let me take him with me. It's my fault for bringing that dip to begin with, and you have enough cleaning up to do as it is. Let me take him and get this out of his system."

She gazed up at him, something like amazement on her face. "You'd do that?"

"Hell, it's not like I've got nice rugs to worry about."

"But you won't get any sleep."

He shrugged, bending to pick up the crate. "Doesn't matter. I'll just give him back to you in the morning when you get to work. How's that?"

She thought for only a moment, then squeezed his arm. "Thank you. That would be a huge help. Let me just clean the crate out first."

Minutes later, after letting the dog relieve himself copiously on the front lawn and putting him in the crate in his car, Dylan returned to say goodbye. They stood just inside the door, his clothes exuding cold from the now-frigid air outside.

"Thank you for coming," she said. It was the same thing she'd said to everyone else, but in a far different tone. She stood close to him. "Did you enjoy meeting everyone?"

He tilted his head and wondered what she expected from him now. A chaste, first-date-type kiss? A boyfriend kiss? He wanted to know what she thought, but did not want to have the conversation to find out.

So he nodded. "I did. Everyone was real . . . down to earth. Friendly. I appreciated it."

She smiled with downcast eyes. "If you had it to do over, would you do it again? Knowing what you know now, I mean."

He laughed. "I can't believe I agreed to do it the

first time. But honestly, I'd have less hesitation, knowing what I know now."

That pleased her, he could tell. She moved an inch or two closer and lightly took hold of the front of his coat, one hand on either side of the open jacket. "Then maybe we'll do it again sometime. Or maybe . . . just the two of us could do something."

Her statement was more of a question. A lead-in to a date. Dylan wasn't sure what he thought of that, though he wasn't surprised it had come up. Inviting him here had been a pretty obvious sign. He just didn't know how she figured it would ever work between them. They were too different. Couldn't she see that? How was it she was proceeding so fearlessly?

Because she didn't know about him. Didn't know the extent of his past or how it colored his present. Didn't know who he really was at all.

Instead of answering, he put a hand to the side of her neck and pulled her in for a kiss. Not a chaste one, no, but a slow, lingering dance of tongues, and lips, and breaths.

Before it could go too far, he pulled back. "Good night, Penelope."

Her eyes turned upward, dark and intent. He could have her again, he thought, despite her having said she wasn't inviting him to spend the night. Right now, right here. He could let her lead him up to what was no doubt a pink, ruffly, pillowed bedroom and make love to this gorgeous woman. God knew he wanted to. In so many ways, he wanted to.

But he wouldn't know what to say or do afterward. And he didn't want the fight between his mind and his body, didn't want the guilt, didn't want the addiction, didn't want the final decision about what was right and what was wrong laid squarely on his conscience once again.

So he avoided the issue, kissed her softly once more, and repeated, "Good night, Penelope."

Chapter 11

She was wired. She'd cleaned the house, loaded the dishwasher and started it. She'd stacked all the dishes that wouldn't fit next to the sink for the next load, and she'd put all the table linens in the laundry. She'd picked up glasses and napkins and appetizer plates from all around the living room, blown out and put away candles, and she still wasn't the least bit tired.

Parties did that to her. Energized her. Especially when it was her own and it was successful. How she wished someone were still here whom she could discuss it with! She and Glenn used to go over who said what, who ate the most, who drank too much, who seemed to be fighting before they arrived.

She thought about Glenn with a little burst of nostalgia. Theirs had been such an uncomplicated romance. He'd been perfect for her; she'd been perfect for him. They'd met, they'd dated, they'd fallen in love, they'd gotten married. Everyone had been happy for them. His family, her family. The only thing that'd been missing was the next step—children. The step at which Glenn had balked.

What were Dylan's feelings on children?

Laughter and fear leaped to her throat. He probably had *no* thoughts about children. He was so busy taking care of himself, building his business, running away from all that stuff he was running away from in Baltimore. Having children was probably the last thing on his mind.

And yet, hadn't it been paternal to take care of Mr. Darcy tonight? And hadn't it been caring—one might even say *loving*—of him to think about her work load after the party and take the sick pup off her hands? Most people thought about children at some point, particularly in their thirties . . .

He had fit in with her friends so much better than she'd even hoped. A deep inner warmth glowed even now as she thought about the moment she'd glanced over to see him laughing with Brady Cole. Good old Brady; she knew the two of them would get along. And Georgia, bless her heart, with her lively, if inappropriate, comments, must have at least assured Dylan he could say nothing as off-kilter as she did. Not to mention Georgia had saved Penelope from mortifying him further when he'd arrived.

Then there was the cozy conversation Dylan and Sutter had had. Who would have thought the two of *them* would get going like that?

She took a deep breath and sighed, smiling. This thing really *could* work out—the evening proved that, she was sure. Maybe even to the point that Dylan could be convinced it would too.

The house was quiet. Too quiet. She had the impulse to take the dog out for his last walk of the night, and then remembered that Mr. Darcy was with Dylan. She should go get him, she thought. Here she was wide awake, she could take care of the sick dog, if need be. If Dylan was still up, maybe the two of them could even take him for a walk, though it was a bit cold.

She stood up and looked for her purse. She'd drive by his shop and see if the apartment light was on. If he was awake, she'd knock and take Mr. Darcy off his hands.

Decision made, she practically danced for the door. A glance at her watch told her it was midnight. That wasn't *that* bad: If he was like her he didn't go to bed until midnight anyway.

At the door she paused. Then, with the feeling of wanting to keep the secret even from herself, she sprinted upstairs, rooted through the drawer in the bedside table and came up with two condoms. Resisting surprise at herself, she stuffed them into her purse, deep down to the bottom so she wouldn't think of them again, and raced to the car.

The streets were dead empty so late on a Sunday, so she drove slowly down Caroline Street, nearing his store about three minutes after she'd left her house. The windows above Mersey Pots glowed dimly, showing at least one light on deep inside the apartment, she reasoned. A reading light, perhaps. She turned up the alley and rolled the Mercedes to a stop at his back door.

He answered the third time she knocked, looking puffy-eyed and disheveled in sweat pants and a tee-shirt.

He couldn't have looked more surprised to see her. "Is everything all right?"

Clearly, she'd woken him up. For a split second she wondered if she should invent an emergency. "Oh everything's fine, yes, I'm so sorry to have woken you up. It looked like your light was on."

He rubbed a hand across his face. "What time is it?"

She looked at her watch. "Twelve-ten. I am so sorry. I can just go. It's just—"

"No, come on in. Is everything all right?"

She laughed a little, since he'd just asked her that. If she hadn't been so mortified to have woken him up, she'd be amused to see him groggy, so unlike his watchful and alert self.

She liked him this way. It gave her a glimpse of how he'd be with his guard down, when he trusted her, when he trusted life.

"Everything's *fine*. I was just wired after the party and thought I'd come take Mr. Darcy off your hands. I'm so awake, there's no sense leaving him here to keep you up."

He eyed her. "You don't trust me with him?"

"Don't be silly. I just thought I'd relieve you of the responsibility."

A wry smile curled one side of his mouth. "I was enjoying the company, tell you the truth. But I guess you missed him."

For some reason this struck Penelope as a revelation. "You were? I'm sorry, then. I'll leave him. You two have a nice night and I'll just get him in the morning, like we planned."

She turned to go but he stopped her with a low chuckle and a hand on her arm. She wished she didn't have a coat on. The moment his hand reached out a longing to be touched by him swamped her. Did he feel it too? Or was her imagination carrying her away?

"You don't have to go. I'm awake now. Come on up." He turned toward the wooden steps and headed up. She took the opportunity to enjoy how his sweatpants rode on his hips, clung to his tight, toned buttocks. All that running, she thought, paying off.

His apartment was, to be generous, Spartan. He had a twin bed with white sheets and a thin blue blanket with a ragged edge. A boom box sat on a cinder block and a small black-and-white TV with rabbit ears was shoved in a corner. He probably couldn't get anything on it from here. The kitchen was clean, spotless really, making her wonder if he even owned any dishes or ever ate at home.

Mr. Darcy's crate was next to the bed, and he whined and wagged and pawed the wire walls noisily when he saw her.

"Look who's here, Bonsai," Dylan said in a playful voice she'd never heard before. He nabbed a sweatshirt off a chair and pulled it over his head, briefly exposing a swath of toned abdomen. Penelope's heart quickened. "Mama missed you."

He leaned down to open the crate door, allowing her a last lingering look at that fine behind.

"I wish you'd stop calling him Bonsai," she said without rancor, bending to pick up the pooch, who ran to her.

"I tried to, but he wouldn't come to me when I called him Mr. Darcy." He rubbed a hand through his hair. "Not that I blame him. He probably gets beat up at the dog park for having such a pansy name." His eyes held a teasing glint.

She suppressed a smile and held the dog close. Then she pulled him away and looked at Dylan. "Did you give him a bath?"

Dylan shrugged. "He got a little messy on the way home. But he seems okay now."

Her heart felt like it expanded in her chest. She looked him in his sleepy, not-yet-defensive eyes, and said the thing that sprang to mind. "I bet you'd make a terrific dad."

If she'd lit his shirt on fire she could not have received a more panicked look.

She burst out laughing. "Don't worry. I'm not volunteering to make you one."

He relaxed, stretched his eyes, blinking fast, and looked at the ground. "Jesus, you do know how to wake a guy up, Penelope."

"I'm sorry." Her fingers moved slowly in the dog's fur as she held him. "There's just something about you that makes me want to . . . shake you up."

His eyes, no longer sleepy, regarded her with a heavy-lidded indolence. Penelope's breathing got short.

"Is that right?" he asked. "And here I was think-ing you were the one needing a new angle in your world view."

"Oh no," she said, eyes on him, heart racing. "It's you. My world view is all-encompassing these days. You're the one clinging to old ideas."

She watched him take a step toward her, closing

the gap between them. He took the dog from her arms.

"I have a new idea," he said quietly, his eyes not leaving hers. Then he turned and put Mr. Darcy back in the crate.

Penelope's heart hammered in her ears as she watched him return to her. There was no strife between them this time, no conflict or challenge, this was simply Dylan looking at Penelope as if he would swallow her whole.

She recognized the look—whole and overt now—as one she had received from him in splinters earlier in the evening. When he'd glanced across the table at her, when he'd watched her talking to Megan, when he'd kissed her at the door.

He moved right for her and without hesitation took her face in his hands and kissed her.

She dissolved against him. Her hands up and hovering next to his body, not touching, as if contact would put her over the edge. She could think of nothing but his lips, his tongue, the warm cotton and all-male scent of him.

He took a step in and broke her suspension. Her hands dropped to his hips, to the top of that fine, toned ass she had been admiring just minutes ago, and pulled him into her.

His body was lean and wiry strong. She arched into him. His hands dove into her hair, he deepened the kiss and she was lost, her brain heating to liquid that coursed down through her body to end in a molten pool at her core.

The kiss ended and he pulled back, long-lashed eyes gazing at her with the question he already knew the answer to. Already knew it because his hands were pushing her coat down her arms, his fingers were moving to the million tiny buttons of her silk tunic.

She couldn't help him, all she could do was gaze at him, her breath high in her chest, her lips parted, her body, every nerve, reaching out for his.

The shirt opened and his eyes dropped to her breasts. He reached out, touched her skin reverently, heat radiating out from his touch. She watched his face, the long sandy lashes atop the angle of his cheekbones, the wide sensuous mouth, the mouth that did not do enough smiling, curving with satisfaction as he lowered the straps of her bra.

When his palm covered her breast, lightly brushing back and forth across the nipple, she was spurred to action. Her fingers found the hem of his shirt, pushed tee shirt and sweatshirt up until her hands found his flesh and slid into his warmth.

Seconds later they were naked and he was lowering her onto the thin mattress of the twin bed.

"This, my dear, is a bed." She could hear the smile in his voice, see the teasing in his eyes. "Preferable for this sort of activity over other hard surfaces, such as Formica."

She laughed. "Hey, the counter was your idea. I remember distinctly."

His lips curved as he kissed her. "It seemed like a good idea at the time."

He reached over to the single lamp that burned by the bedside and turned it off, darkness descending only briefly before light from the street turned them into a study in shades of gray.

Which was just what they were together, she thought, heart pulsing with possibility. Shades of gray. Their lives, so black and white individually, met at the point in between—depended on their seeing the nuances that connected them.

She looked up into his face, found his glittering eyes upon her.

"You're . . . impossibly beautiful." He lowered himself to kiss her again, one lingering, gentle kiss, teasing.

He gazed down at her, and with two fingers smoothed strands of hair from her forehead. The movement was so gentle, she felt as if she could cry.

"So are you," she whispered. Before he could laugh or make any comment, she raised her hands to his face and drew it to her for the same kind of gentle kiss. A promise. She was telling the truth, it said. It was all she could do to stop from uttering the next words that teetered on the tip of her tongue. *I love you.* She thought that she might burst with the feeling, their connection was so strong.

But he would recoil, she was sure. Instead she shifted beneath him, reached low with one hand and held him, moved him toward her, and settled for, "I want you, Dylan." She said his name with every ounce of emotion she could not otherwise express. "Dylan."

He pushed toward her, kissed her again, this time insistently, tongue probing, body moving.

"Wait," she whispered close to his ear.

He froze.

"Just—I have a condom, in my purse. We should . . ."

He pushed up, his look penetrating, she could tell by the corded muscles in his arms. "Aren't you on the pill?"

She swallowed hard. "Uh, no. But I—I brought two condoms, this time."

He rolled slightly to the side, tension radiating from him, his gaze pinned on hers. "What about last time?"

She had no words. She got out of bed, found her purse and managed, through some kind of miracle, to put her hands immediately on the two connected condoms. She turned to look at him, naked in the middle of his room, light from the lamps on Caroline Street grazing her skin with secret, tentative fingers.

Slowly, careful to maintain her balance on unsteady knees, she moved back toward the bed, toward that long angled body and that inscrutable face turned toward her in the dark.

A thousand thoughts raced through her head, a million things to say. *I don't get pregnant. I've wanted to, I've tried before. In my marriage. You didn't get me pregnant, I feel sure, but—but—*

But she did not want to have that conversation. Didn't want that word, so hard and tangible on the tongue, to kill what they had now. The closeness, the intimacy, the understanding.

She reached the edge of the bed and held the condoms out to him. "I want you," she said again, staring at him. "Make love to me, Dylan."

The moment she'd said it, he'd been lost. The ghostly pale goddess, standing in his grim apartment, her dark hair tumbling over feminine shoulders onto breasts that peaked with desire for him, was no contest for his sudden fear, his common sense.

She said it, *I want you*, and his frightened desire had surged back to life, the blood thrashing through his brain erasing any thought but possession. He could have her. For this time, and these moments, she would be his.

Make love to me. He wanted himself inside, needed himself inside her. Here, in his ratty, crappy apartment, she saw nothing but him. She offered herself simply, after gazing at him tenderly the whole damn night as he'd negotiated a social minefield the likes of which he'd never before encountered.

Ironically, what pushed him over the edge was the sudden memory of a moment, earlier in the evening, when she'd taken his hand and leaned against him before they sat down to dinner. That moment of closeness had startled and gratified him. Now it sealed the deal.

He'd reached out and taken the condoms, and he'd taken her places even he'd never been before.

Now . . . now, however, he lay awake in a shabby gray dawn thinking about the last time. When there had been no condoms. Thinking about the surging desire that had poured into her unprotected body, into the unprotected body of a woman he knew to be desperate for a child.

Would she do that to him? Would she trick him? Trap him? Fool herself into thinking it was right?

He rejected it. She'd brought condoms. She needn't have told him anything, hadn't had to bring it up at all, but she'd brought protection this time. Still . . . last time . . .

That's when the phone rang.

Penelope pretended to be asleep. She didn't want him to leave the room, which he would do if he thought she was awake and listening. It wasn't that she planned to eavesdrop; she just wanted him back in bed as quickly as possible. Her back, against which he'd been folded, was cold now that he was gone, and she wanted to wake up with him, to look at him with the new comprehension she felt they now shared, with the intimacy of last night still hanging in the air.

"Yeah." Dylan's voice was low but she could hear it. "Details of what? . . . No, I can't talk now. No, nobody important."

Penelope's entire body froze, the blood stalling in her veins.

"I can't say." He gave a chuckle even she could tell was forced. Then his back tensed. "When? I'm not sure . . . Look, I said I—"

She watched as he ran a hand through his hair. Was this another woman? Did she want to come over? Some girlfriend he left back in Baltimore?

"Of course you do." He said this with the resigned air of a man used to a certain kind of nagging. "I'm not an idiot, I wouldn't do that."

Of course not, honey. I wouldn't cheat on you. Trust me.

She turned onto her back. Tears leaked out of her eyes and ran into the hair at her temples. They were cold.

"What? Tell me what you've done." A long silence, then an uncontrolled, hissing, "*Jesus.*"

Silence.

Then, "I'll be waiting."

The phone flipped shut and he stood motionless. Penelope turned over in bed, her face to the windows. The day was gray, cloudy. Perfect. She wanted to get out of there so badly she pictured herself sailing out the window.

She'd done many stupid things the last few weeks, but this morning was not going to be one of them. She was going to get out of here with dignity. She'd say nothing about the phone call; she'd be cool and aloof. And she'd figure out what the hell to do next once she was out of this bitter, dreadful space.

There was no place colder, she reflected, than the morning-after bed of misspent passion.

Chapter 12

Dylan sat at his potting wheel working an eight-pound block of clay, pressing the wet mass into a cone and then guiding it back into a ball, up and down, up and down, replaying the conversation with Pinky in his mind.

Pinky needed a favor. And it wasn't some risk-free, straight-up action he needed Dylan to take either. It was enough to easily land him back in jail if anything went wrong.

Pinky had a contact who'd knocked over a jewelry store in Baltimore. The stuff was headed for Miami, most likely to be traded for drugs, or melted down, sold, and the proceeds used for drugs. But some of it was apparently estate stuff, the kind that brought real money. The kind that would identify the source of the robbery.

They needed to get the stuff out of Baltimore fast, and Dylan's was the perfect place to hold it until it cooled off, Pinky had decided. Dylan being one of Pinky's only contacts outside of Maryland—hell, outside of Baltimore. Once the cops were off the scent, someone would come pick it up and drive it to Florida. Dylan would never even have to touch it if he didn't want to. And he could make a nice chunk of change in the bargain. Such were Pinky's promises.

Dylan's insides quaked like Jell-O. Not with fear, but with rage. The only way he could keep his hands still was to continue coning and unconing the clay in front of him, letting the slick, spinning mass conform to the shape of his hands, respond to the balance and release of pressure.

Pinky's first call had come when Penelope was there, a spotlight beamed from heaven on all that was wrong with the two of them. He'd let himself forget, for a while, that it would never work. Let himself bask in the bright sunshine of possibility.

Then reality had shown up. Jarring him awake, making him wonder what he'd been thinking, that he could have something real and lasting with someone like Penelope Porter? That he could turn into country-club Glenn?

Or maybe he'd thought his luck was changing,

stupid bastard that he was. A beautiful, sweet woman stood naked in his apartment, oblivious to the barren surroundings, and asked him to make love to her. It would have been Herculean to resist her. And he was no Hercules, as he'd proved.

For a moment his hands stilled, clay slipping beneath his wet fingers. He recalled the feel of her lips, tender and yielding, and the strength of her body as they'd moved together. In his mind she glowed like freedom. A woman untainted by his old life. Someone so far removed from the seamy side of his existence that she would never understand it. For some reason he felt that if he could just reach her, have her, he'd be safe.

He scoffed at himself. A fairy tale. They couldn't sustain closeness for even twelve hours straight. She'd left coolly that morning. Miffed, he could tell. No doubt because he'd been yanked away from her and she felt it, but there was nothing he could do about it. Not a goddamn thing. He owed the favor and it was up to him to either do it or figure out how the hell to get out of it. Either way he was probably toast.

He guided the clay back into a cone. He hadn't wanted to get into it with Pinky, not while she was sleeping in his bed barely ten feet away. He hadn't wanted Pinky to give him even one detail, because once that conversation began he couldn't tell Pinky to go to hell. He'd know something he shouldn't. He'd be complicit.

So he'd cut him off, but not before seriously pissing him off.

The second conversation, once Penelope was safely away, had been the kicker.

"I can't do it," Dylan had said, careful as always not to use Pinky's name on the phone. "I'd help you for old times' sake, but I'm not doing anything illegal. The cops already watch me, they know my past and they're ready to jump down my throat if I so much as park in a loading zone. Which wouldn't do you any good either. Don't ask me to fuck things up here. I've worked hard."

"You've worked hard," Pinky said. His voice was low, deadpan. Dylan remembered Pinky using that same tone of voice on a guy who'd tried to stiff him on profits from some stolen stereo equipment ten years ago. *This is all you got,* Pinky had repeated the fence's words, waiting a mere beat before slipping the knife from his sleeve and slicing the guy's cheek open. "I work fuckin' hard too. I worked hard when I saved your ass in the pen, you forget about that?"

"I believe I thanked you for that," Dylan said mildly. He wasn't going to get into that, not if he could help it.

Pinky made a sound like spitting. "So you're

saying you don't trust me. I've known you since we were kids, you forget that? You forget playin' kick ball in the street? Knockin' over newspaper boxes? C'mon, man. This is safe, I'm telling you. I just need you to hold some stuff 'til I can get it picked up."

"Look, the way my luck's been running, the second it hits my hands the cops'll be all over it. You want to lose the stuff? 'Cause that's the only thing likely to come of it being here."

A long silence on the other end didn't bode well for Dylan. It was Pinky working up another tack to take, Dylan was sure.

Finally, Pinky exhaled. "Shit, they told me you were gonna do this. That's why they made me take out a little insurance."

That spark lit the fuse of Dylan's fury. "What are you talking about? Who told you I wouldn't do it?"

"I can't say. My partners. They said you'd gone soft, but I said don't worry, he's a buddy. He'll trust me. That's what I get for fuckin' trusting people."

"Turns out I'm the one who shouldn't have trusted you."

"What're *you* talking about? I've always had your back. Had your mom's back too, you know. Remember that money she owed?"

Dylan's teeth ground together so hard he thought they might crack. "I paid that back. With interest."

"Yeah, but she run it back up again. Not with me, man, with them. And you know they ain't the kind that take Visa."

Dylan suddenly felt cold. "Are you threatening my mother? What about all she did for you, growing up? You have turned into one ugly piece of shit, you know that?"

"Listen to what I'm telling you. It ain't me. I'm just warning you, they want their dough and you could get it back for her, you just do this one thing."

"I'll get a loan."

"You think there's time for that? Besides, who's gonna give you money?"

"I'll find a way. But I'm not risking jail again."

"This ain't no more risk than anything else you do. You know how easy it would be for someone to turn you in for possession? Candy, ice, they could fuck you over either one without lifting a finger."

"I don't possess shit, and you know it," Dylan said.

Pinky laughed, a sound chilling in its confidence. "Guess again, my friend."

Say what you wanted about Pinky, he didn't make idle threats. So much for childhood friends.

Dylan's throat closed. "Look, I haven't done anything to you. I just want to get out," he said, his voice low.

"Yeah, well, I want a million dollars. Maybe

you haven't done anything to me, but you haven't done anything *for* me either. Do this and I'll let you out. You'll be free, I promise. Freer than you ever been."

"If you keep threatening me, you're going to learn a thing or two about me you might not know," Dylan said, his resolve hardening. "I'm cleaner than you think. Don't push me into doing something you'll regret."

Pinky's voice rose, in both octaves and volume. "Cleaner than I think? What are you saying? You gonna turn *me* in?" He laughed.

"I know an awful lot about you." Dylan's voice went soft with his anger. "And I'm not afraid of you. You could screw me over, you could do me some harm, but don't ever make the mistake of thinking you control me. Got it?"

Silence.

"It's a small thing," Pinky said finally. "And I promise I'll protect you. This is the last time. And you do owe me, remember?"

"I remember."

"Then do this one thing. Make it easy. I'm askin', man."

"Tell me about the insurance."

Pinky inhaled. "The shit's on its way, man. It's coming to you whether you agree to it or not."

Dylan's mouth opened but nothing emerged.

"But you'll agree to it, 'cause these guys I work

with, they got shit on you. I can't go into detail, but they do."

Dylan shook his head. "I haven't done anything. There's nothing they could have."

"Doesn't matter. It just needs to look like you done something. And they got that covered."

Dylan exhaled. *Fuck.* "You're lying."

Pinky's voice got curt. "Don't be stupid. I don't have to lie. Now, the stuff's on its way. Be ready for my guy on Friday."

"Where is it now?"

Pinky didn't answer.

"Where the fuck is it now?" Dylan demanded, knowing even as he said it he was betraying how powerfully Pinky had gotten to him.

Pinky stayed silent. Stonewalling.

Dylan put his head in his hand. "You don't have anything on me."

After a minute, Pinky continued. "Look, I don't wanna ruin your fresh start. I just want you to remember what I did for you. Remember how grateful you said you were? It's a matter of fuckin' honor, man. Do this for me and we'll be square. End of story."

It was the kiss of death. He'd threatened, he'd reasoned, and now he appealed to Dylan's honor. Ironically, this last was the one that stung. It *was* a debt Dylan owed.

When Dylan had gone to prison, his mother had

been left without anyone to support her. Dylan had feared for her safety, with no one and nothing to live on. He'd been young, with an exaggerated sense of his own importance.

Now he understood she'd have been fine. She was an innocent, an idealist, a kitten among bobcats. But like a kitten, she always landed on her feet. He knew that now.

Pinky had made it possible for his mother to keep her apartment. He'd swung some kind of deal with the landlord, who apparently owed Pinky a favor, and he'd had his guys lend her a couple thousand dollars. Money that Dylan had paid back once he got out of jail.

It was pretty simple, but it was no small thing to Dylan. He had always fully intended to pay back the favor, in addition to the debt, but to pay it back with his life . . . not his breath, not his beating heart, but the life he'd built here. The future he was just beginning to see.

It was too much. Wasn't it?

"All you gotta do is get the stuff and hand it over to the guy I'm sending. It'll be over before you know it."

"Why do you even need me? Why can't your two guys exchange it?"

"Look," Pinky snapped, "I'm not getting into the nitty-gritty details with you. They're none of your goddamn business. Just be ready Friday. Call me when he gets there and I'll make it happen." They both were silent a minute, before Pinky added, in a slightly more conciliatory tone, "If you do, I'll make sure they lay off your mother about the dough."

Dylan ground his teeth, gripped his hand into a fist so hard it threatened to cramp. It sounded so simple, but he was all too aware it wasn't. "I could call the cops right now, you know. Tell them what I know, what's happening. They'd watch out for Mom and I wouldn't be risking jail."

Pinky burst out laughing. "You? Trust the cops? Gimme a break. Besides, if these guys wanted? They could get *her* busted."

Dylan exhaled. "So you're saying I've got no choice."

"You got no choice, man."

Dylan's mind spun, figuring all the ways he could get caught. The cops would have to be watching him, suspecting him already. Or watching the contact. Both things were likely. They'd have to know the day it was happening. Nothing hard about that.

The only thing on his side was the fact that if Dylan didn't know he was involved until today, the cops might not either. And Friday was only four days away.

He bent his head to the clay, his thoughts turning over again, like a blanket being folded over and over onto itself. The one thing he'd been trying to forget, since it was nothing he could control at this point, was the one thing that might matter the most.

The last time.

He pictured Penelope's face when she'd pulled out those condoms and revealed she was not on the pill as he'd foolishly assumed. *The last time,* which was the first time, actually, that they'd had sex. If he was bathing in worst-case scenarios, he could wallow in this, too.

What if she was pregnant? What if he became a father?

In the soup of emotion that followed, he could think of only one thing. If he were to be a father, he'd never do what Pinky asked. He wouldn't risk one more moment on illegal behavior, no matter who he owed what to.

With that thought, the penny dropped and something became dreadfully clear. He couldn't do this and be done with it. If he was available to Pinky and his cohorts for this, there was nothing to stop them using him again. If he really wanted out, if he was serious about ridding himself of the past and becoming someone new, he needed to screw them. He needed to make enemies he'd have for the rest of his life and ensure that they'd never try anything like this again.

His mind ran over the things Pinky had said. Needed to let the ice cool. Dylan was his only contact outside Maryland. His buddy'd knocked over a jewelry store a couple weeks ago. A couple weeks ago.

For no reason he could think of, the image of the guy with the chicken, who'd delivered his mother's pottery, flashed through his mind. That had been a week and a half ago.

Mutual friends, Chicken Man had said when they left. They knew his mother through *mutual friends*.

Dominoes fell, clicking against each other in his mind, connecting things he'd never even considered. An idea—no, the *truth*—entered his head and took root. That guy, the chicken guy, had disappeared for damn near fifteen minutes while Dylan and the other guy had unloaded the van.

That guy, Dylan suddenly knew, had planted something here, in the shop. The stuff Pinky now needed picked up.

Someone was coming on Friday. Pinky would call to say where the stash was. It wasn't somebody bringing it, as he'd led Dylan to believe. *It was already here.*

Dylan shot to his feet, eyes scanning the room as if he'd be able to see it, an Easter egg in an obvious place.

He had to search.

He had to find what they'd planted.

* * *

"You ever notice how no one talks about nipple sensitivity?" Georgia asked.

They sat in the dog park on this blustery Tuesday with the smell of wood fires and fallen leaves in the air. Sage, her massive Great Dane, lay at her feet, too old these days to be running around the grass enclosure with Mr. Darcy, Lily's Doug, and Megan's Twister, who was playing keep away with an ancient, mud-blackened tennis ball.

"It's true," Megan said with mock sobriety. "I never talk about it."

Lily laughed. "Okay Georgia, what do you have to say about nipple sensitivity? Are we talking a medical condition?"

"No, I'm talking sexually. It's an important issue. Some women have very sensitive nipples and some, I imagine, don't."

"I guess that tells us which category you're in." Lily pulled her hood up over her hair and tied it. The wind was whipping everything about, keeping the dogs ebulliently chasing one another, the ball, leaves, trash, whatever was moving.

"Why do we need to talk about it?" Penelope watched Twister cut and run right, then left, then right again, tempting both Doug and Mr. Darcy with the ball. A minute later a springer spaniel entered the park and the contest, giving Twister much more of a run for her money.

"Because . . ." Georgia beamed, clearly glad

someone asked. "More men need to know about it. If they're not going to follow through, they should know they can offer a great deal of satisfaction to those with high sensitivity without ever going downstairs."

Megan laughed. "Downstairs? You're being very discreet, Georgia, considering the only person who could possibly overhear is twenty yards away."

They all looked over to the springer's owner, a white-haired man with one of those plastic claws for throwing spit-swathed tennis balls.

"I'm protecting Penelope's delicate sensibilities," Georgia said. "She already looks annoyed with me." Their gazes all shifted to Penelope.

"What?" She sat up straight on the picnic bench. "I'm not annoyed. I'm just preoccupied. Go ahead. High sensitivity. I'm with you."

"Are you going to tell us what happened with you and Dylan after the party the other night?" Lily kept her eyes on Penelope even as her dog, Doug, charged over and leaped onto the bench between them. His tongue curled in the middle of his doggy grin as he panted and wheezed.

"Boy, Sutter really took a shine to him Sunday night." Megan reached over to pet Doug. "He liked him before, of course, but he was impressed with him this time."

"Brady liked him too," Lily said. "I have to say, it seemed like Dylan really rose to the occasion."

"Or did he?" Georgia raised an eyebrow at Penelope's dark expression.

"Oh I don't know," Penelope blurted, exasperation in her sharp exhale. "The guy's a mystery to me, a total mystery. One minute he seems like he's coming around and the next he does something completely off-putting. I just don't know what to make of him!"

She told them the story of what had happened Sunday night—omitting the more salacious details—culminating with his "nobody important" conversation the next morning.

"It had to be a girlfriend, don't you think?" Penelope finished. "What else could that mean? And the 'I'd never do that' part. Surely he was telling her he'd never cheat on her. Lying jerk."

"Penelope," Megan said, "you're making up a whole story around two comments. It could have been anyone. It could have been his mother, for heaven's sake. How many men tell their mothers that the woman they're seeing is 'nobody important' until they suddenly pop up with a fiancée?"

"That wasn't even the worst part," Penelope continued, heart heavy with the memory. "He completely disappeared on me after that."

"He *left*?" Georgia's mouth gaped open. "Weren't you at his place?"

"He didn't leave." Penelope picked at the splintering table with a fingernail. "Not physically. He just withdrew, like it was guilt. He could barely look at me."

"Why didn't you ask him who it was?" Lily wrestled a stick out of Doug's mouth and tossed it across the grass. The dog took off after it. "I sure would have. You don't call me 'nobody important' and not explain it."

"He didn't know I heard." Penelope's shoulders slumped. She leaned her elbows on the table. "And I had too much pride to bring it up. I was hoping once he got off the phone he'd explain, or at least act normal to me, but I'm starting to think there is no 'normal' between us."

"You two looked pretty normal the other night," Megan offered.

"*He* looked great," Lily said. "I mean, I thought he was cute before, but once he loosened up and got social he was *really* cute."

A leaf blew into Georgia's hair and she pulled it loose, nodding. "Shower-worthy, you might say."

Three heads swiveled to hers.

"What?" Penelope asked.

"You know, the attraction test." Georgia pulled her scarf up and over her hair, winding it around her neck. "You meet them, they're nice-looking, but would you want to take a shower with them? You can think all kinds of people are nice-looking, but unless you want to take a shower with them you don't feel the right way for a relationship."

The three of them went silent a minute, thinking, while Georgia smugly arranged her scarf.

"She's right," Megan concluded. "There aren't many people I'd want to shower with."

Penelope could hardly get the image of showering with Dylan out of her head. In fact, in her current state of mind it seemed like the very thing they needed to do, be alone in a confined space, warm water, slippery soap, naked bodies . . .

"Wow," Penelope murmured. Her fingers twitched with the desire to run down his drenched abdomen.

Doug leaped up on the seat between Penelope and Lily again, slobbery stick in his mouth, and Penelope was shaken out of her reverie.

So, apparently, was Lily.

"You need to ask him what he meant," Lily insisted. "Ask him who he was talking to and if he really considers you 'nobody important.' We're too old to be playing these games. Just flat-out put it to him. Ask if he has a girlfriend. Get it all out on the table."

"Lily's right," Georgia said. "He knows what you want. He'd be an idiot not to, and that guy is not an idiot. My guess is, he's got demons he doesn't want to share with you, whether they're ex-girlfriends or a psycho mother or whatever."

"He is bound to have demons." Megan nodded significantly at Penelope, who understood immediately what she meant. Anybody who'd been in jail had demons. They had to.

"You're right," Penelope said. "I should talk to him. I should tell him, for one thing, that I know all about his past. If he thinks he has to try to keep me from finding out he was in jail, that could lead to some misleading secrecy."

"I'll say," Georgia said.

"That could be the whole thing," Megan said. "He has to know you don't date ex-cons as a regular thing. He has to know that would be a big deal to you."

"Ex-con," Lily pondered. "That's such an ugly term. Isn't there something better for someone who's been in jail? An ex-inmate or formerly incarcerated or something?"

"An ex-in?" Megan mused. "An outmate?"

Buoyed by the thought that Dylan's secrecy sprang from something she already knew, Penelope perked up. "Speaking of in- and outmates," —she cast a look at Georgia— "things any better with Leland? Have you asked him what the story is?"

Georgia smiled, her long, mascaraed lashes dipping lazily. "Honey, he's figured out the nipple sensitivity effect. I'm willing to let him stay upstairs a little longer if he continues to play that game right."

Chapter 13

The place was a mess. All of his displays had been taken down, the shelves were bare, the tables empty. The pots stood in a corner and on the counter, carefully placed and padded but not set up in any way that resembled a display. Everything from under the register had been taken out—receipts, rolls of coins, pens, pads of paper, all of it—and scattered across the counter, and Dylan was nowhere in sight.

At first Penelope thought he'd been broken into, until she'd seen the pottery wheel neatly dismantled on the floor. Had he gone on some self-destructive rampage? Gallery Night was two days away. What was going on?

"Dylan?" Her voice sounded dead in the ransacked room. When she heard nothing in reply, she went behind the counter, tiptoed through the minefield of plastic sheeting, unglazed pots, and blocks of new clay toward the back room. There she saw a similar mess, with one large table on its side, and all shelves and cabinets bare. Nothing was destroyed, but everything was disordered.

A rectangular chicken box from Popeyes stood on the windowsill, looking strangely unharmed amid the mess.

"Dylan?" she called again, this time heading toward the open basement door.

Like hers, the basement here used to be a storehouse for the building above, accessible from outside through lean-to doors of the kind Penelope always associated with *The Wizard of Oz*. It contained old hooks, pulleys, doors, and beams scarred with hardware the purpose of which had been lost over the years.

Dylan's head was inside an opening beyond one of these very doors, a rusted two-foot by two-foot affair on corroded hinges with a long metal latch on the back wall.

"What are you doing?" she asked.

Dylan jerked out of the opening and turned, blinking and staring at her as if she'd materialized like a ghost.

"Penelope," he said.

She laughed a little. "That's right. What's going on? What happened upstairs?"

His hair was mussed and a cobweb clung to one side. He looked like he'd worked up a sweat doing whatever it was he was doing.

"I didn't hear you come in."

"I've been calling you. You didn't get broken into, did you?"

He rubbed a hand over his face, discovered the cobweb in his hair and tugged at it. "No. No, I was . . . looking for something."

She crossed her arms over her chest. It was chilly down there. "Did you find it?"

He shook his head, wiped his hands on his jeans. "No, but I think I figured out how your dog keeps getting in here." He gestured toward the rusty door. "Looks like there used to be some kind of tunnel, maybe a grain chute of some kind, between our two buildings. It's lined with metal and looks slanted from your place to mine. It'd be nothing for him to get through. This door wasn't shut all the way. I don't even think it latches anymore."

She walked to the opening and peered into its inky depths. "Oh my God. So all this time I've been locking him in the back room and leaving the basement door open . . . ."

"Suited him just fine." Dylan seemed to be trying to clean himself up as he stood there, brushing at his tee-shirt, straightening his hair, but he wouldn't look at her. It was more a diversion, she felt, than an attempt to look better.

"I wondered if I could . . . talk to you a minute." Penelope bit her lower lip as she watched him. "But it looks like you're busy. Maybe we could meet later. Or . . . you could come by my house for a glass of wine?"

His motions slowed and he finally met her eyes. "We can talk now, Penelope. I guess I needed to talk to you too."

The dread that dropped into her stomach was the intuition that trumped hope inside of her. His tone and demeanor said this was not going to be a good conversation.

"Come on upstairs." He headed for the steps, looking at something stuck to his palms.

She stood motionless, watching him and thinking she might as well hear what he had to say here in the cellar, where it was dank and depressing and perfect for what was to come.

At the stairs he turned back. "Penelope?"

"Yes." She took a couple of steps toward him and stopped. Her knees felt wobbly. "Just tell me what you have to say, Dylan. There's no place to sit upstairs anyway."

He looked at her a long moment.

"I can start," she said, voice weak, "why don't you tell me why you called me 'nobody important' on the phone the other morning?"

He sighed and dropped his head. His palms rubbed down the sides of his jeans. "Penelope. You and I . . . we can't be . . . we can't have a relationship. I probably should have said something the other night. Before we—"

"Is it because you have a girlfriend? Is that who called that day?"

He swallowed, obviously considering his answer carefully. "I have commitments that prevent me from, ah . . ." He raised his eyes, searching for words, and shoved his hands in his pockets. After a second he met her gaze. "Look, you know I'm attracted to you. Every time I see you, it's hard not to . . . not to touch you. But we're just not those people, don't you see? We don't fit. Or I don't."

A lump grew in Penelope's throat. "Those people? What do you mean we're not 'those people'?"

She wished he'd come closer so that she could touch him, even just on the arm, remind him of the power in their contact. A light touch, a reconnection. But she knew he wouldn't. They'd probably never touch again. Maybe that was all they had anyway, and who could build a relationship on that?

"You and I," he said, in a tone that was gentle but resolute, "are not couple material. You know that as well as I do. We're too different. You're— little Cornish chickens and I'm Doritos and bean dip." His laugh sounded forced.

Penelope blinked several times fast. "You didn't have fun at the dinner party."

He sat down on the second step and put his head in his hands. "I did have a good time. I like your friends. But where could this go? You live in a house—a house you probably own—with crystal bowls and—and chafing dishes. I use a cinder block as a coffee table. Come on, Penelope. Do I really need to explain this?"

"You keep mentioning things. But things don't matter, Dylan. I'll share my things with you, if it comes to that. Just don't blow me off because I have stuff and you don't. Who cares?"

"*I* care. It's not the stuff, it's what it indicates. It's the life, period. I'm never going to be country-club guy. I'm never going to—"

"How do you know what you're never going to do?" she burst out. "Sure, you keep saying you'll never be this and you'll never be that and that'll do it. You'll never be those things if that's how you think. But what do you *feel*, Dylan? What do you feel *for me*? Aside from fear of my crystal bowls?"

"I feel . . . physical attraction." His voice went hoarse and he cleared his throat. "But that's not enough. I don't want to hurt you, Penelope, but don't read more into our . . . encounters than that."

"Oh," she said, barely heading off tears. She reached for anger and found it waiting for her. "I get it. I thought it was something else, but no. We were just fucking. Weren't we?" She hated that word, hated using it with regard to herself but also to him. But it was what Georgia would have said, and more than anything right now she wanted to be as impervious to hurt as her practical, earthy friend.

His expression softened. "No. No. Don't do that, don't twist my words. We had a mutual curiosity that we mutually satisfied."

"Ah, so you're satisfied now." She nodded, composing her face.

He raked a hand through his hair and looked away from her, like the words were hard to say while she stood right in front of him. "It wasn't like that. It's not like that. But I'm not right for you and you're not right for me. We both know that."

"I wish you'd quit saying that," she said, her voice breaking. "I wish you'd stop saying what *we both know*. Because I don't agree with it. I think there's something here."

He stood up and came toward her. Close enough to speak softly, but he didn't touch her. His eyes were kind, pained even. As if he knew what he was doing to her but was forced to do it anyway.

"There's physical attraction." He smiled tightly. "At least on my part. But I'm not what you need, or even want. You don't know me very well, but I am not who you might think."

So that *was* it! The jail thing. Hope reinflated instantly.

"You don't know me very well either." She took a step toward him, reached out a hand, but he shook his head.

How could he say they weren't right for each other when they'd connected so completely? Even now they were connecting, the way he looked at her, the way he spoke to her. They weren't strangers. How could he say they weren't right, when his words made her feel like her heart was breaking?

But she could fight. Damn it, she could fight with the best of them. She could call on this thing inside herself, this feeling for him, and she could convince him. For him. For herself, for something within her that needed to acknowledge that what she felt for him was *real*.

"Dylan, you can't even know who I might think you are. What I know is that when we made love the first time I saw something, *felt* something in you that made me do something I have never in my life done before. Then the other night it was only confirmed. Didn't you feel it? That connection? I know you did, I saw it in your face. I believe that part of myself, the part that knows that kind of thing. And I know what I need, what I want, and what I can trust. There's something between us, Dylan. You're not the kind of guy to do what you're doing now. You don't use women. That's what my heart tells me and that's what I believe."

His smile was a cross between reluctant and wry. "You really think I haven't done anything like this before?"

The words hit her like a slap. She took a sharp breath.

He opened his mouth as if to say something, then closed it. Silent. But his eyes looked shattered.

"I didn't say that," she said. "But can you honestly say you didn't feel anything, something you haven't felt before, with me?"

Sweat prickled along her scalp. She was so far out on a limb she could hear it cracking under her weight. What if he said she was a fool, he'd been using her, she was kidding herself that he could fall for someone like her? It would destroy her.

He was silent a long time, studying her as if trying to figure out a math problem.

"Then tell me you felt nothing," she said with far more conviction than she felt. "Just *do not lie to me*."

Finally his gaze dropped and he exhaled. "I do . . . feel something . . . for you. But—"

She brightened. "I knew it! The feelings surprise me too, Dylan. But they're not the end of the world, are they? Why wouldn't we work together?"

"Because, Penelope," he said, his voice and eyes

growing harder, "you're a *good girl.* Do you know what that means?"

"It means I have sex on store counters?"

"It means" —he took a step toward her, his expression darkening— "that you would never understand me. Let me be clear on this, Penelope, because this isn't just about *you* putting up with *my* deficiencies. I have my own concerns about you. You would always suspect . . . you'd never completely trust me. You couldn't. Not being who you are, and me being who I am."

"That's ridiculous. Why do you say that?" She met his adamance with her own. "Because you have a record? Because you were in jail?"

He actually took a step back, mouth open.

"That's right. I know about it. I've known about it since before we made love the very first time, since before we ever kissed. What does that tell you about my deficiencies?"

He shook his head and turned away, running both hands through his hair. His back was tense and he stood a moment not looking at her before turning to her once again. "It doesn't matter what you know—"

"It doesn't matter what you *did*—"

"Of *course* it does, Penelope. Don't be naïve. I was convicted of possession of drugs with the intent to distribute. Do you know what that means? It means

I was convicted of a felony. I went to jail. And I am on every cop's hit list whenever anything bad happens around me. You really want to be a part of that? Is that what you pictured for your life?"

"That isn't your fault. You . . . you . . ." She flailed a hand, searching for words. ". . . You paid—"

He interrupted her with a hard laugh. "Don't tell me I paid my debt to society. That's a fairy tale good white liberals tell themselves when they go to sleep at night. No, my past is more complicated than that. My past is *who I am*. It's part of me in ways you could never understand."

Ways I wouldn't want you to understand, he thought.

"You are who you choose to be, Dylan." When he laughed at this she raised her chin. "Look at what you've done with yourself. You got that grant, you've opened this shop. You've started a new life in a new town. You're a new person. You've risen above all that stuff in your past. Why don't you let yourself believe that? Why don't you let yourself believe that someone—that *I*—can believe that about you too?"

She looked like she was going to cry, but all Dylan could think about was Pinky's call, Pinky's threats, and the whole of his past looming up to throw a shadow over everything. And Penelope was standing in the darkest part.

The fact was, he couldn't find the stuff Pinky planted. He'd torn the place apart, and other than the empty chicken box he'd found in the basement, there was no evidence anything was ever there. But just because he couldn't find it didn't mean it didn't exist. The very fact that the chicken box was in the basement at all meant Curtis had been poking around for some reason.

The problem was, if it was still there and he didn't follow through on Friday, Pinky could turn *him* in. One anonymous tip to the cops and Dylan would be off to jail, for possession of stolen goods or fencing hot jewelry, or hell, maybe even being behind the robbery.

Penelope would drop him like a hot rock if that happened.

"Don't protect me by hurting me, Dylan," she said. "Don't try to save me."

He laughed once. "I'm not saving you. You've got it backwards. I'm saving myself. You think you can get over my past? Good for you. But did you ever think maybe that's not what I need? You think I want someone who needs to *get over* who I am? Forgive me, Penelope, but I want someone who wants the whole package, the good, the bad, and the ugly. And that someone isn't you."

She opened her mouth to speak but he held up a hand to stop her.

"I don't *want* it to be you," he clarified.

She wrapped her arms across her chest. The look on her face nearly crushed him.

"You need someone different, Penelope," he said, gentling his voice to the point of pleading. "Hell, maybe even Glenn. He's the kind of guy whose faults you really could get over. Maybe you could even improve him, the way you think you can improve me. He's a lot closer to what you want than I am."

He recalled what Glenn had said, about Penelope wanting children, about his having a vasectomy, how he hadn't told her yet. Glenn was a dog; she'd be hurt by him in the end. Still, he was closer to what she needed than Dylan was.

Penelope dropped her head and thought for a long time. Finally she looked back up at him, on her face an expression he'd never seen before. Distant. Unreadable.

"Maybe you're right." She moved abruptly toward the stairs. He shifted sideways as she passed, as if touching her would burn.

When her foot hit the first step he couldn't stop himself from saying, "Penelope . . . wait."

She stopped and turned her head back toward him, looking at the wall to their right.

Hell, he couldn't *endorse* the guy. He didn't have to get involved, but he couldn't actually recommend him. She deserved so much better.

"Not Glenn." He took one step toward her. "Just . . . someone like him."

She started to turn to him fully when the chime upstairs told them someone had entered the store. She continued up the wooden steps, Dylan behind her. He turned his eyes downward, so as not to watch her long legs and slim hips as she moved. He'd just burned any right he might have had to appreciate those.

Dylan hadn't anticipated that his day could get exponentially worse. But when they left the back room, both he and Penelope stopped dead at the sight of two plainclothes cops standing in the middle of the mess he'd made.

"Carson, hi," Penelope said to the big one on the right. "Were you looking for me?"

"No, ma'am," the guy said in a deadpan, full-of-importance voice. "We're here to speak to Mr. Mersey."

Penelope turned a worried look back toward him, but Dylan kept his eyes on the cop.

"I'm Dylan Mersey," he said, finally recognizing one of the policemen who'd come the night he'd knocked on Penelope's door. She knew him, knew he was a cop, knew Dylan was in trouble. "What can I do for you?"

The cop, Carson, looked at Penelope. "Best if you went on home now, Penelope. I'm not sure you want to be here for this."

* * *

"Ladies and gentlemen," Georgia declared from Penelope's kitchen, "I have an announcement to make."

She walked into the living room holding a pitcher of sunset-colored rum punch and what could only be described as a shit-eating grin.

"Consummation has occurred!" She poured punch into the four glasses on the coffee table, stabbed one straw in each, and took her seat in the recliner. "And it was *fabulous*."

"Congratulations!" Megan laughed. "How did this occur? And did he have any explanation for why it took so long?"

Georgia settled down smugly and took a sip of her drink. She did glow, Penelope noted, wondering if *she'd* looked that way the morning after she'd first been with Dylan. Probably not. The two of them had followed caring with conflict from the very beginning.

"It's really quite romantic," Georgia said. "We were in the parking garage and things were getting hot and heavy. This was after we'd gone to dinner, you understand, and we'd had some wine. So we weren't really feeling the cold, if you know what I mean."

"Did you have sex in the parking garage?" Lily stopped arranging the throw blanket on her legs and stared at Georgia. "What is it with you and cars?"

"What?" Georgia protested. "When the mood strikes, the mood strikes. And you know what they say, you have to strike while the iron is, well, *iron*."

"So what made the difference?" Megan persisted. "Is he one of those guys who's not turned on until you're in a public place?"

Georgia sucked down a quarter of her drink. "It wasn't like that. Not that there's anything wrong with that, mind you. Not in my book. No, it wasn't until I said . . ." Here she paused and blushed.

"What? What did you say?" Penelope asked. Were there magic words to reach an elusive man?

"I told him I was falling in love with him." Georgia shrugged sheepishly.

Penelope looked at her hands. That would never work, not for her. Dylan, aside from not believing it, would think she was a lovesick, romantic fool.

"Georgia!" Megan squealed. "You're *in love?*"

Georgia looked desperately uncomfortable. "That's what he was waiting for, as it turns out. He wanted to wait for me to feel something for him beyond the sexual. That's what he said."

"What did you say to that?" Lily asked.

Georgia laughed. "I said if I'd known that I'd have said it weeks ago. But it doesn't matter now. He was right, and now it's perfect."

"I can't believe it," Penelope said. "Usually when

you tell a guy how you feel, all hell breaks loose and he's gone before you can form the next sentence. Georgia does it and gets everything she wanted. Are you really in love with him?"

Georgia blushed again and looked down into her drink. "I am," she said quietly. Then she looked back up at them, eyes aglint. "But the funniest thing happened in the middle of it all. There we were, you know, doing—"

"Right. Got it," Lily interjected with a roll of her eyes.

"And we saw this funny little man breaking into cars. He looked kind of like . . ." She paused, tapping one red fingernail against her chin as she thought. "If you took a cartoon weasel and turned him into a man, that's what he looked like. He was going down the whole line of cars parked in the lot using one of those slim-jim things? Opening up the doors and rifling through everyone's stuff. We actually had to hurry up before he got to us!"

"Did you call the police?" Penelope protested.

This could get the cops off Dylan's back. Carson had already intimated to her that he believed Dylan and his "criminal element" were responsible for the recent vandalism. So if there'd been more break-ins, that was probably the reason Carson had shown up at Dylan's shop. She thought of

Georgia's description of the guy. "Wait a minute, I think I know that guy. Did he have slicked-back hair and a pointy kind of face?"

"Exactly," Georgia said with one definite nod. "Like a cartoon weasel come to life."

"That's the guy who offered to find Mr. Darcy for me, that first time he got out. For a hundred and fifty dollars, I might add." She put a hand to her forehead. "In fact, he said he knew who let Mr. Darcy out of the car. Of course he did! It was *him*. And he was able to say he thought he could find him because he'd seen the direction he ran. Oh my God. I hope you called the cops."

"We did! But not until, you know, after we were done. All they did was just ask a few questions and let it go. Didn't even take our names. Thank goodness," she turned, laughing, to Megan, "because I gotta tell you, we probably looked like we'd been doin' exactly what we'd been doin'."

"They probably all know who you are anyway," Lily said, "considering the *last* time you had sex in a car it was with the mayor."

"Oh honey." Georgia waved a hand nonchalantly. "That wasn't the last time."

They all laughed.

"But here's what I want to know," Georgia said, her gaze landing squarely on Penelope. "Did you talk to Dylan about the phone call?"

All eyes turned to Penelope.

"Yes, did you ask him what he meant by 'nobody important'?" Lily seconded.

Penelope took a deep breath. "I sure did. And it wasn't good."

Chapter 14

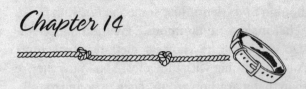

"That's the whole story," Penelope finished telling the girls. She gazed into her glass as if words of advice would appear, like in the bottom of a Magic 8 Ball. *Give up now.*

She hadn't mentioned how the cops had shown up at the end of the conversation. She figured Dylan deserved some privacy.

"He meant it," she continued. "He meant every word of it. So I'm going to forget about him. Forget anything ever went on between us. I'm going to put my efforts back into Glenn and see what happens."

She sighed, wondering how on earth she was going to get her head back around Glenn.

"But here's the weird thing. Or rather, one weird

thing. At the end of the conversation, after telling me I needed someone more like Glenn, he then said it shouldn't *be* Glenn. Just someone *like* him."

"That makes it unanimous," Georgia muttered.

"Do you think he knows something about him? He's been running with him a lot. You know they're both in that marathon group. They're bound to talk. What do you think Glenn could have told him?"

"Chances are he just got to know him," Georgia said. "Glenn doesn't have to say anything specific for people to not like him." She glanced from her drink into Penelope's face and her expression changed. "I'm sorry, honey. That's not fair. He's not immediately unpleasant. I didn't dislike him until I found out what he'd done to you."

Penelope shook her head and sighed. "It's all right. I've actually made peace with all of that. And I have to say, Glenn's been really sweet lately. He invited me to go see a play in D.C. Of course, it was Friday night, when he should have known I had Gallery Night, but he promised to get some for another night. And he's taking me to dinner on Thursday."

Lily's straw slurped as she hit the bottom of her drink. She pulled it away from her face to look at the suddenly empty glass.

"I'll get that." Georgia leaned over from her seat and poured a fresh rum punch into Lily's glass.

In front of them, a fire crackled in the hearth and scented candles flickered on the mantelpiece.

"I don't understand how you can just give up on Dylan." Lily took a sip of the new drink. "I mean, if it was as good as you say, as intense as you say, when you were with Dylan, it seems like there must be something else wrong. Like maybe he's just afraid of getting involved. Maybe he only needs a little more time, some gentle persuasion. He obviously feels something for you. In my experience, sex can't be that good for one person if it's not for the other one too."

"That sounds like a lot of romantic hooey," Georgia said. "How many times have you lied when they said, 'Ooh baby, was it good for you too?'"

"I've never been with anyone tacky enough to say something like that," Lily said.

Megan laughed. "That's not quite the point. I can't believe Dylan would tell her he wasn't interested simply because the sex wasn't good."

Georgia snorted. "I would!"

"That's not exactly true, is it?" Megan challenged. "Look at you and Leland. You stayed with him when you weren't having any sex at all."

Georgia held up a finger. "That's very different than havin' *bad* sex."

"The sex *was* good," Penelope protested, then blushed.

Megan leaned back on the couch and put her sock-clad feet up on the coffee table. "Dylan strikes me as the kind of guy who'd be as honest as he can be. If he said he was preserving himself, I think it might be true."

"But that's just the point." Lily held her drink aloft. "Penelope's a much better person—a much worthier girlfriend—than he thinks she is. He doesn't know he has nothing to fear from her."

"Doesn't he?" Megan asked. "They could get involved and it could be a disaster. They're so different. Completely different backgrounds, completely different *lives* until the last few months."

"Which is why the sex was great," Georgia said.

"Wait a minute," Lily said. "You and Sutter could be described the exact same way, and look at how great things turned out for you."

Megan looked thoughtful. "That's true."

"This is different," Penelope said, feeling the weight of it in her chest. "Dylan has a lot more to hide than Sutter ever did, which makes it hard to disregard what he said. It feels like it would be selfish to force things. And it would be just like the sheltered little 'good girl' he accused me of being."

"Well, it's true, don't you think?" Megan looked down the couch at Penelope, curled up on the other end, her chin on her knees. "I mean, aren't we all sheltered little good girls when it comes to living the life he's led? Breaking the law and going to jail. I know I couldn't relate to that."

"And that's why you were so adamantly opposed to us getting together." Penelope looked at her sadly. "I thought you knew something about him you didn't want to tell. But instead you were just more perceptive about what *he* needed."

Megan shook her head. "I wasn't thinking about him, Pen. I was thinking about you. I was being just as prejudiced as he accused you of being. More so. I figured he would hurt you just because he was an ex-con. I thought he had to be—callous, you know."

"Maybe you were right. I mean, he's nothing like anyone I've ever been with before. And certainly nothing like the perfect guy I always dreamed I'd be with." Penelope shifted so she sat cross-legged and swirled her glass in her hand, watching the straw circle the rim with the pinkened ice. "I mean, who can make a living on pottery? We'd probably fight about all kinds of things: money, lifestyle, activities. I'm sure we have vastly different values. And I like to play tennis and go out to eat and drive a nice car. I used to love going to the club with Glenn. Dylan would probably hate all that stuff. And even if he didn't, would he ever fit in with all those people I know? I can just see him talking to someone like Gerald Fitzpatrick, with his what's-in-your-portfolio and whose-car-is-more-expensive-than-whose competitions. Call me crazy, but I think Dylan's got way too much pride to be polite in a situation like that."

"Hm." Lily extricated the straw from her mouth again. "Pride. And prejudice."

Georgia laughed and refilled Penelope's glass. "It all comes back to Jane Austen, doesn't it, Lil? The woman was *so* ahead of her time."

"It's true." Lily looked at Penelope. "It strikes me that this whole situation mirrors *Pride and Prejudice*."

Penelope tilted her head, thinking back to the miniseries. She'd never finished the book, but she'd watched the series three times. All six hours of it.

"Hm, I can see that. Glenn is Darcy, with his money and prejudice against children and the fact that no one, not even me, has liked him or thought he'd be good for me the last few years. And Dylan is Wickham . . . the good-looking guy who tempts Elizabeth but is ultimately wrong for her. And I'm the girl who just wants to find a good husband."

Her own words struck her in the heart. When had she become so lonely and pathetic?

"I don't think Dylan's the snake Wickham was," Megan added.

Georgia pushed back in the recliner and crossed her feet. "You all are crazy."

Lily shook her head. "No. I'm thinking *you're* Darcy, Penelope."

"Me!" Penelope laughed. "I hardly think Glenn could be Elizabeth. He has too much money, for one thing."

"Not Glenn, no." She lifted her brows significantly.

"Dylan," Penelope said. "He's poor. He's sharp. Gutsy. Impulsive, it could certainly be argued."

"And wary of you being upper class," Megan reminded her.

"And you were prejudiced against his upbringing at first," Lily said. "Remember? You're *still* using it to talk yourself out of him. I'm telling you, you're Darcy. And Glenn is the evil, two-faced Wickham." She looked around the group. "Come on, you've got to give me that, at least."

"Yes, Professor," Georgia said. "But otherwise I don't know what the hell y'all are talkin' about. You're nuts to be talkin' 'class,' for one thing. This is America, last I checked. Anybody can get ahead."

"With pottery?" Penelope asked quietly.

Georgia turned to her. "With *pens?* For pity's sake, Penelope, I can't believe your parents were jumpin' up and down when you told them your idea for a way to make a livin' after your divorce. But look at you, you've made a success of it. Far as I can see, Dylan Mersey's got his act together too. He's opened a shop with gorgeous stuff in it, put it in a great location and priced it right. I bought a bowl from him just last week. What makes you think he won't make a decent livin'?"

She sighed. "He probably will. He'll probably do great, turn into the model citizen, be a raging success, and it'll all boil down to the fact that he's simply not interested in me. All this protecting himself is just bullshit!" Her voice had risen and she suddenly felt the whole impact of Dylan's rejection.

He'd made a mistake with her and he'd needed to get out of it. His speechifying about her being a good girl and him needing someone who wasn't was nothing but a very well-planned put-off.

"Now you've done it. You've got Penelope swearing," Lily said to Georgia, then she straightened and looked around the room. "Hey, where is Mr. Darcy, anyway?"

Penelope put her drink down on the coffee table and stood. "He's in his crate. I'll go get him."

As she walked from the room, she made herself stand straight, pulling her shoulders back and taking a deep breath. She was *not* going to turn into a puddle over this. She'd had her life all worked out before Dylan Mersey came along and cast his twisted spell over her. All she needed to do was get back to her original plan. For all her hurt feelings and wounded pride, the fact was Dylan was right about the two of them. They would not work. She was grown up enough to see that, and even admit it.

Feeling stronger, she opened the wire crate and the puppy shot from it, his whole body wiggling with joy at being free.

"Come on, you rascal," she said, leading him back to the living room with the girls.

"There he is!" Lily exclaimed, patting her legs with both hands. "Mr. Darcy! Mr. Darcy!"

The dog did not even glance in her direction. Instead he bounded from Georgia to Megan, to Megan's glass on the floor, to the coffee table that held the cheese.

Penelope watched from behind the loveseat where Lily sat.

"Mr. Darcy!" Lily said again, more insistently, leaning forward. "Mr. Darcy, come!"

Penelope shook her head and, gazing at her dog, said, "Dylan calls him Bonsai."

Lily tilted her head. "Bonsai!"

The dog spun on his tiny paws, nails scratching against the floor and flew into Lily's arms.

Thursday morning, Penelope was fighting irrational tears as she opened up the shop. She should be relieved, she told herself, taking a fresh roll of paper out of the plastic wrap and threading it into her register. Jubilant. She'd dodged an enormous bullet. A life-changing event.

Dylan had broken up with her, if that was the term for someone cutting you off before you even had a chance to have a relationship. There was no future for them and she'd resolved to put her energies back into Glenn, who was suddenly behaving like a prince.

How would that have worked if she was going to have Dylan's baby?

The very thought brought a lump back to her

throat. *Dylan's baby.* She felt as if she'd never wanted anything more in her life. It would have turned him around, too, she just knew. Nothing made you look toward the future like a baby.

Instead, she'd gotten her period that morning. Right on time.

Mr. Darcy came trotting into the shop from the back room carrying a long, empty box. Two feet of it stuck out on one side, clipping shelves and display cases as he passed. He looked very taken with himself, bouncing along as proudly as if he carried the Olympic torch in his mouth.

Penelope sniffed and smiled at him. This was why people had pets, she thought for the hundredth time. They could make you laugh even when you were at your lowest.

Wiping her eyes, she rounded the front counter and met him in the middle of the store. Hormones, she thought. They made you crazy. That's all this melancholy was. Day after tomorrow she'd probably be ecstatic. She'd *make sure* she was ecstatic.

"Time to put you away, little man." She took the box from him and lifted him into her arms. He licked her chin, curly tail waving. "And this time, I'm onto you. No more escape routes."

She was going to close whatever door was open in the basement, his secret passageway to Dylan's, and in closing that door she was going to cut off the connection she'd longed for and nurtured and harbored between the two of them. No more having to see him to retrieve the dog. No more reinforcement from Dylan that the puppy's name was Bonsai instead of Mr. Darcy. In fact, she was going to call Dog Manners obedience classes as soon as she finished securing the place. She had to teach Mr. Darcy who was boss.

The basement was a place she used only for storage, and even then she just used the front half, right near the base of the stairs. There was a whole rear section that she never went into, mostly because it was poorly lit and kind of creepy. Now, with a flashlight and the dog on a leash—she didn't want him bolting for Dylan's now—she ventured beyond her boxes of stock into the area that looked much like Dylan's basement, with old hardware and beams and mysterious doors that were apparently open.

"Okay, Mr. Darcy," she said, "lead me to your secret passage."

She spent a moment imagining herself sliding through the chute to stick a perfect landing in Dylan's basement. *Ta-dah! I'm here to save you! Even if you don't want saving!*

She squelched the thought. It was time to let go of all thoughts of Dylan.

She spotted the door immediately, and sure enough it stood slightly ajar, but what caught her eye was a plastic bag on the floor just below it. As the flashlight's beam crossed it, something flashed from inside, reflecting the light.

She moved toward it slowly, a chill crawling up her spine for some reason. The bag was not some leftover trash or cast-off from the previous occupant of the building. It was too new, for one thing, and looked fairly clean. No dust, no cobwebs, not even much dirt from the hard-packed cellar floor. And it didn't look like anything she stocked, though she could be wrong.

The bag was full of something and lay heavily on its side, still sealed but sporting a good-sized hole near a top corner.

Mr. Darcy pulled toward it at the end of the leash, bounding like a sled dog in high snow. She held him back with the leash easily. "No, no," she murmured, reeling him in close so she could pick him up.

As she knelt next to the bag, she could see what had flashed inside—something metal. In fact, a bunch of metal somethings, encased in smaller plastic bags within the larger one. It definitely wasn't anything she'd ordered for the store.

Mr. Darcy wrestled in her arm as she reached out to pick it up. It was heavy and smeared with something greasy. She put it down and smelled her fingers.

Chicken. That's what had the dog going crazy. The bag smelled like fried-chicken grease. That also explained why one corner of the plastic was riddled with tiny tooth holes.

She cast her eyes up the wall to the metal door a few feet up. She looked at the dog.

"Did you bring this here?" she asked, then wondered if sound carried through the chute as easily as the dog had.

She picked up the bag and stood. Upstairs, in the light, she'd investigate it further. In the meantime, one thing was certain. Mr. Darcy had retrieved this from somewhere, and the only place it could be was Dylan's.

It was at times like these that Penelope was glad her store didn't get a ton of traffic. She desperately needed advice but couldn't leave the shop.

"Megan," she said into the phone, "you've got to come here. It's an emergency."

"Penelope? What is it? Is something wrong?"

Penelope swallowed. "I'm okay, but I have a problem and I really need to talk to someone."

Actually, it was Dylan who had the problem; that much was clear. He was into something bad; that also seemed clear. What was unclear was what Penelope should do about it. Because she had to do something.

She might be an idealistic fool, but she was smart enough to know that what she held in her hands was potential dynamite for Dylan Mersey.

But was she a fool to think she could save him, even from himself?

"I'll be right there," Megan said.

Twenty minutes later, the bells rang as Megan pushed the glass door open.

Penelope had her left hand up, fingers out-stretched, to admire a three-carat square-cut dia-mond ring in a platinum setting that just happened to be on her ring finger.

"Oh my God!" Megan gasped. "Penelope! Is it—was it—are you—not *Dylan?*"

Penelope dropped her hand and looked soberly at her friend. With her other hand she reached under the counter, pulled up the plastic bag and dropped it heavily between them. Inside were dozens of little bags, each of them holding a ring the same size or bigger than the one Penelope wore.

"Yes," she said, "I believe they are Dylan's."

She told Megan everything. Starting with Dy-lan's obvious search for something that he couldn't find the day she'd gone over there and gotten her heart broken, and ending with finding this bag just under the door where Mr. Darcy came and went from Dylan's shop.

"Oh, and one last thing." She took the ring off her finger and looked at it reverently. "Just before I left Dylan's the other day, Carson and another cop—that is, I think he was a cop, neither of them was in uniform, but it was obvious—the two of them came into Dylan's shop and said they wanted to talk to him. Carson, in typical alarmist fashion, made a big deal of the fact that I should go. Like they were going to do something my delicate sensibilities shouldn't witness."

Megan stood with one hand over her mouth, the other arm wrapped around her waist. "Do you think they were there to arrest him?"

"I don't know. But his shop's open today, so I doubt it." She tilted her head toward the front, and Megan looked out across the street at Mersey Pots and the "Open" sign in the window.

"They might have been there to search the place. Did you see a warrant?"

"I didn't see anything. I was so intent on getting out of there. Dylan was . . . well, he was not the same person he's been the last couple of weeks. Something was clearly bothering him. He was agitated and closed off and angry. And he was obviously looking for this stuff." She hefted the bag again. "How many engagement rings do you think are in here? It weighs a ton. It's got to be worth a fortune."

Megan picked up the bag, eyes widening. "This has got to be thousands and thousands of dollars worth of stuff. Look at the size of those diamonds. I don't see anything under a couple carats in there."

"I know." Penelope stroked the ring she'd taken out with one finger. "They're gorgeous."

"Oh honey." Megan reached out a hand and

squeezed one of Penelope's. "This isn't the way you wanted to get a diamond, is it?"

Penelope laughed sadly. "The whole day's been a cruel joke." She told Megan about not being pregnant.

"Well, that's a relief anyway. Isn't it?" She peered into Penelope's face, though Penelope wouldn't meet her eyes.

"You're going to think I'm crazy, but I've been kind of . . . sad about it. I mean, I know it wouldn't have been good for Dylan. Probably the worst thing ever, in his opinion. But it would have been a baby, Megan. It would have been *my* baby, no matter what happened with him. Not that that's what I want, but . . . you know."

Megan smiled and squeezed her hand again. "I do know. When I discovered I was pregnant with Sutter's baby, part of me *knew* it meant disaster for the relationship. But the other part knew . . . well, like you said, it was my baby. I was . . ." She shook her head, her eyes distant. "Happier than I'd ever been."

Penelope studied her. "But it wasn't disaster for your relationship. You're getting married."

"That's the part that's the miracle."

They both laughed.

"Well, I'm not getting married." Penelope picked up the ring she'd chosen and put it back in its little plastic bag, squeezing the plastic zipper lock in two fingers. But she couldn't put it back in with the rest of them. It was exactly the ring she would have chosen, if she would ever in her life be in the position to choose again.

"Glenn could afford that ring," Megan offered.

Penelope shrugged. "Do you think so? He's got alimony and child-support payments. And you should see the house. It's dead empty. Like he can't afford a stick of furniture."

"You know men. They don't decorate."

Penelope put the bag down and looked at Megan. "Here's the thing. I don't care if he can afford the ring. And I don't care that Dylan can't. In fact I don't really care about getting a ring at all. What do you think I should do? What if this stuff puts Dylan back in jail?"

"If he stole it, doesn't he deserve to be back in jail?" Megan's voice was soft, her face troubled.

Penelope shook her head. "I don't think he stole it."

Megan looked at her and sighed.

"I know. I know. I'm being naïve but I just can't condemn him. I can't believe he really would do something so . . . stupid."

"I have a hard time believing that too. But he sure as hell didn't buy it," Megan said. "There aren't many people who could afford a bag like this. Plus I'm pretty sure he put everything he had into that shop."

It's who I am, Penelope.

Had he meant that as literally as this bag of diamonds made it seem? He'd gone to jail for drugs, and now had a bunch of stolen jewels. Did he mean he was a compulsive criminal?

"No," she said again. "I refuse to believe he stole it. I don't know what happened, why he's looking for it or what it means, but—but I can't believe he would do this."

Megan was silent a minute, then said, "Penelope, regardless of what he did, what are *you* going to do? Give it back to him? Take it to the police?"

Penelope felt helpless, her mind spinning with questions and dangers and repercussions. But the bottom line was, there was nothing she could do to save him if this was what he was into.

"No," she said slowly. "I'm going to go to him, I'm going to let him know I have it and I'm going to ask him what's going on. Then I'm going to tell *him* to take it to the police. It's the only thing to do, whether he's guilty or not."

Chapter 15

Dylan closed his shop at six and took off running at 6:04. He'd called Glenn to run with him—mostly because he needed to get outside of his own head—but Glenn said he was going out with Penelope.

Fast work, he thought, running too fast, too soon. His muscles protested, the cold air burned his lungs.

So much for worrying that he'd hurt Penelope's feelings. She was obviously able to shift gears without missing a beat.

He clenched his teeth against a bone-deep anger. It wasn't Penelope's fault, for God's sake. He knew that. What did he expect her to do? Pine for him?

No, he was angry at life. At the circumstances that prevented him from taking even what was set before him on a platter. At Pinky and the missing jewelry and the fact that he had to worry about some asshole he'd never seen before showing up and giving him shit about stuff he didn't know he had, a heist he'd never even heard about and a deal he had no part in.

And yeah, the cops who were onto the whole thing. They'd come to search the place, that same clown who'd picked him up drunk the night he'd met Penelope, and another guy who was all full of street lingo and threats. He'd told them to go right ahead, which had clearly thrown them for a loop. Apparently they'd just wanted to threaten him with a search warrant, see what he'd do. They'd stumbled all over themselves promising to come back later and do the job. It would have been comical if it had been happening to someone else.

But no, it was happening to Dylan. The guy who would never be able to escape his mistakes.

Any other guy who'd met Penelope and had the kind of chemistry they had could have let the relationship take its natural course.

Which would be what? he asked himself. Dating, marriage, kids? Did he really think he was that kind of guy?

He stepped up his pace, replacing the voice inside his head that played devil's advocate with the sound of his own breath, his own blood rushing in his ears.

So she went back to Glenn. Lying Glenn. Was she really better off with a guy who would lead her on about something as important as children? Or had Glenn possibly confessed by now about the vasectomy?

And what about that first time he and Penelope had made love, would she tell him if something had . . . happened?

As his thoughts boiled along these and related lines, he slowly became aware of running footfalls a small distance behind him. Turning his head he noted a guy in a red windbreaker. He'd seen this guy before out running—those in this particular line of exercise tended to be out at the same times on the same routes—but there was something else familiar about him.

He'd been at Penelope's dinner party.

"Dylan?" the man asked.

Dylan slowed his pace until he caught up. "Yeah, hey," he said, reaching for the name.

"Leland Brown." The older man smiled and held out a hand. "We met at Penelope Porter's house. And I think I've seen you out here before."

"Yeah." Dylan reined in his thoughts and took the man's hand. They shook briefly. "I think you look familiar too. I mean, other than from the party."

"You usually run with another fellow, don't you? Tall, dark hair?"

Dylan laughed wryly. "Glenn Owens. Penelope's ex-husband."

Leland looked surprised. "Well that's . . . open-minded."

"Not really. Penelope and I, we're just friends." *Hah!* his mind countered.

"Really?" Leland's tone was skeptical.

Dylan looked at him askance. "Yeah. Really."

"Sorry, I didn't mean anything by that. I was misinformed. I thought there was more there."

Dylan picked up the pace. "Nope. Nothing there."

They jogged on for a quarter mile or so in silence, Dylan reflecting on how rude he himself was and how he hoped it got back to Penelope. *He's an asshole! A jerk! He deserves to be lonely.*

Then he thought how it might reflect badly on Penelope.

"Leland, listen, I'm sorry. I've had a bad couple of days. I don't mean to be rude."

"No, not rude at all. It's none of my business." Dylan glanced over at him and the older man smiled. "But you do seem like something's troubling you. Care to talk about it?"

Dylan laughed softly to himself. All these do-gooders, and him with problems none of them could solve.

"I'm quite good at listening," Leland added. "And very discreet. I'm a counselor by trade."

This took him by surprise. "I thought you were some kind of professor."

"I was, once upon a time. But I found myself more interested in helping the kids through the rough spots in their lives than in the actual teaching, so I went back and got a master's in counseling."

If he believed in God, would Dylan believe that He'd sent him a therapist at exactly the right moment? Dylan couldn't help it. He laughed.

"Is that funny?" Leland asked, but he didn't appear offended.

Dylan drew himself to a halt, bending over his legs and touching his fingertips to the ground. Leland stopped too.

"It is, actually." Dylan straightened. "I mean, it's great for you. You seem like you'd be real good at it. It's just . . . what I need now is more of a miracle worker than a therapist."

"You'll probably laugh at this too," Leland said, "but what I've noticed is that miracles tend to come more from within than from someone else."

"I'm my own miracle worker." Dylan went to a nearby stone wall and sat down on it. They were next to the college athletic fields, but at this hour on a Thursday night, they were empty, the street-lights already on.

"Sorry to be the one to break it to you." Leland

sat next to him, stretching one arm across his body and holding it with the other to warm up the muscles. "That's never what anyone wants to hear."

"Guess not. Though it does throw the control back into your own hands."

Leland beamed. "Exactly the point."

Dylan sat, quietly stretching, before thinking, *What the hell.* "It's just, I owe this guy a favor. But the favor he's asking . . . well, it could end up really bad for me. I mean *really* bad. But I do owe him."

"Because he did you a favor?"

"Yeah. It was a while back, but I don't believe in forgetting these things."

Leland thought a moment. "This favor, did it cost him a lot when he did it for you? Because it could be he's asking for something disproportionate to the debt."

Disproportionate to the debt, Dylan thought, a tiny light dawning.

"You can't give more than you can afford to give," Leland added, "no matter what you owe. It's true for Visa, it's true for friends."

"I wouldn't call him a friend, exactly. He used to be."

"Back before he started trying to ruin you?"

Dylan slanted his eyes toward Leland and smiled. "I'm not sure he sees it that way. We both used to be in the, uh, life-ruining business, but I got out. He hasn't quite accepted that."

"I hope this doesn't have anything to do with why you and Penelope are just friends." Leland stood and propped one foot on the wall, stretching a hamstring and trying, obviously, to make the question seem casual.

"If I'm not paying you, are you still obligated to keep what I say to yourself?"

"You bet." Leland continued stretching.

Dylan took a deep breath. "I have feelings for Penelope. I do. And . . . a lot of regrets. Not for things that have happened, necessarily. Mostly about things that can't happen. Why it won't work. We are so incredibly different. She's the type of girl who, if she knew about my past, about *everything* in my past, she'd be running for the hills. And now, with this favor cropping up, it's obvious my old life isn't going anywhere. At least not soon. So I have to . . ." He shrugged. "Protect her. That's not as noble as it sounds either." He gave Leland, who was watching attentively, a hard look. "It's a lot of work protecting someone when they're close to you. Much easier for her to just be . . ." He made a pushing motion with his hands. "Over there. Away from me."

Leland was nodding, a frown line between his eyebrows. "Does she agree with this?"

Dylan laughed. "Not hardly."

"Why do you want to protect someone who doesn't want protecting?"

"Because she's an innocent. She has no idea what she'd be in for with me."

"Nor you with her. But let me ask you this. If this favor weren't in the way, or better yet if you could erase the past you have, what would you want from Penelope?"

Struck by the question, Dylan's mind flew to an image of her face, a specific look that she'd given him the night of her dinner party. She'd gazed up at him and smiled, glowing, and for a second they seemed to share a secret.

Dylan stood up. "Her dog," he said, grinning at Leland. "That's one cute pooch."

Leland chuckled. "She might just give him to you, if you asked the right way."

"Hey, I appreciate your help, Leland. Thanks for taking the time. I mean it." He held out a hand and, while shaking Leland's, added, "I better get going, my muscles are tightening up."

"Sure, sure. I'll just be going this way." Leland tilted his head in the direction of the soccer fields. "Old knees, you know. I like running on the grass."

Dylan nodded. "Right. I have to go back to the shop. I'll see you around."

As they ran off in separate directions, Dylan let himself imagine, just for a moment, what he would want from Penelope if he could erase his past. He thought of her sleeping in his bed, how calm, how peaceful he'd felt for those few hours before the phone rang. He thought of having multiple nights like that, no fears about the future, no worries about the past. He thought about kids, about how he wouldn't be as anxious, or as scared, of Penelope being pregnant if this cloud wasn't hovering over his life. He thought about how great a mom Penelope would be. Would he be as good a father?

As he headed down the steep hill on Hanover Street, he thought of something he should have gotten Leland's take on. Should he tell Penelope about Glenn's vasectomy? Not that he'd have used details, but he could have couched the question to preserve their anonymity.

By the time he reached Kenmore Avenue he'd answered his own question. It was none of his business. If Penelope wanted to believe her ex-husband, that was her business. She'd married the guy, after all. And divorced him. Surely she knew better than to trust him.

Way to "protect" her, his inner critic said.

Dylan sprinted the rest of the way home.

Penelope had been about to pack up her purse and head to Dylan's to ask him about the jewelry when Glenn's BMW pulled up out front.

Oh no, she thought. She'd forgotten all about their dinner date tonight. What did that say? she thought, not really wondering. That she could completely forget she was supposed to see him did not portend anything good about a possible future.

The heart can't be forced, she thought, mustering a pleasant expression for him as he walked through the door.

"Hey, beautiful!" His smile was genuine, she could tell. It hadn't occurred to her to worry about it before, but it was obvious Dylan hadn't mentioned her dinner party to Glenn. He wouldn't have been able to act as nonchalant as this no matter how much he might have tried. "Are you ready?"

"Hi Glenn." She gave half a thought to cancelling on him, but knew she couldn't with him standing right in front of her. Besides, she needed to plan out exactly how she should approach Dylan, what she should say. That would take time. "I'm ready. I just need to leave a light on for Mr. Darcy."

"Who?" Glenn frowned. "Oh yeah, the dog. How's he doing, anyway? You trained him yet?"

On the way to the back room, she turned. "I've been training him all along."

"I know. That's what I meant. But last time he was a little rowdy, you know? Humping legs and all."

"He's a puppy, Glenn." She could barely keep the irritation out of her voice. "He'll be a puppy for months, you know."

"I know, I know!" He held his hands up in mock-surrender, a gesture suddenly so familiar she felt her irritation blossom into outright animosity. She turned away before he could read it on her face.

He took her to Olde Towne Steak & Seafood, one of their favorite restaurants when they'd been married and still one of her favorites for prime rib. He ordered a bottle of wine, a Shiraz, another one of her favorites, and then leaned his elbows on the table and beamed across at her.

"You look gorgeous tonight," he said. "Of course, you look gorgeous all the time, but tonight you're with me, and that makes you all the more beautiful."

She started to laugh, then realized he wasn't joking. Did he mean it as a compliment to himself?

He reached across the table and took the hand that lay near her water glass, flipping his fingers on the other side for her other hand, which lay in her lap. She gave it to him.

"I've been wracking my brain, Pen, trying to figure out why we broke up when we're obviously so perfect together." His palms were warm.

She squelched the urge to look around and see who might be looking at them. With this kind of display, if she knew anyone at the restaurant there could be talk all over town tomorrow about how they were getting back together. "I don't know if we ought to think too hard about that. It might spoil dinner."

He laughed. "No, it won't. It seems to me it was something to do with children."

Something to do with children? If he hadn't been holding her hands she might have used one of them to smack herself in the forehead. Or him.

"But as you know," he continued as she looked on incredulously, "I've had to have a little change of heart on that score."

"Yes, how is little Brittney?" Penelope asked, removing her hands from his. "You barely talk about her."

"Well, not to you. That doesn't seem . . . prudent." He smiled sheepishly at her. "But I'm a proud daddy to everyone else, let me tell you. I just go on and on."

"Have you got any pictures?"

"Pictures?"

"You know, in your wallet. I haven't seen her since that time I ran into you and Abigail in church. She was just a baby then."

He cleared his throat. "No, I don't have any pictures. Abigail was supposed to get me her latest and she never has. So . . ."

Penelope nodded, rearranging her napkin in her lap. The waiter arrived and produced their bottle of wine with a flourish. Glenn joked with him about how it "better not be a screw top. We're paying real money for this one," with a wink at Penelope.

She sighed.

After the waiter poured the wine, they ordered,

and Penelope realized she was not looking forward to the meal so much as its being over. She took a long sip of the Shiraz. It was good. Glenn expressed his appreciation too, and she knew that at one time she would have taken that as a sign—albeit a small one—that they were meant to be together. So much in common . . . so much the same tastes . . .

"As I was saying." Glenn put his glass down. "I've had to rethink the child issue and I wanted to tell you, well, just that I'm enjoying being a father. You were right about it, all those times you said I would love it once we actually had a baby."

Penelope looked into her glass, nodding. "I'm glad you feel that way. Glad for you and for Brittney."

"No, I'm serious," he said, as if she'd contradicted him, "I've learned a lot these last few years. I've changed a lot." He gave her a deep, significant look.

Penelope felt herself blushing, as if he'd just exposed a little too much skin.

"Glenn, that's great. I'm happy for you." She tried to sound sincere. "I've learned a lot too. I think we've both done a lot of changing. And growing."

And falling for other people . . .

"That's true. That's exactly it." He leaned back in his chair, sipped his wine. "You always knew me so well. Do you remember the time we were having that party, and just before everyone was supposed to show up we got to feeling kind of . . . amorous? I'll never forget having to throw on our clothes to go answer the door. And I had my shirt buttoned wrong! I always was kind of an idiot like that, wasn't I? Always giving us away." He laughed at the memory.

Penelope did too, if only to mask how sad it made her. All of it, this attempt at rekindling and how desperately it wasn't working, made her wonder what the point of everything had been. Why had she started this? They'd been *fine* before she'd stopped by his house that night. Of course they'd barely talked. But she could have just rekindled the friendship, not tried to date the man again. Good God, had she forgotten how self-centered he could be?

She supposed she could be too. But the only way that worked was if each was as interested in the other as they were in themselves. And that just wasn't true anymore.

Penelope steered the conversation toward Glenn's work, a topic that he usually took and ran with, and was relieved when the food finally came. Her prime rib was perfect. She figured if she wolfed it down and didn't order dessert, they could be out of there in half an hour.

Glenn, however, had other plans. He lingered over his meal, debated getting another bottle of wine—which she talked him out of—had coffee and pondered dessert until she pointed out he didn't want to undo all the good his running was doing. At that point he inhaled, sucked in his stomach, and looked immensely proud of himself.

As he should, she considered. He was working hard, and that little pot belly she'd noticed a month ago was significantly diminished.

When they finally made it to the car, Penelope's face hurt from stifling yawns. So many of the reasons she'd given up on Glenn and their marriage had come back to her over the course of dinner. She now understood another of the many layers of meaning in the phrase, You can't go home again.

Glenn pulled up in back of her shop, where she'd left her car, and turned off the BMW. He twisted in the seat, one arm around the back of hers.

"I had a good time tonight," he said, eyes glinting in the dark.

"Me too. Thanks, Glenn. I haven't been to that restaurant in ages." She leaned over to kiss him on the cheek, but he turned his head and caught her lips with his.

His left arm went around her waist and pulled her toward him. Her knee hit the gear shift.

"Glenn, I—"

He dove in for another kiss, this time with his mouth open, tongue probing. Something about the fact that she had started all this, that Glenn had wanted nothing to do with her at first, stopped her from pushing him away. But she couldn't make herself get into it.

Maybe she just needed time. Maybe it was too soon after thinking things might actually work out for her and Dylan. Then Glenn said the one thing she never thought she'd hear him say.

"Penelope." He breathed heavily, resting his forehead on hers. "I've been thinking about another child . . . about a child of ours . . ."

She pulled her head back. "Really?"

His expression was serious. "I have. I know it's probably been too long, that it's possible you've changed your mind, but . . . it's just what I've been thinking about lately."

She held her breath. Was this a dream come true or a nightmare unfolding?

"I, uh, well, that's . . ." She inhaled deeply. "That's something I'd need to think about, Glenn."

Inside her head a riot was going on, as if there were thousands of tiny protestors on one side screaming, *But we want Dylan!* against thousands on the other side yelling back, *But we've always wanted a child!*

"Glenn, I have to go now." She leaned back in her seat and undid the seat belt. "Can we talk about this later?"

"I'll call you tomorrow," he said with an indulgent smile.

"No, not tomorrow. It's Gallery Night and I have a lot to do. But maybe this weekend."

He leaned over and kissed her once more soundly on the lips. "You got it."

She gave what she hoped amounted to a smile—it felt like a malformed grimace on her shocked face—and got out of the car.

She opened up her own car door and got in as Glenn drove off, staring straight ahead without seeing, past the cloud of her own breath in the frigid air of the unwarmed vehicle to some magical, mystical place where dreams came true.

A baby. Could she have a baby with a man she didn't love?

The thought surprised her. She hadn't known she didn't still love Glenn.

What was less surprising was what she saw in that magical, mystical place where dreams came true: Dylan. And no one else.

Chapter 16

Dylan was half glad for the crazy day. Women from the Gallery Night committee had shown up before noon to set up drinks and food, requiring him to rearrange many of his displays. The women had brought wine—both red and white—cookies, cakes, hot cider in a crock pot along with little meatballs in another crock pot, and piles of napkins, forks, plates, and cups. Between moving his merchandise and setting up plugs and extension cords so that they wouldn't trip people in the shop, he hadn't had a moment to spare to think about who was coming and when, and what he was going to do if they expected something to be here when they arrived.

Foot traffic that day was good too, so in the midst of all the figuring out and setting up there'd also been a fair number of customers. He sold two of his mother's bowls before noon.

His mother had shown up about three o'clock with the same two guys who'd driven her pottery down. Curtis and . . . he'd forgotten the other guy's name. The less chatty one who drove the van. She'd also brought another vanload of merchandise.

"Look at my baby!" she'd exclaimed, running to Dylan and giving him a big hug. Then she'd backed up, put a palm against one of his cheeks and beamed, saying, "You just grow more handsome every day. Curtis!" She flitted like a bird, her quick eyes and frail hand beckoning to the beefy Curtis. "Doesn't he look good? I think he's really digging his new place. It's so good for you, honey." She glanced back at Dylan with a laugh. "Look at you, rolling your eyes at your old lady."

Curtis snorted and shuffled off to the food table, only to be swatted away by one of the ladies setting out cookies as delicately as if she were building a house of cards.

"Mom, how do you know these guys?" Dylan asked, standing close and watching Curtis, a.k.a. the chicken guy, wander around the store touching things he should not.

"Through Pinky, hon. Why?" Before he could answer she spun, her long blonde hair fanning out around her. "You haven't told me how you like my new outfit. I bought it special for tonight. It was a little expensive but I wanted to make sure you could be proud of me."

She was dressed in her typical style, though the clothes were a bit flashier than usual. A long purple peasant skirt brushed her ankles and was topped by a clingy, low-necked sweater that glittered with sewn-on gold spangles. Large hoop earrings graced her ears, multiple bangle bracelets her wrists, and an ankh symbol on a piece of leather was around her neck. She wore blush and lipstick, but no other makeup, and she still looked more like his sister than his mother.

"You look real pretty, Mom. As usual." Then he reached out and hugged her around the shoulders. "I'm always proud of you."

Her smile glowed. "I'm proud of you too, honey. Look at what you've made of yourself. I bet you sell everything in here tonight. Every last piece!" She threw up her hands and cast her smile around the room. She believed every word, he knew.

He couldn't help but smile with her, albeit wryly.

A couple hours later his mother was still shooting sunshine around the shop, charming customers and making the Gallery Night ladies laugh, when the door opened and Penelope entered. It was past five o'clock, already dark out, and he happened to know her shop was open tonight too, so he was surprised to see her. Truthfully, after their last meeting he'd have been surprised to see her come through his door under any circumstances.

Her dark eyes caught his immediately. She looked . . . amazing. Something jammed in his throat as his eyes drank her in. In sharp contrast to his colorful, flamboyant mother, she looked sleek. Her dress was ivory, her hair smooth and long, her jewelry consisting of one thick cuff bracelet in gold and long spearlike earrings that accented her graceful neck.

"Oh, hello!" his mother enthused, going right over to Penelope and taking her hand. "Aren't you beautiful? But you must be freezing, walking around like that without a coat. Come in. These nice ladies here have some hot cider, I think."

Clearly confused, Penelope turned her attention from Dylan to her. "I only just came from across the street."

"Thank goodness! Otherwise you'd be courting pneumonia. Is there something you're looking for in particular, sweetie? My son, here, has the finest collection of ceramics you'll find anywhere on the East Coast. Maybe even the country."

"You're Dylan's mother?" Penelope's surprise was genuine. As was everyone's.

Dylan's gaze shifted to Curtis, who lingered next to the sushi sets, openly eyeing Penelope's ass.

Dylan walked over to him, cutting off Curtis's view. "I have a question for you."

Curtis picked his teeth with a fingernail. "Shoot."

"What were you doing in my basement last time you were here?"

Curtis's eyes flicked sideways. "What're you talking about?"

"I'm talking about you being in my basement, for no reason I can think of, the day you brought down my mother's stuff."

Curtis shrugged and gave him a dead-eyed look. "I don't know."

"You don't know why you were down there?"

"I don't know what you're talking about."

"Dylan, honey, this young lady wants to talk to you!"

Curtis's lips thinned into a yellow smile. "I think I hear your mama calling you."

Dylan fixed him with a hard look, then turned to his mother and Penelope.

"Aren't you the lucky one?" his mother said with a wink. "This beautiful girl says she wants to speak with you."

Penelope smiled down at his petite mother. "It was so nice to meet you, Mrs. Mersey. I hope we get to talk again."

"Oh, Sara, *please*. I've never been a 'missus' in my life." She patted both Penelope and Dylan on their backs as they headed for the back room. "You two just run along now, I'll keep track of things out here."

Dylan turned back and pointed a finger at his mother. "Do *not* give anything away. No matter how nice someone is."

"But it's good business!" she protested. "If they get a little something, maybe they'll buy a little something."

"They're *here* to buy things, Mom. They're here to support the arts."

"Oh, well then."

Dylan shook his head and they moved into the back.

"Your mother is so sweet," Penelope said, wonder in her voice, as if she expected any mother of his to have several snarling heads. "And she's so proud of you."

Dylan shrugged. "Mothers."

Penelope smiled, but it wasn't like her smiles in the past. This one was sad.

"Was there something you needed?" he asked. "I mean, I know you're open tonight too, so I don't want to keep you."

She looked down. "I . . . oh gosh, now that I think about it, now's not really the best time." She looked up through her lashes. "Can I just ask . . . when those cops stopped by the other day, were they here to search the place?"

Even if she'd known they were cops because of Carson, her question surprised him. It seemed to reflect more knowledge than he was comfortable with her having. Had Carson told her what was going on or had his own search clued her in?

"Yes," he said.

"And did they have a warrant?"

He studied her. Knowledgeable questions. He didn't like it. "No. They asked if they could search and I said yes."

Amazing how that made it sound like a civilized conversation.

She exhaled, seemingly relieved.

"Not that they couldn't have gotten one," he added, taking his own honesty too far.

Her gaze was sharp. "I think I might have what you were looking for. Or rather what *they* were looking for."

Dylan stilled, so much so that he thought his blood might have stopped flowing in his veins. "What?"

Her eyes were so dark he thought he might drown in them. "I found . . . something valuable. Very valuable. In a bag. In my basement. Right where Mr. Darcy would come through from your place."

Dylan's mouth opened, then closed, then opened again. He didn't know where to step first, there were land mines everywhere. Admit? Deny? Go get the stuff? Cling to ignorance? He didn't even know what, exactly, she'd found.

But he needed to get it. Forget what that would mean for him and Penelope—that he would have to admit he knew about it, reveal to her he was part of it, in no matter how warped a way—his only choice now was to pass it on and be done with it. And he had to keep her out of it, at all costs.

"I can see by your face you know what I'm talking about," she said. Was it his imagination or did disappointment drip from every word?

"It's not what you think."

"I don't know what to think."

"But I need it back from you. Don't go get it, not in front of those guys out front. I'll come by later and pick it up. I don't want you involved in this at all."

She swallowed, her expression set. "That's all very noble, Dylan, but I'm not giving it back to you. Not unless you promise to go to the police with it."

If she'd slapped him across the face he wouldn't have felt more stunned. The breath left him. "You want me to go back to jail?"

Her face clouded. "No! Of course not. Don't you see you'll be *less* likely to go to jail if you don't commit the crime? You have to do what's right here. I know you've been trying to start a new life. I know this isn't really what you want to do, this— this—lawbreaking. I understand it must be hard to stop, but—"

"*Quiet,*" he commanded.

Penelope startled.

Curtis wandered through the stockroom door

toward them, looking as nonchalant as a bull in a china shop.

"Someone's here to see you," he said, scratching the side of his neck. "Says you got something for him."

Dylan's blood ran cold. "Yeah, tell him to wait."

Curtis's brows rose. "I'll tell him, but he won't like it."

"Yeah, well, I don't like it that he's here. Tell him that."

Curtis frowned, then left the room muttering, "You a crazy motherfucker."

"Penelope," he said urgently, leaning toward her and taking her by the shoulders, "you have no idea what you've stumbled into here. Don't get involved. If you care about me at all, you'll walk out that door and not look back. Just give me whatever you found. We'll go to your place right now. Then we can talk about the cops, all right?"

"You're going to give it to that guy, aren't you? The one who's waiting. You're selling it." She looked, for God's sake, as if he were doing it to hurt her feelings.

"I *have* to, don't you understand? I'm just a pawn in this game."

"I thought you were getting out of the game. Now's your chance, Dylan. Take a stand. Let them know it." She extended a hand toward the front of the shop. "And how can you do this with your mother right there? I'm sure she didn't raise you to be a criminal, Dylan. How can you do this to her?"

"My mother," Dylan growled, "is the reason I have a record at all, Penelope. Now don't fuck with me. I need that stuff and I need it *now*."

She took a step back, bumped into the wedging table, and caught herself with her hands behind her back. She looked afraid. *Afraid of him*.

He closed his eyes, while his soul turned to ashes.

He'd scared her. She actually thought he might hurt her. And hadn't he already? Red marks showed on her arms where he'd grabbed her.

"I'm sorry." He shook his head, backed up. "I'm so sorry, Penelope. I don't mean to hurt you. You're right." Something settled deep inside him. Resignation. "You're right. We'll go to the cops. I don't—I don't—give a—"

"What the *fuck*, man?" Some guy Dylan had never seen before strode into the back room, followed by Curtis.

The new guy looked unexpectedly formal, dressed in black dress pants, a dark blue shirt and black tie. His overcoat was long, black and open. Dylan eyed its deep pockets.

Though he was probably not yet thirty-five, he had a craggy face with a scar that split his left eyebrow in two and ran up into his short cropped hair. His blue eyes were small and sharp as blades.

"Dude, I don't have time for this shit. You Mersey?" He jutted his chin at Dylan, his eyes cutting to Penelope. "Who's this? Get her outta here."

Dylan turned to her, his face frozen. "I'll get that bowl wrapped up and bring it over to you as soon as possible. Thanks for shopping with us today."

She leaned toward him and hissed, "I'm not leaving you—"

"This your girlfriend?" the new guy's voice was mocking. "Let me guess, she don't approve of what you're doing."

"She's not my girlfriend," Dylan stated. "I know why you're here, but she doesn't. She has to go."

"Nobody leaves." The guy hunched his shoulders under his coat, then straightened them, working a kink out of his neck. Or doing a De Niro impersonation, one or the other.

Dylan stared him down. "Yes. She does. She's not involved in this. Besides, the stuff hasn't even arrived yet."

"Yeah, it has." Curtis's words sealed Dylan's fate, as of course he'd known they would.

Dylan closed his eyes.

Curtis glanced at the new guy and jerked his head toward the basement door. "It's downstairs. Come on, Kane, I'll show you where."

Kane laughed. "You think I'm stupid? I ain't going down there. You get it and I'll wait here with these people." His eyes scanned Penelope's body.

Curtis had to get past Dylan to get to the basement steps, but for a moment Dylan couldn't move. His limbs were paralyzed. If they'd both gone down he could have persuaded Penelope to leave. As it was, there was nothing he could say to her in front of them.

Curtis glared at him. Dylan shifted slightly and the man passed, though he paused at the top of the stairs, looking at him.

"Let me just show her out," Dylan said to the new guy and dragged Penelope toward the door, whispering to her quietly as they turned, "Get out of here, now, Penelope. I'm begging you."

"Get moving," Kane barked to Curtis.

Penelope's face was alarmed but she stopped. "What will they do when they don't find the bag?"

"I don't know. But don't worry, I can handle them. I just need you to go." Dylan pushed Penelope toward the door.

Curtis disappeared. Kane turned back to them. "I told you, she ain't going anywhere. Both of you, get back over here."

Ominously, the guy's hand went to his pocket. Dylan's heart sank. There was no mistaking the threat implied by the gesture.

"Come on. She'll only be in the way," he reasoned.

"She's *already* in the way. Nothing you can do about it now." Kane peered at the basement door.

Below them, Dylan heard the iron door latch

grinding as Curtis tried to work it open. It had taken Dylan quite a while to get it shut the other day, both the latch and hinges being rusted in place for God knew how long.

After a minute Curtis called from the basement. "Kane! Get Mersey. I can't get the goddamn door open."

"All right, come on." Kane strode toward them and ushered Dylan toward the basement. "You too, sweetheart." He took Penelope by the wrist and pulled her with them.

Dylan moved, but didn't stop talking. "I'm telling you, she's just a customer. You don't want—"

"Shut up," Kane commanded.

"No, I'm not going to shut up." Dylan stepped between Kane and Penelope, shoving the other man's arm off of her. "You may have all kinds of shit on Pinky, but you don't have anything on me. I'm clean. I'm not part of this. I didn't even know—"

"*Mersey!*" Curtis's voice rang out from the bottom of the steps. "Get down here now and open this goddamn door."

Dylan's heart hammered in his chest. Maybe he could push Kane down the stairs. Or hit him in the head with one of the old pulleys. Trip up Curtis and lock them both in the basement until the cops came. He'd have damn sure given it a shot if Penelope hadn't been there.

Kane pushed both Penelope and Dylan toward the stairs, and the three of them stomped down the wooden steps like cattle on the way to slaughter.

Curtis carried a penlight and shone it on the iron door on the back wall, his eyes glittering in the dim light. For the first time the chicken guy actually looked dangerous.

"You had to close it, didn't you," Curtis said to Dylan, his voice low but harder now, more determined crook than dumb lackey. "I left it open. You found the shit, didn't you?"

Dylan returned the same dead-eyed look to Curtis that Curtis had given him earlier in the evening, and repeated his words, "I don't know what you're talking about."

Curtis grabbed his arm and pushed him toward the door. "Open it."

Dylan worked the iron lever, remembering how hard it had been to force closed. All to save Bonsai, he reflected. He should have been thinking; he should have left things as they were.

Sweat broke out on his brow, but he got the lever up, releasing the latch. The moment he opened the door, however, he knew that whatever they were hoping to find wouldn't be there.

He stepped back without opening the door. "You want to do the honors?" he asked Curtis.

"Just get on with it, for Christ's sake," Kane growled.

Dylan backed up toward Penelope as Kane moved forward and grabbed the lever.

"When it opens, *run*," Dylan said low to Penelope.

The door opened.

Kane screamed like a little girl.

Out of the door sprang a fuzzy white ball of fur. It hit Kane squarely in the chest, knocking him backward, where he tripped over a wooden crate and landed on his back.

"Mr. Darcy!" Penelope squealed, running toward the dog.

"What the *fuck?*" Curtis spun, then started shouting, "Ice storm, Ice Storm. Get in here *now*."

Dylan tried to grab Penelope and direct her up the steps, but Kane, after scrambling to his feet, stepped in front of him, both hands fisted in Dylan's shirt.

"Who's Darcy?" Kane yelled. "Who the fuck is Darcy?"

Dylan whipped his arms up and over Kane's, breaking his grip, and backed away.

Kane yanked his coat around himself and shoved one hand into his pocket.

Dylan lunged for Penelope, who had followed the dog to the corner and was now trapped between the back wall and Kane. Throwing himself in front of her he spun to see Kane directing his pocket at them. There was no question what was inside of it.

"Where is it, asshole?" Kane's voice shook and his eyes shot sparks. "If you don't want your little piece of ass here watching you bleed to death on the floor, you'll tell me what you did with it."

"I don't even know what you're talking about." Dylan's voice was steady, his muscles coiled, ready to spring at the guy. Kane might get one shot off but it would be enough time for Penelope to get away. The adrenaline surging through Dylan's veins made him feel super human.

He had it all worked out until Penelope shouted, "*I've* got it! The bag! The jewelry—it's at my—"

"No! She's lying." Dylan retreated into her so hard Penelope's back hit the wall. He could feel the dog squirming between them. "Trying to save my ass, because I lost it. I'm telling you, the stuff might have been here, but I never saw it and I don't know what happened to it. I don't even know what it is."

"Oh right. She's got it," Kane said, moving closer. "A bag of fucking diamond rings? What better way to impress a chick? So you double-crossed old Pinky, eh? I'd say good for you, but nobody fucks with me. Come on, bitch, we're going to your place."

He reached out to grab her arm, but a clatter

of footfalls sounded on the wooden steps behind
him.

Kane spun, yanked the gun from his pocket and
fired it. A chunk of one of the ceiling beams rained
down on four men on the steps, three of whom had
weapons extended, double-handed, and aimed at
Kane.

The front one reached the floor and knelt, gun
aimed. "Police! *Freeze!*"

Chapter 17

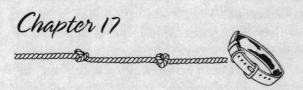

Penelope's hands shook as Sara Mersey handed her a cup of hot cider. The gun had worn a silencer, thank God, but she'd still never been so close to such violence before in her life. Just before he'd fired, Kane had had the gun pointed *at her*. He hadn't been bluffing and the gun had been real.

She shook more just thinking about it.

When it had gone off, and wood chips and splinters had rained down from the ceiling, it had taken Penelope a moment to figure out what had happened. That's when the shaking had started. She'd held Mr. Darcy so tightly he'd squealed.

Dylan had lowered her down to sit on the floor. He'd taken the dog, held him in one arm and instructed her to put her head between her knees, all while the policemen who'd saved them shouted and swarmed around Kane and Curtis.

But that was another odd thing. It appeared as though the sloppy guy, Curtis, was a cop too, because he hadn't been arrested along with Kane. Instead he had left with the man who'd handcuffed Kane, helping to drag the thug off to who knew where.

Through all of it, she kept expecting them to come drag Dylan off too, but they seemed to be ignoring him. Maybe because he was taking care of her.

"I must not have closed the door on my side," Penelope babbled, "when I found the bag. That's how Mr. Darcy got here. I didn't close the door. Even though I meant to. That's why I went into the basement. I never go down there, all the way back there, to that part of the basement. It's creepy. Then I left Mr. Darcy in the back room to come talk to you."

"It's all right, Penelope," Dylan said. "It doesn't matter now."

He'd stroked her hair, ran the back of his fingers across her brow, and tried to make her focus on his face.

"Penelope, look at me. Everything's all right now."

She looked around. They still weren't coming for Dylan, even as they all went up the basement stairs.

"I know, I know," she said, but her voice was high-pitched and not her own. She didn't know how to get back to her regular voice so she just kept talking. "I didn't know, Dylan. You were right, I didn't understand—anything. I had no idea how dangerous it was. I shouldn't have tried to tell you what to do. I nearly got you killed!"

"No you didn't. None of this was your fault."

"I'm such a fool—"

"Stop it, Penelope. You were caught up in this by accident. You didn't do anything wrong."

"I shouldn't have interfered. Though I didn't mean to. It was Mr. Darcy. See, the bag smelled like chicken grease."

That made Dylan laugh. "Make sure you tell Curtis that."

"Why?"

"He likes chicken." Dylan helped her to her feet and guided her up the stairs. "Look, I have to talk to these guys a minute. I need to find out exactly what happened. Will you be all right?"

"I'm fine. I'm fine," she said again, but she still had that weird voice. Maybe she'd have it forever.

Once upstairs, Dylan's mother had taken her by the arm and sat her down in a chair. Dylan had gently handed her the dog, and then went to talk to the cops, who still were not arresting him.

Two of the policemen went to Penelope's to get the jewelry. She called and told Lucy, in a strangled, quaking voice, to show them where the safe was. She gave them the combination. She really didn't think her knees would hold her to go with them.

Dylan stood with the last of the four men who'd come to their rescue, both of them leaning against the high table on the back wall. Dylan's arms were crossed over his chest and he looked at the floor, casting surreptitious worried glances her way every now and again.

The other guy tapped a cigarette on the counter and took a lighter out of his pocket.

"Man, I told you I had your back. When will you ever learn to trust me?" The stocky man was missing a finger on his right hand, Penelope noted as he lit the cigarette.

"You could have told me," Dylan said. "I was completely in the dark. Had no idea it was a sting. After you called me I lost a couple years off my life trying to figure out how to screw you over."

The short guy laughed, expelling smoke toward the ceiling and revealing a gap-toothed smile. "I know, dude, but I couldn't tell you. Besides, it was better for you not to know. This way it was obvious to Kane you weren't in on it. And you know how those guys talk. And the cops, they know you're clean. Curtis was wearing a wire."

Dylan rubbed the back of his neck and twisted his head to look at his friend. "No kidding?"

"Caught the whole day. *And,* since he was the

one planted the shit, they know you had nothing to do with that either."

Penelope hardly knew what to make of this information. She wished *she* was wearing a wire, so she could play back the entire conversation later and figure out exactly what they were saying.

Dylan ran the same hand he'd been rubbing his neck with through his hair. "I guess I owe you. Again."

"Nah. I'm outta the debt-keeping business."

"You shock me, Pink," Dylan said. "I never thought you'd cooperate with the cops."

The guy lifted a shoulder. "They made me an offer I couldn't refuse," he laughed cynically.

Dylan chuckled. "I'll bet."

Dylan's mother sat beside Penelope and put an arm around her shoulders. "Are you okay, honey? I wish I had some chamomile tea, that would calm you down."

"I'm fine," Penelope said, but her body was clenched together like a fist, and if she didn't hold her cup with both hands she would spill it.

Dylan watched her closely, then shifted his gaze back to the four-fingered man. "Do me a favor, though."

His friend laughed. "Another one?"

"Don't involve me in anything like this again. Ever. I don't care if you are working for the good guys now."

"Hey, I did it for you. They coulda got someone else, but I picked you. Had to get someone Kane didn't know, and you been out so long he never heard of you. Plus he wouldn't come into Maryland, too many cops knew him. So when they got cooperation from Virginia I picked you. This'll get the cops off your back forever, don't you see? I just guaranteed your fresh, goddamn, start!"

He laughed, but Dylan merely dropped his head.

"I can't say it's quite so 'fresh' now."

The guy continued to chuckle. "But, dude, I gotta say, even I didn't expect you to fight me so hard. And moving the shit? Man, I did not see that coming. Were you really gonna go to the cops with it?"

Dylan's eyes darted to Penelope. She dropped her gaze to the paper mug in her hands.

"It was kind of a . . . last-minute idea."

There was a bustle in the front of the shop—which had been closed, much to the shock and consternation of the Gallery Night ladies. They were now in the process of packing up their cookies and cider and moving across the street to Penelope's.

It made Penelope sad, to think of all Dylan's beautiful creations sitting, waiting for the admiring masses, only to be locked away behind police tape.

Despite herself, she began to shake again. Dylan had been right. She'd had no idea what his past—what his present—was like. She couldn't relate to his problems. She couldn't even understand his friends. She glanced furtively at the guy with the missing finger. Dylan had grown up with that tattooed thug. He looked like something out of a Mafia movie. One of the lesser henchmen. One who'd get killed in the opening scene.

Beside him, Dylan's lanky good looks, his clean jeans, and button-down shirt worn for Gallery Night suddenly seemed suspect. Like a disguise to mislead the audience into thinking he was one of the good ones.

But he was very different from the character she'd created in her head. The one with the shady past who was now just as "normal" as she was. She'd treated his memories and experiences almost as if they'd occurred in a particularly moving book they'd both read.

The two cops who'd gone to her shop entered Dylan's back room with the now familiar plastic bag.

"Got it," one of them said, holding it aloft. "Looks like it's all there, but we'll go through it with the list from the victim."

For a second Penelope thought they meant her; then she realized they were talking about the jewelry store, the one that had been robbed. She wasn't a victim, just a naïve girl who'd thought she had all the answers. No wonder Dylan hadn't wanted her in his life.

A tear dripped down her cheek.

A second later Dylan was squatting next to her, handing her the portable phone. "Call Megan. Or one of your friends. Someone should get you home." His voice was gentle, his hand warm on her knee. "I'd take you but I have to go with these guys, file a report."

"But, but my car is here, at the shop." She motioned across the street. She was fine, wasn't she? She could get herself home.

"I'll bring it over later." He looked at his mother. "She should go home."

"I know, honey, you're right," Sara Mersey said. "Do you want me to call your friend?" she asked Penelope. She took the phone from Dylan's hand. "Tell me her number."

Penelope laughed breathlessly and for a moment thought she might hyperventilate. "No, no. She'll think I've died. I'll call her."

So she did as Dylan asked, called Megan—caught her on her cell phone, and breathed her first unhindered breath at the sound of her pal's voice—then waited for her to show up, her brain numb, her body cold.

Ten minutes later, after the committee ladies had cleared out and gone to Penelope's, and the two cops with Kane had left for wherever it was they were taking him, Penelope was alone with Dylan. His mother, Curtis, and the four-fingered man were in the front room. Curtis was going to drive them to the police station for Dylan to give them a statement.

Dylan pulled up a chair across from her, sat with his elbows on his knees and said, "I'm so sorry I got you into this. Are you going to be all right?"

Penelope swallowed, wishing she knew what to do. He looked so sad, and she felt so weak. "Of course I'll be all right. Will you? I mean . . . they didn't arrest you or anything?"

She was still confused about what exactly had gone on here tonight. It seemed as if Dylan was set up to catch someone else. Did that end up making him innocent?

Dylan sighed and dropped his head, his hands threading through his hair. She looked at the straight blond locks, his long fingers strong and yet so vulnerable-looking. She wanted to reach out and take his hands, but hers were icy cold, and what if he resisted?

She had acted just like the sheltered little girl he'd always believed she was. Because she *was* sheltered. Just like Megan had said. What did she, or any of her friends, know about living in a bad neighborhood, getting mixed up in crime, and going to jail?

"It's complicated." Dylan raised his head. "It's kind of like what I told you before, or tried to. A life, a lifetime of being a certain way . . . it's not so easy to scrape off. Bits and pieces, they cling to you. Every now and then, I guess, that stuff crops up, whether from inside or outside. Tonight it was outside. I was used because of what I used to do, who I used to be. I was just lucky to be used by the good guys this time."

"You mean the cops used you because they believed you'd do something illegal?"

He dropped his gaze again. "That's right. And . . . I was going to. I was going to hand over the stuff to whoever came to get it and cross my fingers that it never came back to haunt me again. Until you intervened."

She saw one corner of his mouth rise in a wry smile, but he still didn't look at her.

"You were . . . going to let them use you." She held her paper mug so tightly between her palms it started to give. "But it was because you didn't have any other choice. Isn't that right?"

He gave a sound like a laugh, but it was not amusement. "Don't give me an out, Penelope. There's always another choice." He looked up at her, his eyes frank. "I could have done what you said I should do. I could have gone to the police immediately and told them exactly what was going on the minute I learned of it."

"But you didn't have the bag!" she protested. "How could you have gone to the police? And when I said I wouldn't give it back to you, you agreed to turn it in."

"Only after you wouldn't give it to me. Don't you see? *That's* when I had no choice." He clasped his hands together in front of him, elbows still on his knees. It brought him closer to her, she could reach out and touch his cheek . . . but she didn't. "When I had a choice, I . . ." He shook his head.

"I'm so sorry, Dylan. I had no idea what I was asking you to do. Not really. You were only trying to save yourself. Save yourself from something that wasn't even your fault. It had nothing to do with you! Who wouldn't do that?"

"My point is, Penelope, that I haven't changed, not really. I was accidentally saved tonight, but before that happened, I nearly got you killed. And for that, I'll never forgive myself."

"But—"

"Mersey!" the abrupt voice at the door made them both jump. Penelope turned to see Curtis— former hapless flunky turned beady-eyed cop— waiting impatiently. A gun holster now adorned his sweat-stained shirt, beneath the grimy jean jacket. "C'mon. We gotta go."

Penelope sat up straight. "Where are you going? They're not—they didn't—"

"I'm just going to give a report." Dylan stood slowly, looking down on her with what looked like regret.

"At the police station?" She stood too. For some reason adrenaline rushed through her veins again, as if he were leaving for some foreign country and she'd never see him again.

"Yeah, my mom will stay with you until Megan gets here." He lifted a hand, as if he might touch her hair, but didn't follow through. He pushed the hand into his pocket.

"I should go with you," she said. "I know people down there. Maybe I can help."

"Penelope, no." His voice was firm. "You're no longer involved in this. I don't want you anywhere near it."

"But—"

"No." He took her arms. "Penelope. Thank you, for all you did tonight. You tried to save me when—when . . ." His voice seemed to get thick and he stopped. She took a step toward him.

"*Now*, Mersey. You can make up with your girl-friend later."

Dylan turned to glare at the man. "Give me a *minute*."

"You've had a minute. They're waiting for us."

"They're not going anywhere anytime soon and you know it," Dylan said and turned back to Penelope as if Curtis weren't there.

"I'm sorry, Penelope. For all I got you into, for all you had to do tonight. I'm sorry you had to see—what my life is really like." He held his hands out helplessly. "I hope you see now what I've been trying to tell you. I'm not who you think I am."

"Stop it," she cried. "Just stop it. You're not—"

"That's it." Curtis strode into the room. "The squad car just pulled up. We're outta here. Don't make me cuff you."

"But he's not arrested!" Penelope protested. Mr. Darcy started barking and nipping at Curtis's shoelaces.

"Get off me." Curtis kicked his foot out and the pup went flying.

"Oh!" Penelope knelt to the floor, hands out for the little dog.

Dylan grabbed Curtis by the collar. "Damn it, I don't care if you are a cop—"

"It's okay!" Penelope grabbed the dog and rose to her feet. "It's okay, Dylan. Just go with him. We can talk later. We have plenty of time now. You go."

Dylan slowly let go of Curtis's jacket. He sent one last inscrutable look at Penelope, then left with Curtis and the four-fingered man.

Sara Mersey bustled back into the room with another cup of cider and what looked like a flask.

"Here we go, honey," she said, looking pleased. She set the cup on the high table and poured a generous dram of whatever was in the flask into it. "I had to go ask those nice ladies for more cider, but this ought to calm you down some."

Penelope walked toward her, eyeing the flask and getting a good whiff of something strongly alcoholic. "Mrs. Mersey—"

"Sara, please!" She turned with a bright smile and put a hand on Penelope's arm. "You and I are going to be great friends, I can tell. You obviously mean a lot to my Dylan, and he has very good taste."

Penelope looked into her twinkly blue eyes and felt sad. For Dylan and for Sara. She was like some kind of elfin woman, always smiling, always bubbling, but beneath the surface something lurked, something like fear.

"Sara, then." Penelope smiled. "Did you know Curtis was with the police?"

Sara's laugh was like breaking glass. "Me? Heavens no. I would never have let him drive me here if I had." She leaned conspiratorially toward Penelope, even though they were the only two in the whole shop. Her voice was soft and sweet. "You can't trust the pigs, honey. Remember that."

"The—pigs?"

Sara gave a great sigh and put the back of her hand to her forehead, wiping a few strands of hair back. "The cops." She leaned toward her again. "You probably don't know this like I do, living here in this pleasant little town, but you can't trust the law. They're out to get you no matter what you think. They get *points* for arresting people, Penelope, so they don't care much about guilt or innocence. Just bring 'em in and lock 'em up." She shook her head and took a sip. "So. Curtis, a cop?

That surprised me. He seemed like such a nice young man."

Penelope frowned and watched the woman down the cider, polishing it off.

"Oh!" Sara laughed brightly. "I poured this for you, didn't I? Well, no matter. I'll just go get some more."

Penelope touched her arm as she started off. "Don't worry about it, Sara. I've had enough."

"Oh. Well, then." She poured more from the flask into the now empty cup. "Goodness, I don't know how I'm going to get home tonight. I certainly can't go with Curtis. Maybe I can sleep on Dylan's floor."

Someone knocked on the shop door.

"That must be my friend, Megan." Penelope smiled and put a hand on Sara's shoulder, gently taking the cup from her hand and placing it on the table behind them. "Come meet her."

"Of course, dear." Sara was happy again. She was like a puppy. Any distraction was fun; her mind could be guided from one thing to another, as long as it wasn't expected to stay in one place too long.

It was actually Megan and Georgia, both of them wearing frantic expressions of concern. Penelope smiled and waved as she and Sara moved through the shop from the back. She unlocked the door and let them in to a flurry of concern.

"I ran into Georgia—almost literally," Megan gasped, shivering off the cold, "as I was racing over here. She was crossing the street down by Goolrick's, so I made her come with me."

"She didn't *make me*, for pity's sake," Georgia said. "I had to come. In fact I was on my way here already. Are you all right? Someone at Hyperion said there was a drug bust here! Is that why the store's closed?" She looked around, caught sight of Sara Mersey and extended her hand. "Hi, I'm Georgia Darlin'."

"Hello, sweetie. I'm Sara Mersey." She smiled up at Penelope. "Everyone here is just so nice! I should move to the South. I think I'm a Southerner at heart."

Megan sent Penelope a startled look, as she took off her coat, and turned to Sara. "Are you related to Dylan?"

"I'm his mother. Do you know him too? Of course you do, if you're Penelope's friends. Can I get you some hot cider?" she asked, holding up her hand and looking at it in confusion. "Now what did I do with my cup?"

"That'd be great," Georgia said. "It's colder than a polar bear's weenie out there."

"Oh yes, me too," Megan concurred, rubbing her hands up and down her shoulders. She wore a tee-shirt and jeans. "I left the house as soon as

I made sure Belle was taken care of. I didn't even think to put on a sweater."

"Belle's her daughter," Penelope explained to Sara.

"Oh you have a daughter!" Sara exclaimed, coming to take Megan's hands, much the way she had Penelope's when she'd entered the store. She was intense, Dylan's mother. "Children are the biggest and best comfort you'll ever know. Take my word for it. My Dylan has been the pride of my life. Such a good boy. And he always took such good care of me."

Unbidden, Dylan's earlier words rang in Penelope's mind. *My mother is the reason I have a record at all.*

"Sara," Penelope said, "did Dylan ever do drugs? When he was younger, I mean."

"Dylan?" Sara looked aghast. "Never! He's been clean as a whistle his whole life, my boy. He's kept me on the straight and narrow too." With that she swept to one side, and picked up one of Dylan's celadon bowls. "And look at what an artist he turned out to be. Isn't this gorgeous?"

Penelope, Megan, and Georgia exchanged a look.

"I bought one of those myself, last month," Georgia said. "He's got talent, all right."

"He does. I taught him the wheel early on, but he learned to do things I never could. Which is just as it should be." She turned to them, eyes shining with pride. "The children should exceed the abilities of the parents."

Whatever her faults as a parent, Penelope thought, she did love her son—that much was obvious.

"But Sara," Penelope persisted. "Dylan went to jail on a drug charge."

Sara turned away again, her skirt flaring like a flamenco dancer's. "He told you about that? Well, that's my boy. Never could keep a secret. He's as honest as the day is long."

"So he did do drugs?" Penelope pushed gently.

"Oh no!" Sara briefly met her eyes, then looked away, her fingers playing with one of the spangles on her shirt. "He just got caught up in something that wasn't his fault. I . . . don't really remember the details. But he's been clean ever since then anyway. He never does anything wrong, and he gets so mad when I—oh! I was going to get you girls some cider!" She fluttered toward the door. "It's just across the street at Penelope's adorable little store. They had to move it, you know, when the pigs showed up."

"The pigs?" Georgia repeated.

"Don't go out in the cold just for me," Megan protested, glancing at Penelope.

"Don't be silly," Sara said, swinging the door open with a wide smile. "It couldn't be closer. Me and the ladies over there are already great friends.

They'll probably be filling cups the moment they see me. I'll be right back."

She darted outside and dashed across the street.

Megan, Penelope, and Georgia looked at each other silently for a long moment.

"Well," Georgia said finally, one brow raised analytically, "that explains a lot. Who calls cops 'pigs' anymore?"

"She's like a little child," Megan said wonderingly.

"A little child with a drinking problem. You should have seen what she just polished off in back." Penelope watched the woman disappear into her own shop, where Lucy was manning the till and the Gallery Night ladies were handing out cookies and cider to customers.

Penelope gave them a quick rundown on the evening while Sara Mersey was gone. Her friends responded with gasps and exclamations and bouts of hand-holding sympathy.

"Dylan's down at the station now," she finished, "giving them a report, and he wanted me to call you because I was so shaken up he didn't think I could get myself home." She shook her head, her eyes on the door to her shop. "He's obviously used to taking care of fragile women."

"That woman is beyond fragile," Megan said. "She's living in a completely different world."

Penelope felt resolve forming within her. "You

know what? When he had me call you, I *was* fragile. I was so shaken up I didn't feel like I could stand up without my knees buckling. But now . . ."

"Now you've got to babysit Mama." Georgia rolled her eyes. "Lord, Penelope, you've landed in the middle of an episode of *CSI*."

"I'll say." Megan laughed, but looked with concern at Penelope. "Are you sure you're all right? I mean, gunfire! That alone gives me the shakes."

Penelope shook her head. "I'm fine. I'm more than fine; I'm ashamed of myself for reacting like such a ninny. I mean, even Sara Mersey was calmer than I was." She tossed a hand in the direction the woman had gone.

"That's because she's three sheets to the friggin' wind," Georgia said.

"Why *should* you be able to react to something like this calmly?" Megan asked. "What in the world could have prepared you for that?"

"Nothing. You're right." Penelope squared her shoulders. "But I can respond better now. Which is why I think what I need to do is stay here, and open the shop back up. Dylan worked so hard. Look at all this gorgeous stuff! Why should he miss out on all the business of this night because of something that wasn't his fault?"

"I agree. And I'll help." Georgia stood up. "Now where's Dylan's mama's flask?"

Megan laughed.

But something had occurred to Penelope. She turned quickly to Megan. "Did you tell Sutter where you were going? Or rather, why? That Dylan was in trouble?"

Megan fiddled with her purse. "I did, yes. I was rushing around—he went to get the nanny—I had to tell him. Should I not have?"

Penelope's heart sank. "No, no. Of course you had to. But . . . he isn't—that is, is he very disappointed in Dylan? He wouldn't take back the grant money, would he?"

"Penelope, no!" Megan looked astonished. "In fact we both left Belle with the nanny. Sutter went down to the police station. To support Dylan and see if he needed anything. He didn't believe for one second he was guilty of anything."

Penelope's gaze dropped to the floor. "Then he was ahead of me. I was sure he was guilty."

Chapter 18

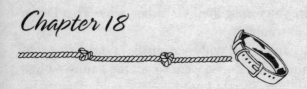

When they reached closing time and Dylan had still not returned, Penelope insisted Sara come to stay at her house for the night. It was only nine o'clock and, after thanking Georgia and Megan profusely for their help, Penelope had decided this was a golden opportunity to understand Dylan a little better.

So she left him a note explaining that she would bring Sara back in the morning when she came in to open the shop. Sara didn't have a ride back to Baltimore anyway, she'd added, and Penelope didn't want to think of her sleeping on Dylan's floor when she had an empty guest room.

They stayed up talking until late in the evening,

and with every story out of Sara Mersey's mouth—some ringing true, others more like dreamlike fabrications—she got a clearer picture of how Dylan was raised.

Or rather, how he had raised himself. His father had left when he was ten and from that point on it seemed he'd had to grow up way too fast. His mother, sweet as she was, was a weird combination of cynicism and naiveté. She'd instilled in her son a mistrust of the system, police in particular, while at the same time exhorting him to trust people, give everyone the benefit of the doubt, let the universe guide his life and provide for the future.

She depended, much like Blanche DuBois, on the kindness of strangers. And yet she didn't seem to have any common sense at all, let alone be a good judge of character.

Dylan, it was clear, had grown up taking care of his mother.

"He was the sweetest little boy in the world." Sara sighed, smiling. "His whole life he's been sweet. Came out of the womb that way. I think it was because when I was pregnant with him, I was doing a lot of meditation. His father and I traveled with a group who studied under the Maharishi Mahesh Yogi. You probably don't remember him but he was the one who started Transcendental Meditation."

"How fascinating. Did you teach Dylan how to

meditate?" Penelope imagined the boy-Dylan sitting cross-legged, beautiful eyes closed, concentrating on goodness and peace. What had happened?

"Oh no." Sara shook her head and tilted it to the side, looking into her wineglass. "I probably should have, now you mention it. But by then we were into other things. Still exploring our minds, you understand, but in other ways, through . . . through altered states of consciousness. Hypnosis, acid, you know, all that stuff. Dylan was such a good soldier in those days, because when you're doing mind work like that you sometimes . . . sometimes lose track of things . . ." Her voice drifted off and she looked pensive, as if trying even now to remember those things she'd lost track of.

Penelope frowned, imagining a young Dylan trying to understand a mother tripping on acid. "What do you mean, 'a good soldier'?"

Sara's head snapped up. "Oh, well, hm." She leaned forward, poured herself a fresh glass of wine, and settled back again. "Once—this was just after his father had left, so Dylan was about ten—I'd gone out—I was such a free spirit in those days."

Those days? Penelope thought.

"Everyone was. We had parties and jam sessions and rap sessions, poetry slams. It was the most wonderful time for community and sharing. But that night I got home a lot later than I thought I would. So I let myself in to the apartment in the morning, real quiet like." She put a finger to her lips, *shh*. "And I tiptoed into the kitchen to find Dylan asleep in the chair at the table. I'll never forget it; his little head was tilted at this uncomfortable angle, so I straightened him up and kissed him awake. Turns out he had made dinner for me the night before, and set the table and everything. It was so cute! I was delighted. We were such pals, even back then." She beamed nostalgically. "So we had it all for breakfast. And it was such a great joke, hamburgers for breakfast! We laughed about that for a long time. That was just one of our private little jokes."

Penelope could barely speak for the lump in her throat. Dylan, age ten, cooking for his mother, who never came home. She blinked rapidly to dispel the tears.

There were several stories like that, with Dylan's no doubt devastating disappointment being blown off—or worse, retranslated—into some warm, fuzzy memory. Dylan was never the bad guy, never once, but neither was Sara. She seemed to have no concept of the fact that she was a criminally negligent mother.

And yet, at the same time, angry as Penelope felt at that stupid young girl, she felt a tug of protectiveness toward the sunny, childlike woman sitting across from her who wanted only happiness for everyone, most especially for Dylan.

You couldn't speak to her of bad things without her dancing around the subject or recasting it into something more benign. When Penelope tried to engage her about the "pigs" who'd arrested Dylan the first time around, years ago when he'd gone to jail, she wouldn't—or couldn't—elaborate. Instead she disseminated into some version of "I don't exactly recall all the details" or "You'll have to ask him about that," then began talking about how she'd sent him cookies every week while he was in prison and how much he said all the other inmates loved them too. He was always so good about sharing . . .

In the two hours they spent talking, Sara Mersey polished off an entire bottle of wine by herself. It occurred to Penelope that perhaps the drugs Dylan had gone to jail for had been his mother's. Or that he'd been dealing so that she could afford her drugs. Based on his quickly bitten off comment earlier in the evening, and everything Sara Mersey said and did as the alcohol kicked in, Penelope knew what she had been seeing in Dylan every time he'd pulled away from her, the sad little boy who didn't want to be responsible for anyone anymore.

It struck Penelope that she might well have come across as another fragile female who needed protection, much like his mother. And hadn't she been? Like when she was with Glenn? She'd loved his protectiveness, his good, secure job, his money, and his ability to handle things. She hadn't even had to work.

Dylan had known it, had seen it in her. He'd almost said as much, when he'd told her he didn't want someone who could get over his past, but someone who understood it, who accepted it wholly. Someone, in other words, who could handle it—not someone who was used to being protected from the harsher realities of life. And definitely not someone looking to remake him in the image of her ex-husband.

She'd been looking for exactly that when she'd initiated trying to get together again with Glenn. Comfort and security. But maybe that wasn't who she was anymore. Or who she was supposed to be. She was stronger than that. It was that inner strength, that part of her that could handle more, that knew it *should* be handling more, that had stepped into Dylan's world and refused to step out.

Well, she wasn't stepping out now. She'd had a taste of Dylan's old world and she'd come out on the other side. She understood what she was accepting and she'd seen how it could manifest itself. She'd also seen his desire to be out of it.

And *she could handle it*. This was the amazing part. She'd proved to herself that she was ready to take it on, ready to learn and become something new, someone new, someone who didn't see things through the same single lens she'd been brought up with.

She only hoped she could prove it to him.

Dylan had never been so tired in his life. He'd returned to his shop nearly disoriented with fatigue. In fact, it had taken him a long time to figure out that he had not been robbed. The missing merchandise had all been sold and his till was full of cash. There were even some credit card sales—surprising, since he didn't yet have a credit card machine—marked in a meticulous, feminine hand on sheets adorned with the Pen Perfect logo.

Penelope, he thought, closing his eyes and inhaling through his nose as if he could pick up the subtle flowers of her fragrance in the air, the clean smell of her hair, the sweet scent of her skin.

Then he'd found her note. She'd taken his mother home with her. He hadn't an ounce of energy left to worry about Sara, so with a grateful sigh he'd retreated to his apartment and had slept solidly for nine hours.

The woman was amazing, he thought upon waking, Penelope springing immediately to mind. He didn't have any other word to describe her. She'd come to his rescue in more ways than he could count. If she hadn't found the jewelry and kept it from him, he'd have had to go through with the deal and the cops could well have charged him with collaboration no matter what Pinky said. And even if they hadn't, they would still have believed him capable of it in the future. This way it looked like it was his idea not to cooperate with criminals, making him damn close to squeaky clean as far as the authorities were concerned.

Penelope had saved him. And she'd done it by standing up for her convictions. When in the world had Dylan ever done that? He'd never felt free enough. Until now.

As he got out of bed, Dylan felt as if a hundred-pound weight had been lifted from his chest. His fresh start was fresh again. He was off the hook with the cops. He was off the hook with Pinky. He was off every hook he'd ever been on. He almost didn't know where to put his thoughts.

So he put them on the one thing that stood out like a beacon in his mind. Penelope.

As much as she'd been his savior last night, he was afraid it was also the undoing of her feelings for him. She'd stayed and kept the shop open—along with Megan, Sutter Foley had told him at the station—but most likely that was simply her generous nature. Or maybe it was her attempt to feel normal again after such a harrowing evening. Or maybe it had been Megan's idea.

In any case, he couldn't believe that after experiencing the darkest part of his past Penelope could want any more to do with him. But when he thought about standing by his convictions, about doing what he believed in and taking that first positive step forward in this life that was suddenly so free, the first thing he thought of was her.

Dylan put on his jacket, locked the front door behind him—he'd never had so much cash in the shop before—and walked across the street to Pen Perfect, steeling himself every step of the way.

She was inside, alone, setting merchandise into the glass case next to her register. She turned when she heard the door chimes.

He knew, from the warming of his face to the thundering of his heart, that he had never been happier—or more afraid—to see anyone in his life. He tried to detect her mood from her expression. She was smiling, but she was a smiley person. She didn't seem angry, but then she'd probably be more sorry for him than angry.

"Hi," he said.

"Hi." Her voice was soft, her eyes gentle on his.

"Where's my mother?" he asked, groping for the first thought he could lay his hands on, or at least verbalize. The rest of him just wanted to touch her, to grab her and hold her and ask her never to give up on him.

He glanced around the shop. It appeared empty but for the two of them. His pulse accelerated.

"She wasn't awake when I had to leave, so I left

her a note and let her sleep. Bonsai's in the back."
She clasped her hands together in front of her.

"You—'Bonsai'?" He smiled at the slip. "Don't
you mean Mr. Darcy?"

She tilted her head, splayed her hands. "It was
the name he picked. And he had plenty of chances
to change his mind. So Bonsai it is."

He chuckled, looked at the floor, and silence de-
scended.

Time to belly up to the bar, he thought. *Be a man,
say what you think. Fight for what you want!*

"Thank you," he said finally, lifting his head.
"For opening the shop back up last night. And for
doing so well. I know I could never have sold so
much no matter who came in."

"That stuff sold itself, Dylan. You should have
heard people's comments. They loved it. Of course,
I'll have hell to pay with my accountant when we
figure out the credit-card receipts, but . . ." She
shrugged.

Was it his imagination, or was she more reserved
than usual? It wasn't like her to be detached . . .
unless she'd changed her mind about him.

And why wouldn't she? Who would get into bed,
so to speak, with problems like last night's?

He cleared his throat, took a step toward her.
"Penelope, I also wanted to thank you, for—"

"Don't, Dylan." She dropped her head and he

noted that her hands were gripped together hard. He could see the whites of her knuckles. It boded ill to him. "You have nothing to thank *me* for, that's for sure. In fact I wanted to apologize to you."

His mouth dropped open. "For *what?*"

"For causing so much trouble. For refusing to give you back the bag. For nearly getting you killed! If I hadn't been such a coward, if I hadn't . . ." She squeezed her eyes shut.

"A *coward?* Penelope, you—"

Her dark eyes flew open to stop him mid-sentence. She held up a hand, her expression anguished. "Let me finish. Please. The truth is, Dylan, when I found that bag, I thought you were guilty. I—I didn't believe in you the way I should have. I should have trusted you to know what you were doing. And I'm sorry. I'm so, so sorry. You have to believe me when I say I will never, *ever* doubt you again."

"Penelope." Dylan strode toward her, but stopped short of touching her. "Why *wouldn't* you have thought I was guilty? I've spent months trying to convince you I was exactly that kind of person. Then you come in, find me searching my own place—Penelope, you'd have been an idiot not to believe the worst."

"But—"

"You *saved* me last night." He leaned toward her, his eyes seeking to hold hers with the intensity of his feelings. If nothing else, he needed to convince her that he saw her actions as heroic. She would be too hard on herself otherwise. "I had no idea what the hell I was doing. As it turns out I wasn't guilty—they'd planted the stuff at my place to get Kane—but the fact is I would have been guilty of something if you hadn't intervened."

He put his hands in his pockets to keep from scooping her up into his arms. That was probably the last thing she wanted now.

"The truth is," he continued, "I just wanted it over with. I didn't know Pinky was working with the cops. Or that Curtis was one of them. Or that any of what happened was going to happen. I had no idea at all." He made an incredulous sound, staring down into her warm, dark eyes. "As for being a coward . . . are you kidding? Penelope, you stood up to them. When you told them you had the bag, my heart just about stopped in my chest. You were going to take the rap for me. Nobody has *ever* taken the rap for me."

"But you've taken the rap for someone else, haven't you?" she asked quietly.

He jerked back. "Did my mother tell you that? I didn't think she even realized . . ."

"I don't think she does," Penelope agreed. "But I do."

Dylan turned halfway away and spoke in a low voice, mortification clogging his throat. "You've met her. After spending last night with her you can probably see she wouldn't have handled prison well."

"I do see that, but Dylan . . ."

"No." He cast her a sideways glance and a wry smile. "Don't make it bigger than it was. They could have had other stuff on me, the cops. Fencing, buying and selling stolen goods. I just added something more so she wouldn't have to suffer too. It wasn't the wrong thing to do. It might not have been the smartest thing, or even the right thing, but it wasn't wrong. I wouldn't have been able to live with myself if I hadn't done it."

"So they were her drugs you went to jail for."

He shrugged. "Hers and her boyfriend's. But they wouldn't have gotten him without getting her too."

Penelope started to move toward him.

Dylan's heart quickened as he watched her. Was it his imagination or was her expression tender, her eyes shining. Could it be that last night hadn't—

She smiled. "Dylan, you are . . ."

The door chimed and Dylan startled. They both turned to see Glenn striding into the store with a storm cloud on his face. He swung his briefcase like a sledgehammer and it landed on the counter with a hard *thwap*.

Dylan stepped back, away from Penelope.

"What in God's name were you *thinking*, Penelope? What happened last night? It's all over town that you were involved in some kind of drug bust!"

Penelope folded her arms across her chest. "It was stolen jewelry, actually. And how could it be all over town already? It's not even nine o'clock."

"Apparently it got an early start last night. Why didn't you *call* me?"

"I . . . had Gallery Night to attend to. I was working."

"Working? After a drug bust?"

"I told you, it was stolen jewelry." She glanced at Dylan.

Dylan didn't think it was just his wishful thinking that made her sound annoyed with her ex-husband.

Glenn spun and glared at Dylan as if noticing him for the first time. Then he marched toward Penelope and wrapped her in a bear hug. "Thank God you're all right. It scared the hell out of me when I heard about it this morning."

"I'm all right." Her words were muffled by Glenn's shoulder.

Dylan's hands clenched into frustrated fists.

"And you!" Glenn turned, his arm still around Penelope's shoulders, pulling her close to his side. "I should have known you were up to no good. Are you here to apologize, I hope? How did you post bail?"

"Glenn!" Penelope ducked out from under his

arm and stepped between them. "Dylan was as much a victim as I was. More so."

"Is that what he told you?" Glenn's face was set like a bulldog's. Dylan recognized the expression. A man coming to the rescue of a woman and making a show of it for all it was worth. "I never trusted you, Mersey. But you've gone too far, involving Penelope in your illegal scams. I suspected all along you might still be engaged in something criminal."

"No you didn't," Penelope objected, hands on her hips. "In fact, when Carson was talking about him a few weeks ago you defended him. You're quite the fair weather friend, aren't you?"

Glenn, who'd reached out to take her arm, retracted his hand. "What are you talking about? This guy nearly got you killed. I heard there were dozens of cops there to arrest several heavily armed drug dealers. It's a wonder Mersey's not in jail too. How *did* you get out?" He turned again to Dylan.

"He's not in jail because he was not involved either. Not really. And there was only one dealer and as I keep saying it wasn't drugs he was after. Why can't people get their facts straight before talking about something?"

She took a sidestep toward Dylan, which he noticed and Glenn seemed not to. Dylan had also noticed her tone. Calm. Collected. Not at all the kind of voice someone simply putting on a brave face would be able to come up with.

She really was all right.

Dylan's relief was almost tangible.

Glenn threw his hands up. "I can't believe you! You're acting like nothing happened!"

She shrugged halfheartedly. "I know. Maybe after last night I'm out of adrenaline. I woke up today feeling calmer than I've felt in weeks."

Glenn twisted, pounded a fist on the counter, and Penelope jumped. Dylan took a step toward him, ready to drag the guy out the door by his silk fucking tie, if need be.

"Damn it, Mersey, I could kill you for getting her into that."

"I would say the same thing, if I were in your position," Dylan said, "but do you really think *this* is what she needs right now? Someone coming in and berating her for—"

"He *didn't* get me into it," Penelope interrupted. "In fact, he wanted me out of it even more than you do. He did everything in his power to get rid of me last night. Actually, he's been trying to get rid of me for weeks. I got myself into it." She turned back to Dylan. "And I'd like to stay in it, as long as he'll let me."

Glenn didn't seem to notice the change of topic, but Dylan did. His pulse, which previously had been racing, suddenly felt as if it'd stopped. *Stay in what?* he wanted to ask. *Stay with me? In my life? Stay?*

He gazed at her, let hope dance in his heart for the first time in his life.

"Penelope," he said cautiously.

"Oh come on, Pen," Glenn spat. "You're not the kind of woman who'd even know *how* to get into something like that. You shouldn't be exposed to that kind of thing."

She laughed, flipping her hair over her shoulder. "That's what I told them, when they dragged me out of my ivory tower."

Glenn's expression turned fierce. "I know you're making light of it for *his* sake." Glenn jerked his head in Dylan's direction but didn't look at him. "God knows why. You were always taking care of one sort of stray or another. But Penelope, you're not the kind of woman who should be dodging gunfire and risking arrest. You're the kind of woman who should be pampered and protected, the kind—"

"I am *not* the kind of woman who needs protection," she snapped.

"I'll say," Dylan murmured.

Glenn shot him a murderous glance.

"And as for *you* being protective, it wasn't *you* stepping between me and a loaded gun last night, Glenn. And I have to say I'm not entirely sure you would. But Dylan would. Dylan *did*. You cannot imagine how that feels. No one could, until it happened to them."

Dylan's heart blossomed at the words.

Clearly at a loss, Glenn stepped toward her, taking her hands in his. "Penelope, what's gotten into you? You know I'd do anything for you. Anything."

Penelope lowered her head, her shoulders slumping. "I'm sorry, Glenn. I shouldn't have said that. You've always been very protective of me. I know you're only expressing your concern, which I appreciate. It's just . . . I've come to the conclusion that I'm not the kind of woman I thought I was. I don't need someone to stand between me and the world anymore. I need someone who trusts me to be able to handle it myself. Someone who respects me."

"What the hell are you talking about? I respect you."

Dylan didn't know about Penelope, but he thought Glenn's tone was distinctly disrespectful.

"I know you do." She squeezed his hands together in hers.

Glenn—posturing, Dylan thought—turned his head away from her.

"I know I initiated things between us . . . again," she said softly.

I should leave, Dylan thought. This was between *them*. But he was afraid that Glenn was too fine an actor and knew his audience too well. Could he possibly convince Penelope—guilt her—into staying with him? What about the enormous lie he was

perpetrating? She should be told about the vasectomy, shouldn't she?

"You didn't want to get back together until I
showed up at your door that night," Penelope continued. "But Glenn, we're not right for each other
anymore. Don't you see that? Hasn't it been obvious ever since that night?"

"Don't be silly, Pen, of course we're right for
each other. We're the same kind of people, you and
I. We want the same things."

"Do you?" Dylan couldn't resist, then took a step
back. "I'm sorry. I should go."

"No." Penelope shook her head. "I have something to say to you, too."

"I think he should go." Glenn glared at Dylan.
"I'm trying to have a conversation with *my wife*. I
don't think this has anything to do with you."

"*Ex*-wife," Dylan said.

Glenn turned incredulous eyes on Penelope.
"Why would you ask this guy to stay? We don't
need some *convict* refereeing for us."

"*Ex*-con," Dylan said.

Penelope, he could see, tried to stifle a laugh.

"This is between you and me, and the future we
have if we just reach out and take it." Glenn turned
his back on Dylan, closing in on Penelope. "Remember how good it was, in the beginning? Just
you and me. We got along so well. Remember playing tennis? Golf at the club? Remember how happy

you were, fixing up the house? We could have that again, the two of us."

"The two of us," Penelope murmured, looking at him sadly.

"Yes! Like we used to be."

"Why don't you tell her exactly what you mean by 'the two of us'?" Dylan interjected. Once Glenn confessed, he *would* leave, he told himself. Let them hash it out and come to whatever conclusions they were going to come to without him. But he couldn't let Penelope fall under Glenn's thrall, into his lies, so he would stay until the truth came out.

Then he would tell her his own truth. His feelings. That he had finally realized he couldn't live without her, and he was not going to let her go. After pushing her away for so long, he was now determined to fight for her. She deserved it more than any woman he'd ever known.

He only hoped that despite his confession about the jewelry, she had one last ounce of trust in him.

"Would you get out of here?" Glenn snarled.

"I was here first." Dylan lifted his brows. "I'll go when Penelope asks me to go."

Penelope kept her gaze on Glenn. "I actually would like the answer to that question, Glenn."

"In front of him?" Glenn's voice rose to a near squeak. "I'll talk to you about it, but only in private. It's nobody's business but ours."

"I'm sorry." Penelope gave him a steady look.

"But I don't want him to leave. Glenn, I know you were trying hard with me this time around. I'm so sorry I put you through it. But it's obvious we've grown too far apart. The truth is, I know you still don't want kids, no matter wh—"

"God *damn* it, you *told* her, didn't you?" Glenn exploded, whirling on Dylan. "I told you about that vasectomy in confidence. That's what I get for trying to make friends with a felon!" He marched toward the counter and his briefcase, then turned to glare at Dylan. "I thought you could be trusted. Well, you can see what kind of friend he *is,* Pen. The kind who can't keep secrets, who doesn't honor a confidence, who . . ."

His words trailed off as he faced Penelope again and saw her thunderstruck expression.

"I didn't tell her," Dylan said into the ensuing silence. "But I wanted to."

Penelope's eyes moved to Dylan's and the hurt in them warmed to something different. After a moment her lips curved upward and the tears that welled in her eyes seemed, inexplicably, to be tears of happiness.

She shifted her gaze, and her smile, to Glenn.

"Thank you," she said. "Thank you, Glenn, for making this so much easier for me. I had the feeling you were just talking when you said you wanted another child, but now I know. And I also know you haven't changed at all since our divorce.

So I thank you for revealing yourself to me so completely today. You know I don't handle guilt very well."

"You . . . he . . . I . . ." Glenn sputtered. "You can't believe *him*. He's an ex-con, for God's sake. He'll say anything!"

Penelope laughed. "You're the one who said it, Glenn."

"I mean—don't throw this all away because of one little misrepresentation. I was going to tell you, I really was, I swear. I just . . . I was waiting for the right time."

"When? After you'd slept with me?" she asked wryly.

Dylan laughed. She did know the jerk, after all.

Glenn whipped the briefcase off the counter so hard it whacked him in the thigh. He stumbled but regained his balance quickly. He gestured emphatically at Dylan. "I can't believe you humiliated me like this in front of *him*. What's he to you anyway?"

"You really want to know?"

"Oh don't tell me." Glenn's words dripped sarcasm but his expression said the horse he'd bet on had just dropped dead on the track.

Penelope sent Dylan a smile that made his blood hot. "He's the guy I'm in love with. And I have been almost since the day I met him."

"I can't believe it," Dylan murmured, but inside

his chest a fireworks display was bursting into the light and fire.

"I'm outta here. You're making a big, *big* mistake," Glenn said. The chimes exploded as he yanked open the door and went through.

Penelope barely blinked. She walked right up to Dylan, put her hands on his chest, rose up on tiptoe and kissed him square on the mouth. His hands went around her waist and he kissed her back.

"I love you too." Dylan fingers tightened on her warm, solid body. She was *real*. And she loved him still. "Penelope, you have no idea . . ."

As he looked down at her face he could hardly believe his luck. This beautiful woman was gazing up at him with love, actual love, blazing in her eyes. She saw the whole man, too, he knew. The past, the present, even the future.

And she loved him.

"There is one thing I need to tell you though," she said, her fingers clenching his shirt and her eyes dropping to the buttons. "I—I don't know if you've been worried about it, but I'm not pregnant. From, you know, that first time."

Dylan brought a hand up to her cheek and stroked the soft skin, an odd sadness springing up inside him at the news. How strange that it wasn't relief. And yet, not strange at all. He wanted to be bound to this woman, body and soul. Already was bound by his heart.

He let his mouth curve into a small smile. "Maybe, someday, when the time is right . . . we could plan on remedying that."

Tears did spring to her eyes then, and she beamed at him. "Do you mean that?"

He grinned. "Well, I had a lot of time to think about it, when I thought it might actually be happening." He kissed her gently on the lips. "And I think I liked the idea. I've never felt about anybody the way I feel about you."

She threw her arms around his neck and hugged him close. "I knew we were meant to be together."

He laughed. "Now let's get that dog out here— Bonsai, Mr. Darcy, whoever—and tell him we're opening up those doors we closed between us. And we're never shutting them again."

Epilogue

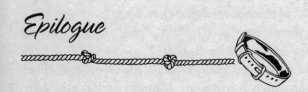

Penelope leaned in to Dylan, snaked her arm snugly through his and said, "Have you seen the bride?"

He clasped her hand. "No, but there's Megan. And I think that's Sutter at the bar. Please tell me this is the last wedding we're going to have to go to for a while."

Penelope smiled up at him. "I know, it's been a few. But aren't you glad we bought this nice suit? It's got to be more comfortable than your old one."

"My old one was fine."

"Fine!" She laughed as Megan joined them. "It was swimming on you ever since you ran that marathon. And this one looks so good." She patted his lapel with one hand, loving the glint of her diamond in the candlelit room.

"Where's the bride?" Megan asked. "I saw the groom inside, but—"

"I guess she's not here yet, but—oh!" Penelope glanced toward the door of the reception hall. "There's Lily, maybe she knows."

Lily and Brady sauntered over to them, shedding their coats. "Where's Georgia?" Lily asked.

"Where's the bar?" Brady asked.

Megan gestured behind her. "Follow Sutter, he's on the trail. I think he's wedding'd out."

Dylan made a commiserating sound somewhere between a laugh and a cough.

"I never saw Georgia leave the church," Penelope said. "Surely she rode over here in the limo with Leland."

Lily snickered. "Do you think they incarcerated her there? I mean, she hasn't exactly been a model member of the flock. Maybe they staged an intervention."

"She did it for Leland, even though *she* wanted to elope to Bali," Penelope said. "His father was a pastor there, you know."

"Would you *ever* have believed Georgia would marry the son of a pastor?" Megan grinned.

"Hey, he knows upstairs from downstairs and can run a flight of steps in the car," Lily said. "I think that trumped everything."

Sutter approached bearing a server's tray with six champagne flutes on it. "Champagne cocktail, anyone?"

"Did you steal that from a waiter?" Megan accused, grinning.

"He relinquished it happily" —Sutter passed the tray around the group— "when I told him he was going to have a riot on his hands if he didn't make the rounds quickly enough."

"I'll say." Brady snagged a glass.

The tray reached Penelope and she blushed. "I, uh . . . no, thanks."

Dylan's hand squeezed hers and he sent her a private smile. Penelope felt Megan's eyes on her.

"It's pretty good," Brady said, eyeing the glass appreciatively, "even if you don't like champagne."

"Come on," Lily said, "this is Georgia's wedding! Not to mention the fourth one we've been to in a year—"

"Fifth, for us," Brady amended, then added, to the others, "My brother Keenan got married a few months ago."

"Oh yes, Tory and Keenan." Lily sighed. "That was a lovely wedding. Did I tell you Barbra Streisand was the ring bearer?"

"Really?" Dylan asked, shocked.

"'Barbra Streisand' is the name of their dog," Penelope explained.

Dylan laughed. "That's worse than 'Mr. Darcy.' "

Penelope mock-scowled at him. "Someday we will have a dog named Mr. Darcy. He'll be Bonsai's best friend."

"In any case," Lily continued, "I know we all loved our own weddings, but let's drink to the organza siege being *over!*" She raised her glass. "To Georgia and Leland."

Penelope picked up a glass, raised it, but did not sip.

"To Georgia and Leland," they all chorused.

Megan slid closer to Penelope and said, with a penetrating look, "Penelope Porter, is there something you're not telling us?"

"That's Penelope Mersey to you," she said primly, trying to suppress the smile that threatened to swallow her face.

"Oh my God!" Lily breathed. "Is it—are you—?"

Penelope looked up at Dylan, who was gazing at her with a subtle smile and the devil in his eyes. "I told you."

"Leave the poor girl alone," Sutter said. "If she had something to say, she'd have said it on her own. Penelope, can I get you a juice or something?"

"Thank you, Sutter, but I'm fine." Penelope looked around the group, feeling happier than she'd ever felt. "I'm not going to steal Georgia's thunder. It's her day. That would be tacky."

"So you mean . . . ?" Megan gripped her arm hard, her face looking nearly as ecstatic as Penelope felt.

"Quick! There's Georgia," Lily said, leaning close. "Tell us now and we'll tell her later, when it's not her day."

"And she calls me incorrigible," Brady said.

"Too late." Penelope smiled past the group as Georgia joined them. "There's the belle of the ball! You look so beautiful!"

"Oh my lord, I can't tell you how glad I am that's over with." Georgia gave an exasperated laugh. "Now we can drink!"

"Here." Penelope handed Georgia her glass. "The ceremony was so lovely, Georgia. And you two look so happy."

"Oh yeah, yeah, what*ever*. I'm just glad all that plannin' and arrangin' and reservin' and anticipatin' is *done*. Who knew gettin' married was so much work? I for one can't wait to think about somethin' else for a change."

Lily raised her brows. "If you mean that . . ."

"Lily, stop," Penelope admonished, blushing again.

Georgia downed half the champagne and looked at Lily, then Penelope, suspiciously. "What's going on? Is there somethin' you're not tellin' me? I didn't have my dress caught up in my panty hose or anythin', did I?"

Megan laughed. "No, you look absolutely stunning."

"Then tell me, for pity's sake. Oh wait." Georgia took a step sideways and snagged a passing waiter. "We need a couple more of these over here." She took another champagne for herself and one for Penelope.

As Penelope held up a hand, Lily said with just a hint of smugness, "Penelope's not drinking tonight."

Georgia looked at her, delight spreading across her face. "*What?* Is there somethin' we should know, Miss Penelope?"

She took a deep breath. "All right, but the conversation about this ends here, right now. Then we're going to talk about how gorgeous Georgia looks."

"Oh the hell with me." Georgia swatted that subject away with a hand. "I'm sick of me."

Penelope glanced up at Dylan. "Do you want to tell them?"

Dylan laughed. "Only if you don't want to."

Penelope looked around the circle at her nearest and dearest friends in the world and couldn't think of anything she wanted to do more.

"It's official," she said, beaming. "I'm pregnant."

Next month, don't miss these exciting new love stories only from Avon Books

Between the Devil and Desire by Lorraine Heath
Olivia, Duchess of Lovingdon, would never associate with such a rogue as Jack Dodger, a wealthy gentleman's club owner. Yet when Jack is named sole heir to the duke's personal possessions, Olivia is forced to share her beloved home with this despicable, yet desirable man . . .

Simply Irresistible by Rachel Gibson
Georgeanne Howard leaves her fiancé at the altar when she realizes she can't marry a man old enough to be her grandfather, no matter how rich he is. Hockey superstar John Kowalsky unknowingly helps her escape, and only later does he realize he has absconded with his boss's bride.

The Highland Groom by Sarah Gabriel
To claim her inheritance, Fiona MacCarran must marry a wealthy Highlander, and soon. Arriving in the misty Highlands as a schoolteacher, she despairs of finding an acceptable groom . . . until she meets Dougal MacGregor.

Wild by Margo Maguire
For Grace Hawthorne, the new stranger is unlike any man she has ever known. Proud, defiant, and mesmerizingly masculine, he flouts convention and refuses to enter into proper society. Is he the real Anthony Maddox, heir to a glittering earldom? Or an arrogant imposter, sworn to claim what doesn't belong to him?

Visit www.AuthorTracker.com for exclusive information on your favorite HarperCollins authors.

REL 1208

At Avon Books, we know your passion for romance—once you finish one of our novels, you find yourself wanting more.

May we tempt you with . . .

- **Excerpts** from our upcoming releases.

- Entertaining **extras**, including authors' personal photo albums and book lists.

- Behind-the-scenes **scoop** on your favorite characters and series.

- **Sweepstakes** for the chance to win free books, romantic getaways, and other fun prizes.

- Writing **tips** from our authors and editors.

- **Blog** with our authors and find out why they love to write romance.

- **Exclusive content** that's not contained within the pages of our novels.

Join us at
www.avonbooks.com

AVON *An Imprint of* HarperCollins*Publishers*
www.avonromance.com

Available wherever books are sold or please call 1-800-331-3761 to order.